The Name and the Key

The Darkening Gate

Kristina Elyse Butke

OHB

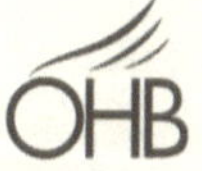

Cover Design by Dar Albert at Wicked Smart Designs

Illustrations and symbols by Ecem Sila KARSLI (Jell Witch)

Published by Oliver-Heber Books

0 9 8 7 6 5 4 3 2 1

To my Seton Hill WPF family who contributed so much to the first creation of this work: Tim Waggoner, Scott A. Johnson, Anne Harris, and Jennifer Loring. A lot has changed since I've rewritten my thesis, but the lessons you taught me, and the encouragement you gave me, linger on.

I also dedicate this book to the enduring memory of my father, Henry Butke. I love you and miss you so much.

FANTASY NAME PRONUNCIATION GUIDE

Andresh Zatavier – ANN-dresh zuh-tay-VEE-er

Jolan Zatavier – JOE-luhn zuh-tay-VEE-er

Sindalia – sin-dall-YUH

Bellamy – bell-uh-ME

Evandra – ee-VAN-druh

Imelda – ih-MEL-duh

Vindal – Vin-dall

Milanie – mill-UH-knee

Celderond – SELL-der-ond

Astacia – uh-STAY-shuh

Paradis d'Azur – pair-uh-DEE dah-SZHUR

Capua Cora – cap-OOH-uh COR-uh

Basseter – BAZ-eh-ter

St. Oliman's – saynt O-lee-mawn's

Aineiron – eye-NEAR-on

Nigredo – nih-GREH-doh

Albedo – al-BEE-doh

Citrinitas – sit-ree-NEE-tus

Rubedo – roo-BEH-doh

St. Briscol – saynt BRIH-skull
Rinnea Abbey – rih-NAY-uh AB-bee
Adanya Caliday – uh-DAWN-yuh CAL-ih-day
Cendelamon – sen-DELL-uh-mawn
Stultus – STOOL-toose
Hirutânvolya – HERE-ew-tawn-VOLE-yuh

CHAPTER 1

Sometime in the chill of the new spring night, Mother left us.

It had been a month since her last flight of fancy, and she gave no indication she would disappear again. Not even when the Zataviers, our neighbors, visited us last night after returning from two years in their native country of Sindalia.

Although she dismissed herself after dinner, claiming illness and a desire to go to bed early, Mother thanked Andresh and his father Jolan for the presents they brought us all from abroad. She laughed when the Zataviers joked; she smiled when they shared their stories from overseas—like all of us in the Bellamy family had done. There was no sign of distress or a desire to flee.

All in all, it was a wonderful evening, and I was glad to see Andresh, my childhood friend, again. At fourteen, he was a year older than me and had grown two inches since I last saw him, finally besting my height. He'd also grown out his jet-black hair. It was now long enough to wear in a short low ponytail, and he had flattering layers cut around his face.

I couldn't help but stare at him as our families shared dinner together. He was starting to show signs of his impending manhood, and he no longer had a weird, wild grace about him, but a sturdier, more confident posture than before. I'd always thought he was cute—he had lashes like a girl's—but now I realized he had cheekbones and a jawline and a face that had grown from adorable to...dare I say it...handsome?

Andresh gave me a big grin from his seat across the table. "Whatcha looking at?"

"You're so different," I said. "Your hair!"

"They wear it long in Sindalia," he said. "You should see the capital city, Evandra. The men and women there keep their hair at such a length, they braid it down their backs in thick plaits. Someday mine'll be like that."

"I don't know if I can imagine that," I said. "But it looks nice now, so I'm sure it'll be even better once it's the way you want it."

His sapphire-blue eyes—a color so deep they almost seemed black at times—glistened for a second. "Thanks, Lily. If you come with me to Sindalia, I'll braid your hair."

My own reddish-brown hair was long, and so glossy and straight that it kept no style and slid out of every pin and clip I used on it. "I doubt it'll keep a braid," I said to him, "but you can try."

My little sister Nell (only I was allowed to call her that) butted in: "Why don't you braid my hair, Andresh?" She was nine years old but still small for her age, and her high-pitched voice made her seem even younger. While it would have been acceptable to call her cute, she was in truth a beautiful child, an image of our mother: rosy cheeks, pink cupid's lips, and long, wavy golden-blonde hair.

"I can, Eleanor. Come here," Andresh said with a grin. He handed her a small gift box, her souvenir from Sindalia, and she ripped it apart to reveal a thick green ribbon with a gold sheen to it. The color matched her eyes.

"Quick! Use it on me!" she cried, rising on her tiptoes. She removed the pins from her hair and shook out her head until all her curls fell down. Andresh gently took her hair in his hands, split it in three sections, and swiftly braided it. He used her new ribbon to tie her hair in place.

"Go show everybody," I said, smiling. Nell nodded and darted off to our parents, grandma, and Uncle Jolan.

Andresh reached into his pocket and pulled out an unwrapped box that fit in the palm of his hand. "This one's yours."

Warmth pooled in my cheeks as I accepted it. "Thank you so much." It contained a silver ring of spun wire braided together into a rope-like pattern, with lilac and pale green beads marking the center of the ring. "It's gorgeous."

It did not fit. I slid it on every finger, never making it past the knuckle, until I got to my pinkie finger. Only then did it slip on all the way.

Andresh frowned, embarrassed. "I'm sorry. I guess I should've asked for your size."

"Oh no, this works!" I said, holding my finger out to him. "I really like it." I laughed. "I'll never take it off."

Andresh smiled back. "Promise?"

"Promise."

That was my last conversation with Andresh before he and his father left us for the night. And then, by morning, Mother had gone.

Usually, when Mother left, she'd be back early in the day, her hair knotted and wild, the hem of her dress muddied and torn. But she always returned. When Father woke to an empty bed, he tried to reassure the rest of us: "It's been some time since she's done this. I'm sure she needed the fresh air. She'll come back soon."

The night came. And another morning that blossomed into day, and still, she had not appeared.

Father looked for Mother in all of her usual places—the woods behind our house, which we called the Derry; the area surrounding Lake Loaman; and the stretch of fields known as Bentley Green. He even went into town to see if she'd gone there, though it wasn't likely, since she preferred wild places.

He contacted the constable when the sun started setting on the second day of her disappearance. The best answer the uniformed figure could give was, "We'll watch out for her." Father said they couldn't spare the men for the time being because highwaymen had started to populate the older, wooded sections of the King's Road and the law was needed there.

"What if she went in that direction?" I asked him.

"The constable's men will be at the ready," Father said, but he sounded as though he needed reassurance.

Father determined that Mother was out in the Rookwood. There was Rookwood, the village, and then *the* Rookwood, which was named for the expansive forest that stretched on for acres and acres. No one knew why that land was called the Rookwood, as rooks preferred fields to forests, but the name had always been that way as long as anyone could remember.

The forest was enormous, and there was no way Father could cover that much ground on his own. That meant Mother couldn't either, so we would find her easily. Nonetheless, Father had the Zataviers over for breakfast the third morning she was gone, and they planned at the table what to do.

"Of course you can rely on us," Uncle Jolan said. He set his teacup on the table with a hard *clunk*, which startled us. I guess he was as emotional as we were. "We'll load up the wagon and loan you our horses, and we'll all ride out as soon as we're packed."

"I'm coming too," I said after I finished a bite of toast. They needed all the help they could get, and I was growing more and more frightened at the thought that Mother was lost in the woods.

"You should stay here with Eleanor and Grandma Violet, in case your mother comes back," Father said.

"You need as many people as possible searching. Andresh is going, so why can't I? You can have four people searching instead of three."

Father thought about it and tucked a lock of brown hair behind his ear. "I'm worried that you might...that it might be difficult for you...because your mother..." He clenched and unclenched his hands, frustrated. "I think it could be hard for you to see her like that, wild and weird."

"She's come to us that way before," I said. "I won't ever be used to it, but I can handle it." I stared Father down. Maybe I was glaring; maybe I looked determined. Father gazed back at me, but nowhere near as full of conviction as I was.

"I'll watch out for Lily," Andresh said.

"I want to go too!" Nell cried.

"No, I need you to stay with me," Grandma Violet said, wiping her mouth with her napkin. "We need to keep this house warm and safe for your mother to come home to. I can't do everything by myself."

"Fine," Nell grumbled, resting her chin in her hand.

"Can I come?" I pressed Father again.

He hesitated, with a sigh. "You and Andresh are to stick together through all of it. Don't leave each other's sight."

"That still only makes three groups. Four would be better—"

"Stop. It's enough that I'm letting you come along. Don't push it further."

"Fine." I didn't mind staying with Andresh the whole time, but I thought I was old enough to go into the woods on my own and search. But I should've appreciated that he was allowing me to ride along, so I thanked him and started collecting everyone's dishes to put in the sink.

A little over an hour later, I packed a small bag with clothes—we had to prepare in case it was an overnight trip—and Grandma made food to take with us. She sent it out with me, and Father and I headed out to our front yard, where Uncle Jolan had prepared his small wagon for us, along with all four of his horses. Two were hitched to pull the wagon, while Andresh and Jolan had applied tack to the two others.

"I was thinking Andresh could drive the wagon and Lily could ride with him, while Kale and I go on horseback," Uncle Jolan said. "When we get to a good spot in the woods, we can make camp and split up,"

"Remember, you're staying with Andresh the whole time," Father said. "And you'll stick to the known paths. Only Jolan and I will go off them."

"I understand." And I would listen to Father—I was sure another member of the family wandering off somewhere would frighten him even more, and it would be cruel of me to do so.

Father and Uncle Jolan mounted the horses while Andresh stepped up to the wagon seat and grabbed the reins. I scootched up next to him. I didn't want to be by myself, although inside the wagon was far more comfortable—we put bedding for the four of us in there with plenty of pillows. But I was happy to keep company with Andresh.

We waved goodbye to Nell and Grandma Violet as we

headed off, Uncle Jolan and Father flanking us, as we departed down the gravel path away from our home.

When we'd made camp in a small clearing near the Old North Path that ran through the Rookwood, Father and Uncle Jolan went on their way, leaving Andresh and me alone together. Unless the trail deliberately directed us to a landmark like a pond or river nearby, we had to get right back on the path as soon as we were finished exploring—only marked land for us.

I thought we were going to walk there, but once Father and Uncle Jolan were out of sight, Andresh grabbed the saddle for his horse, Imelda. She had been one of the animals pulling the wagon, and her companion, Vindal, was already tethered to a tree with a bucket of water at his feet.

Andresh finished tacking up Imelda and had her guzzle some water before he pulled her along. "You can take Vindal."

I was embarrassed to say it. "I never got a chance to ride, even with Father minding your horses and stables while you were gone. I was...afraid to."

Andresh's jaw dropped a little. "After all this time? Oh. Well, you can ride with me. I'll help you up." He mounted his horse easily and held his hand out to me. "Put your left foot in the stirrup there and slide your right leg up and over. You can grab onto me as you do it."

I took his hand and did as he said, my right foot grazing his back and one of my arms flying to his shoulder as I nearly toppled over.

"Scoot close to me, as close as you can. Don't want our weight to get off-balance; Imelda wouldn't like it."

I gripped him around his waist with both hands, and we rode off in a pleasant gait into the woods.

We varied our pace and stopped sometimes for Imelda, travelling for two hours. We only ran into other people passing through once. It was a small family: parents and a young boy. I asked them if they'd seen anyone with my mother's description, and they said the forest had been empty of people as far as they knew. Andresh and I continued onward, our eyes scanning the distance ahead of us and the woods surrounding us for signs of any beautiful, yet wild, woman alone.

"Do you need a break? I need a break," Andresh said. "You've been doing a good job on the horse, by the way. Can't tell that you're nervous about it." He glanced to the side. "How about that little opening in the woods right there? I think it's called The Traveler's Square, if I can remember the old map correctly."

"That's the smallest field I've ever seen. Do you think it was cleared away for people to camp?"

"Likely. Let's go."

We headed to the little grassy meadow, and he pointed to the remnants of a fire pit in the ground, the wood ashen and gray. "You're right. It's a camp."

"Do you think Mother could've made it out here?"

"It's possible. But I don't know. There's supposed to be marshlands out here close by; could she have gone there?"

He dismounted and shook his legs out, holding his hand up to me so I could lower myself easily. Well, it wasn't so easy—I was clumsy about it and crashed into him. He caught me awkwardly as my chest smashed into his, and he tottered a few steps backward.

"Careful, Lily."

I stepped away from him and smoothed out my skirts as he tethered Imelda to a tree. She went right to chomping on the grass as Andresh headed to the pit. He sat down and stretched his legs out, then reached into his bag to hold out an apple for me. "Want one?"

"Sure." I'd left most of our food back at camp, but Andresh packed snacks while I handled our drinks. As soon as he passed me my apple, he got one out for himself, and I grabbed a flask of water for him. We both sat down on the cool, soft grass.

"I'm sorry about your mother," Andresh said quietly.

"I don't know why this keeps happening," I said. I swallowed, my throat suddenly dry while my eyes grew misty. "I thought she loved us—so why does she keep on leaving?"

"It's happened for years, hasn't it? I know she started running off by the time Father and I moved to Rookwood."

"Yeah. The earliest I remember this happening was when I was six and you were seven. I...I don't know if she dislikes us or if something else is...wrong...with her." I hadn't meant to, but I started crying. No heaving or sobbing, but silent tears that flowed freely down my face.

Andresh wore a pitying expression. He reached out to me and patted my back. We sat there in silence for what felt like forever, but perhaps it was only a few minutes.

"You know, there's something I've been dying to show you," Andresh said after my tears had stopped and the silence became overwhelming. He spoke carefully and seriously. "You can't tell anyone about it."

"Sounds dangerous," I said with a weak smile. I started wiping the streaks the tears left on my face, and Andresh handed me the kerchief he'd kept in the pocket of his tailcoat. I wiped my face off and refolded the cloth. When I went to hand it back to him, he shook his head. "Keep it."

"I will." I tucked it into my apron pocket and scooted a little closer to him. "What's this big secret you have for me?" I worked hard to make my voice sound brighter, but I wasn't sure it worked.

"It's something I learned in Sindalia. During my visit I learned more about the old ways, the traditions passed down through the centuries, through the family. The Zataviers are really old in Sindalia, you know. And they have a lot of secrets." He suddenly put his uneaten apple back in his bag and hopped to his feet. "There's one I want to show you."

He headed over to the fire pit. "I'm going to call this fire out." And he got down on his knees, leaning over the old, burnt-out kindling, holding his hand above it. He closed his eyes and started muttering to himself, repeating words that sounded nothing like I'd ever heard before, like the whoosh of air through the trees, or rocks tumbling down a mountain. It wasn't so much the sound, but the sheer force and momentum of the language he used that summoned those images to my mind.

"Is that Sindalian?"

"Shh," he said. "Yes, and no." He added a bit apologetically, "I need to concentrate."

I had no idea what he was doing, with his eyes squinched shut, his hand out and shaking, and his lips barely moving as the words poured out of him.

After a moment, he opened an eye, his brow raised. "Hmm. I'll try one more time."

He repeated the same strange cadence of words as before, his voice coming out stronger, and...nothing happened.

"Damn it. I thought for sure it would work since I learned its name. Guess I'll have to do it the oldest way."

"What do you mean by 'learned its name?'"

"I'm talking magic."

"Whoa, whoa, whoa, what?"

"That's why you can't tell anybody. It's a secret."

"But magic's not real, though. It's a mere sleight of the hand, or a showman's illusion."

"You'll believe me when I show you."

"That you learned magic in Sindalia?"

"My relatives in Sindalia happen to keep it alive. They showed me three ways to do magic—by Word, by Deed, and by Will. I tried to do magic by Word. It's where you use the full name, the true name, of what you want to call. I used the true name for fire, but it didn't work. And that's because it's more complicated than simply speaking. It requires a lot of strength behind it, to use the right word and mean what you say when you say it. So, most people who do magic go by Deed. A series of actions to, uh, wake the magic up, so to speak. And that's what I'll do now."

"Does everything have a true name?"

"Yup. That's the oldest magic there is. After all, the first thing to bring life into the world was the Word, and words are names, aren't they?"

"How do you know your true name?"

"Well...I'm not sure about that. It's a secret to everyone, but if you hear it, you know. Some say it's the first word your parents thought when they knew they would have you, or the first words uttered when you were born. But not only the words, the feelings, too. I can't explain it very well."

"One last question before you do whatever Deed you're planning. In magic by Will—do you think something, and it's done?"

"Pretty much. Magic by Will is all about intention. You can change the shape of things or change their course. It's the most powerful magic there is."

"Can your family back in Sindalia do that?"

He gave me a secret little smile, then clapped his hands, as if he was preparing to do something big. "Don't laugh. I'm going to dance."

I laughed anyway. He was doing a great job at distracting

me from the real reason why we were in the forest. "I've never seen you dance!"

"Quiet, and watch," he said, grinning. He stood still, raising his arms above his head, and his wrists flicked and beat the air to an unheard rhythm. He alternated one foot in front of the other, gliding the bottom of his boots along the grass in a fluid motion as his legs crossed each other, ending it with a well-timed clap of the hand.

His hands turned circles in the air, still moving by the wrists, and added his hips to it, rolling them to match the movements of his hands. He ended the hip roll with the slightest thrust of his pelvis, something subtle but noticeable at the same time.

My face grew warm as a strange flutter tickled my stomach. I tried to concentrate on Andresh's face but couldn't. I looked past him, over his shoulder, to keep my eyes from wandering downward.

That stopped him. "What is it?"

"The dance is a little..." I struggled to find the right word. I mumbled, "Intense."

"There's a reason I'm moving my body this way. I'm not trying to, well..." He cleared his throat. "When we do this, we're fire." His wrists moved again as his hands pulsed in the air: "We flicker." He did the glide steps: "We flash, and we move." He clapped his hands: "We crackle..." His hips moved once more, then came the thrust: "...and we pop. Same as the fire." He lowered his arms. "This is how we wake the flames up. This is what the magic chooses to answer to."

"Does Uncle Jolan know you've gotten into this stuff?"

Andresh hesitated. "He does, but he's not very, uh, enthusiastic about it. He'd probably kill me if he knew I was showing you this."

"So why are you?"

"I trust you," he said simply. "We've known each other for like seven years, ever since we were little. You're my best friend. Of course I'd trust you."

For some reason I couldn't bring myself to come right out and say he was my best friend, too, when a weird little thought popped in my head: *Is he only your friend?*

Andresh nodded his head at me, with a smile at the corner of his mouth, and started over again from the beginning. After he rolled his hips, he bent forward at his waist and held his hands out, palms facedown and fingers spread wide. He drew his arms back to his body, then thrust them out again. He wiggled his fingers rapidly as he raised his arms above his head and ended it with a loud clap once his hands reached above his crown. His waist circled again, but instead of the pop of his hips, he clapped his hands above his head one more time.

He repeated the sequence again, and the ashes on the old kindling twitched. The ground in the pit also crumbled, as if something long buried there was trying to break out. An orange-red sliver, the size of a finger, sprouted from the ground —a flame.

"It needs more power." He waved me over. "Come on. Dance with me."

I froze. "But I don't know what to do."

"You've seen me do it twice now. Copy my moves. It doesn't have to be perfect. The effort and intention are what count."

"I don't know if I can move my hips like that," I said, suddenly shy.

"I won't tease you, promise. I was a little embarrassed myself when I first did it. But when you do the dance, it's amazing—it's like you can feel this energy pulsing through you as you do it. You should try it. Here. Go on the other side of the pit, facing me." Once I was there, he called, "Are you ready? Start!"

I copied him move for move. It wasn't as hard as I thought it would be, but I didn't share his skill. He looked like he had trained all his life for it, whereas I was always a half-beat behind him, completely unable to control what my body was doing. When it came to the hip rolls and thrusting, I kept it demure, for Mother's sake.

But there was joy in it, and a warm, buzzing energy that enveloped my body. We kept repeating the steps, and I couldn't stop laughing as I failed to mimic Andresh's grace. He grinned at me, pointing to the pit. I hadn't been paying attention. Fire the size of a fist brewed there—it wasn't spreading or growing from that little shard of orange earlier but kept coming up directly through the ground.

"Let's get it roaring," Andresh said. "Keep going!"

We moved again and again until we were out of breath from giggling and dancing. The kindling and old wood blazed now, a perfect bonfire.

I rushed over to the spot where we sat down earlier and made a great show of swooning and crashing to the ground. I stretched out on my back, crossing my legs over each other, like a dancer who moved on the tips of her toes. "I'll never forget this, for as long as I live."

Andresh circled around and joined me. His face was rosy from exertion as he sat down next to me. "Yes. And we have a strong fire burning." He leaned over me, and his lips were on mine.

It was a simple kiss, a light velvet touch, but I jerked my face away from his. All my muscles tightened, and my face grew hot as I sat upright and stammered, "What did you do that for?"

"It just felt like I should." He paused. "You didn't like it?"

"I… I don't know." It was true. I didn't know. I was far too stunned to understand what happened. I didn't hate it, but I had no idea what made him want to kiss me.

"I can try again," he offered.

"Oh, no you don't," I protested, but he took my arm and pulled me toward him. Before he could kiss me again, I hit him as hard as I could on the head with my fist. That stopped him. He let me go.

"Ouch! You didn't have to—" he started, rubbing the side of his head above the temple. Before he could finish, I hopped to my feet and took off running. I wasn't sure if what I'd done was smart or stupid, but I needed to stop him. I couldn't handle another kiss from him. Not on a day like this one.

"Lily! Come back here!" Andresh hollered after me. I moved quickly, darting through the tiny meadow and through a cluster of trees, as he was coming up to me fast. There was another clearing up ahead, filled with all sorts of plants and varying shades of green and yellow and brown.

"Lily! I'm sorry, alright? I should've asked first. I wasn't a gentleman." He sounded genuinely apologetic, but I felt like the wind had overpowered my legs and propelled me forward without any thoughts in my head. "Let's head back," he said. "I'll put the fire out. I'm really sorry."

"I can find my own way back," I said stubbornly. He was a few feet behind me.

"But you don't know where you're going! The marshes!"

Andresh's warning came too late. I barreled recklessly into the wet mire, unaware of its depths until the cold water was up to my navel. Gold and green algae surrounded me on all sides as my feet sank into the muddy floor. Several water lilies floated ahead of me while groups of tall cattail reeds hovered above them and blew in the wind.

I lifted each foot up from the bottom of the marsh, trying to shake the slime off them. The water rolled against me in small waves as I moved. The golden algae that encircled me curled itself around the green and brushed up against my waist.

I stared at the gold. It seemed lighter than the other plants, more fluid. It shone brilliantly in the water against the dull greens and browns of the marsh. It moved in its own pattern, separate from the darker tufts of algae that floated with it. I seized a handful of it, rubbing it between my fingers. My heart stopped.

I was holding her hair. My mother's beautiful cornsilk hair.

CHAPTER 2

Arms slid underneath my shoulders and lifted me up. Water rushed down from above, and my nostrils burned as my head slumped back on my neck. When it no longer hurt, I opened my eyes. Andresh's hazy form came into focus.

"I've got you." His voice trembled, betraying his attempt to be calm. He pulled me to my feet and steadied me by wrapping my arm around him, and he walked us out of the marsh.

Though I could see Andresh, everything around us was still a blur. "What happened?"

"You... You were screaming. And then you fell. You went under but I got you."

"Did you—could you—?" I couldn't bring myself to say it.

"Yes. I saw it."

A frenzied, desperate hope overcame me. "It isn't—it isn't!" I freed myself from his grasp and hurried back into the sludge towards the floating mass of yellow. My hands shook as I reached out to the golden hair that twisted and twirled in tiny ripples.

My hands stopped. In the brownish water, amid all the gold, was my reflection; a hazy, dim figure that looked like myself...

And beneath the surface, my mother's white nightgown billowed around her. Her arms slowly floated upward, as if she were reaching for me to hug me.

Andresh stepped towards me. "Lily, no!"

Without registering him, my fingers stretched to hers, and I felt the solidness of her hands. I reached into the water, wrapping my arms around my mother in an embrace, lifting her up.

A mistake. A terrible mistake.

As soon as she broke the surface, a cloud of putrefaction—the smell of decay, coupled with the muck and mire of the marsh—enveloped me. The air seemed to turn a thick and sour greenish brown, and the odor was so sharp, it felt like hot needles pricked the inside of my nostrils and stuck themselves in the back of my throat.

Her bloated form, her beautiful eyes gone, her lips chewed away—I dropped her body and moved aside to vomit into the water. "Oh my God, oh my God."

Andresh held his arms out to me, stepping into the marsh's edge, shaking. "Please," he said, his voice wavering, "come back."

I ran to him, sobbing; my knees buckled. Once again, he had to prop me up, and he hurried me out of there. "We've got to go. We've got to tell your father."

Andresh went to the fire we'd made and said something in another language, then tapped the ground with his foot.

The fire went out.

I was too horror-struck to remark on the additional evidence of magic before me. In fact, I was now an automaton, except one that was broken down, unable to perform the most basic of movements, a lifeless metal doll. I could not think on my own; Andresh had to think for me. I could not move on my own; Andresh had to move for me.

He took me by my shoulders again and gently pushed me forward, walking me over to where he'd kept Imelda. He looked at me with worry, the corners of his mouth turned down while his brows furrowed. He eyed his horse. "Do you have it in you to ride with me like last time? I'll be going faster."

I didn't answer him.

"Hold on to me tight, like you did before."

After untying Imelda, he climbed up onto her easily while peering at me with concern. He held out his arm to me once more, and I latched onto him as I struggled to put my foot in the stirrup and slide my leg over the back of the horse.

Once I was up there, Andresh made a clicking sound, tongue against teeth, and he lightly kicked in his heels. Imelda broke off into a trot. Andresh coaxed her into a gallop as we rejoined the Old North Path, heading south this time to retrace the steps we'd taken.

I swallowed, my throat thickening. I could taste the marsh and decay, and a wave of the foul odor that had come from my mother's body swarmed my nostrils.

I weakened, my grip on Andresh loosened, and I teetered on the horse.

Imelda snorted, and Andresh shouted back at me, "You need to hold on. If you move too far off, it'll mess up our balance, and she'll buck."

I scooted forward towards the saddle and squeezed Andresh's waist, hard. I buried my face in his back, taking in the smell of his jacket, something warm and grassy, but with the faint trace of a musk. I breathed him in, trying to drive out the scent of death that I couldn't dispel, but a wave of rot—so thick I could almost see it—surrounded me. I let go of Andresh and waved frantically at the air. I teetered back on the saddle as a cold chill climbed up my spine and settled at the back of my neck.

Andresh shouted at me as Imelda's ears flicked back on her head and she snorted again, speeding up her pace. "Stop it! Stop moving!" Andresh tried to shift forward in his seat, but I couldn't stop myself from clinging on to him. I tried to push myself towards him, but instead I drew him back towards me. I knew I had to let go of him so we could regain our balance, but the smell of the marshes seemed to chase after us, like an invisible cloud hovering close by.

Imelda snorted again and jerked her head down toward the ground. "No, Imelda, no!" Andresh yanked hard on her reins to bring her head up. He squeezed his legs against her body, tighter this time. "Come on, girl. We're fine, we're—"

Imelda defiantly lowered her head, and we were thrown forward. I slammed against Andresh's back and in the next second lost my grip when the horse reared and started to buck violently. Andresh shouted my name as I flew off her.

White lights flashed in my eyes when I landed face-first against the trunk of a tree. A wave of heat and nausea flooded me as I sobbed from the pain, which wove itself in knots around my skull. Blood gushed from a large, pulpy wound in my forehead. I wiped my eyes, frantic to clear the red from them, but the blood flowed too fast. I held them shut as Andresh grunted and Imelda kicked and stomped.

There was an awful, fleshy smack, and Andresh cried out as the horse galloped off, heading down the path at full speed. He moaned before uttering a pained, "Damn it."

I tried to move but my head felt so heavy. It dropped to the ground like an anvil, my body barely attached to it as I fell. "Andresh!"

He took a shaky breath. "Ugh..."

My heart thumped in my head as I rose to my feet and stood propped against the tree. I wiped my eyes and searched for Andresh, who lay sprawled on the ground further up the path.

"Andresh!" I stumbled towards him. Lightheaded, I fell back down to my knees. I crumpled at his feet, retching as the scent of the marshes burned through me. I had already expelled everything I had in me earlier; this time a clear, thin liquid came out.

I wiped my mouth on my sleeve and brushed the crimson from my eyes. "I am so sorry. Are you hurt?"

"Lil-ly," he panted. He rolled onto his left side. His right shoulder was dislocated, and his entire arm hung at a horrible angle. "Hold on." He propped himself up with his good arm and grunted from the effort. He squeezed his eyes shut and took a pained breath before opening them again. "You're bleeding," he said. "It's bad..."

"I know. You are too." Red painted his mouth and chin from a gash on his bottom lip.

The immediate danger we were in, and the injuries we had, broke me out of my stupor. I was almost thankful I wasn't thinking about Mother. My thoughts were only of Andresh.

"I'm sorry," I sobbed. "I didn't mean to get you hurt."

The pounding in my head and another wave of dizziness knocked me over.

"Lily!"

I couldn't move. My vision clouded with blood, and I blacked out.

My mother's bloated body plagued my sleep. I let out a garbled scream as I woke up. I was lying on the floor of the wagon, buried underneath blankets, my father kneeling at my side. He finished applying a salve to my forehead.

"It was only a nightmare," he said gently. "Sit up. I'm almost done." He held my hair back and wrapped a bandage around my head, securing it tightly. There was a pounding soreness to my wound, as if my heart was beating in it, but luckily the rest of my head didn't ache anymore.

Uncle Jolan approached us from the back, carrying an empty bottle. He sidestepped me and Father as he tucked the bottle into a drawer in a run-down cabinet nailed to the bottom floor of the wagon.

"I gave him another valerian draft," Uncle Jolan said quietly to Father, "so he can sleep through the pain."

"Andresh?" I turned and spotted him in the bedding at the back of the wagon. He was shirtless, his arm in a makeshift sling. He blinked at me in response, looking completely out of sorts, and closed his eyes.

"He carried you all the way back here, with a dislocated shoulder. Imelda never came back. But we don't have time to search for her. You're much more important."

My face crumpled as tears flowed freely. "I'm so sorry. It was all my fault. I made her buck until she threw us off. It's just —after what I saw—" and Father cut me off by grabbing me in a tight embrace. Uncle Jolan nodded and stepped away.

"I'm glad you weren't more seriously hurt," Father said, his voice breaking. "I couldn't bear to lose another."

"Did you... Did you see her?" I had to swallow in between my words. I could barely get them out.

"Andresh warned me not to look. The undertaker and his men took her from the marshes. They're cleaning her up now, but they say they can't—they're not able to fix—" He started weeping. "I don't know if I will ever be able to look at her after hearing what happened to her. I'm sorry you had to see her that way." He wiped his eyes and let me go. "We'll be heading back. Jolan will drive the wagon, and I'll follow along on Vindal."

My nose had started running along with my tears, and I wiped my face. I was greeted with the terrible scent of rot and mire. I gagged and tore my hands away. "The smell. It's still there."

I scrambled out of my bedding and searched the wagon for water and a washing basin. There was one at Andresh's feet, used, but I didn't care. I thrust my hands in the water and started rubbing my fingers furiously, despite the absence of soap. I dragged my nails across my palms, trying to get those cleaned, too, along with Andresh's ring.

Uncle Jolan came to me with a jar of powder he pulled from the cabinet in the wagon. He quickly dumped some of its contents in the water, and little soap bubbles formed the more I scrubbed. The faint smell of lemons permeated the wagon, and I was grateful for it. I wiped my hands on a towel Uncle Jolan handed to me and took another sniff of my fingers.

It smelled mostly sweet, but there was an underlying sourness, a darker scent, beneath it all. It would take more than one wash to get rid of it, but at least it wasn't flooding my nostrils anymore.

"I appreciate it," I told Uncle Jolan.

"I'm surprised it still works, to be honest," he said. "I only swapped out some supplies before leaving. That scrub must be at least two years old." He placed the jar back in with the other items in the cabinet. "I think we're ready to go, you two."

Father nodded. "Stay with Andresh. Keep an eye on him. If he wakes up, see if he needs more medicine. Jolan's got it marked in the cabinet; it's in the green bottle." He kissed my cheek, then eyed my bandage. "Lily. It's going to scar," he said, his voice solemn.

My mouth opened, and it took a moment for the sound to come out. "How bad is it?"

Father gave me a sad look. "I know you must be overwhelmed, going through so many emotions right now. But please, stay here and take care of Andresh," he said. He headed out the front of the wagon. Uncle Jolan joined him, and soon the wagon lurched to a start.

I sighed and took a seat at Andresh's bedside. I wasn't sure how much help I could be to him, especially with him asleep. I watched his chest rise and fall, suddenly fearful he'd stop breathing, and once I recognized the rhythm of his breaths, signaling he had no trouble at all, I relaxed a little.

Andresh. With such long, thick eyelashes. Nicer than mine. Even nicer than Nell's.

My gaze wandered to his mouth, and I flashed back to the moment he kissed me.

No. Don't think about it. It doesn't matter now, not when Andresh is hurt, your father is suffering, and your mother is dead.

That thought snapped me out of it as the words echoed once more in my mind: *Your mother is dead.*

The tears welled up inside me and fell freely. I gasped, and I hiccuped, and let out a moan, then slammed my hands over my mouth. I needed to quiet down or I'd wake Andresh.

I took some slow breaths, and with that, the tears still came, but I'd calmed down enough to try and think about what all had been going on with Mother.

My relationship with her was never as warm or as close as I wanted it to be. I always wondered if she felt trapped by all of us, and that's why she took to her disappearances—to get away from her family. And with such thoughts, I couldn't help but feel the pain of rejection every time she left. But that never erased the love I had for her. Over the past few years, I missed her greatly as she continued to distance herself from us, and now, she was gone forever.

What led her to her death? Was it an accident? Was it on purpose? Something about all of it didn't sit well with me. I replayed the last moments we had together in my mind.

My mother had been sitting in front of her vanity, combing the lustrous yellow hair that cascaded down her back in waves. She repeated the strokes absentmindedly, one solitary gesture, and her green eyes seemed as dead as a doll's—gazing ahead into the glass. Her warm, peachy skin seemed two shades paler than usual.

"Mother?" I called her from the doorway to my parents' bedroom. She didn't look up; she didn't answer. "Are you alright?"

I crossed over to her, stood behind her, and watched her combing for what felt like forever. "Do you see something in the mirror?" I asked her, for she kept looking into it.

"I see myself," Mother said, sounding wistful and far away. "I look different. My skin is like crepe paper, my bones are jutting out of my face. I'm older now. It's too late for me..." She set her comb on the table but wouldn't meet my eyes, and my visit to her room ended with her telling me to leave.

I would never know the meaning of her words. The time to ask was gone.

I bowed forward, burying my face in my hands. Lemon and death. I pulled my hands away and decided I would say nothing about my last meeting with Mother, nothing at all.

I sat there uselessly for a few minutes, my mind jumping from one thought to the next. I smoothed my hair back from my forehead and my palm met the bandage there. My injury pulsed where I touched it.

Father said it would scar. He wouldn't tell me how bad it was, so it must have been truly awful.

I debated with myself as to whether I should take a look at it, undoing Father's careful work, but I couldn't keep my curiosity at bay. I needed to know the extent of it.

I searched the wagon for a mirror of some kind; any reflective surface that might show me what I wanted to know. At the back of the wagon, all sorts of things were stored, but piled up like it was junk rather than something valuable: extra saddles, lots of rope, two wooden chairs haphazardly stacked, and an old toolbox. I couldn't see any mirrors there.

I headed to Uncle Jolan's cabinet and started sifting through the drawers. In the middle one, I found a small hand mirror with a crack in the corner of it. I untied the back of my bandage and unraveled it from my forehead, then held the mirror up to my face.

The fissure in the mirror lined up exactly with my forehead, the lines of my wound matching the mirror's own. It was as though I was made of glass, and my forehead had cracked on impact. Ragged lines jutted out of it in a circular motion, like the rings on a spiderweb.

The mirror clouded up. My reflection was clear, but the space behind me was empty, save for a blooming cloud of dark, swampy colors.

A greenish-gray hand clutched my shoulder. My body jerked as I felt the fingers dig in, but when I reached to tear the hand away from me, I touched nothing.

Nothing was there, and yet in the mirror, the hand remained.

Another one climbed up my back—oh God, I could feel it—and from behind me, the woman in the marshes appeared, the thing that was my mother but at the same time wasn't. Her lips chewed away. Her eyes gone. Her face and body showing signs of bloat. Her hair, stringy and floating around her in the air.

She made a sound between a gasp and a choke, and vomited water, but only in the mirror. Yet I could feel the coldness splash over me and smell her putrid odor.

I gagged and swallowed back bile as the woman croaked out, “Save me. Please.” Still gripping my shoulder, she pointed at us, at our reflection. “Open the door. You’re the only one who can.”

I tried to wriggle out of her hold on me, but her fingers dug into my skin. There was a low hum that grew to an angry buzz. It seemed like it was coming from the woman, yet at the same time, all over the wagon. The sound grew deafening, and my hands flew to my ears as I winced. The woman opened her mouth again, and hundreds of flies escaped from her, swarming us. I threw the mirror at one of the wooden columns supporting the wagon roof, and the glass shattered.

I felt my arms where she’d gotten me—sore, but no blood. I looked over to Andresh to see if he stirred, but he was still.

I stood there for what felt like forever, trying to catch my breath. Then I realized it was dangerous to leave glass strewn about, so I found a brush and a bin and placed the now-empty hand mirror into it. I swept the glass up.

At first, I saw nothing. The walls and ceiling of the wagon were the only things in the pieces. Nothing happened...until I saw my reflection in the glass once more.

The woman gaped up at me. “Save me.”

I scrambled to get the remaining glass up, then headed to the end of the wagon to the back door and tossed the bits of mirror out into the dirt road behind us.

I fell into a heap on the floor, burying my face in my hands as I sobbed. “Oh God. Mother.”

CHAPTER 3

When we arrived at home, Father had the task of telling the family what happened. Grandma Violet's face crumpled, while Nell looked peaked, but said nothing. She stood there, pallid and silent, as if she were shocked into a stupor. Meanwhile, Father and I both cried as he told them Mother was dead.

Father asked me to go upstairs with Nell as he needed to speak more with Grandma. I didn't know what to do for us to pass the time—neither one of us felt like playing—so I decided to grab Nell's favorite book from downstairs, *Marcy in the Garden,* for her to read to me. She often read by the fireplace, so the book was likely there.

And that's when I heard it. On the stairwell I stood, unseen, while Father spoke in a hushed voice: "...Stones in her pockets."

Grandma Violet's voice broke. "She meant for it to happen." It wasn't a question.

Mother killed herself.

I turned on my heel and rushed up the stairs, but my feet

clomped on the steps and that drew Father and Grandma's attention.

"Lily!" Father called after me.

I came back down, wiping tears from my eyes.

"You *cannot* share this with your sister," he said, grabbing my shoulders. It was firm but didn't hurt me; not like the visions I had of Mother in the mirror.

"I won't. I wouldn't dare."

"I'll tell her when she's older," Father said. "She has a right to know, but it can't be now."

"I understand."

Father pulled me into an embrace, and I asked him, "Why did she do it?"

He let go of me. "I don't know. She must have... She must have been very sick."

The thought crossed my mind: *Was Mother mentally ill?* It was a painful thought, and I couldn't say if it was true or not. But something had always been off about her. Was she so desperate that she wanted to die?

And it hit me that I would never know. None of us would. And that was going to be something we'd all have to live with.

I kept my thoughts to myself and headed back up the stairs with Nell's book in my hand. She took it from me, and we headed to the bed we shared in Grandma's room, where she curled up at my side. She propped the book open and read it to me, each of us trying to distract ourselves from reality.

The next morning was the burial at St. Briscol's Cemetery. Father said goodbye to his "one and only love, Estella Anna," and Nell and I said farewell to our "beloved Mother, who we will always love." The casket was closed at the funeral, but every time I pictured Mother in the box, I could only see her image from the marsh and in the mirror.

The mirror. Every time I looked into one, it was only a

matter of seconds before she reappeared, begging me to save her somehow, and to "open the door." I had no idea what she meant by any of it, and I started to wonder if I had something to do with her death, because of how she haunted me. She wanted *me* to save her—did I let her down somehow? Did she ask for help from me, in her own way, before she died? Why couldn't I see what had been happening?

The problem was, before I could ask her about any of it, the images and sensations in the mirror would get worse. The flies would appear and crawl over my body, and I felt the bites and their attempts to get inside my nostrils, my mouth, my ears. I could never look into the mirror past that point. I always had to turn the glass facedown or run out of the room.

It wasn't only mirrors, either. Any reflective surface was a danger to me. The first time I went to take a bath since the mirror incident in the wagon, I saw her again when the water had stilled, and I could see my reflection. She appeared behind me and reached out to me, as though she was going to come up out of the water. I screamed and jetted out of the tub, scaring everyone in the house.

Grandma Violet and Father treated me like a fragile porcelain doll. In a way, almost like they had treated Mother before she died—speaking to me in hushed, gentle tones and escorting me to places I could easily manage to get to, like the chair or down the steps. They looked at me with concern and hugged me more often, too.

They must have thought I was going mad. And I was, a little. Well, more than a little, given what I saw whenever I looked at myself.

The visions weren't all that plagued me. No matter how often I washed and scented my hands, I would always smell an undercurrent of death on them. For a while I thought it was Andresh's ring, like something from Mother must have attached to it, but Father cleaned and polished it and told me nothing was amiss, and that I could continue to wear it if I wanted.

I wanted to wear it because Andresh gave it to me. I wanted him to know I cherished it, and that no terrible memory would ever stain it. So I kept it on my finger, even when I scrubbed my skin raw and red.

Nell noticed something was wrong with me immediately. And it was good for her to, because I distracted her from feeling sorrow for Mother. Of course she felt awful losing her, but with me clearly falling apart, she had something to focus on instead of her grief.

Nell noticed I'd stopped looking at myself. "You're sad," she said wistfully, wrapping her arms around me. "I know you feel bad. I feel bad, too." She'd take a brush and go through my hair, trying to keep its sheen and discourage tangling. Not that my hair could curl or tangle or frizz—it was stick-straight. I continued to wear my hair long and loose. Nell brushed it for me, but when she tried to style it, the most I'd let her do was tie a ribbon on a lock of it.

I was sadder than I admitted, and it wasn't all the horrors in the mirror.

Looking back to the day of the funeral, I remembered Nell seemed to be the toughest one of us all. Silent tears ran down Father's cheeks; Grandma Violet kept dabbing her face with a handkerchief; my body shook with all my sobbing. Meanwhile Nell held onto my hand and patted my back.

She looked upset—her eyes were glassy, but she didn't cry. Her mouth was a thin line most of the time, but when she gave me a "there, there, Lily," she managed a tired but honest smile. I had no idea how she had the energy to comfort me, but she did.

Andresh and his father were at the funeral, too. Andresh's

face mimicked Father's and Grandma Violet's, where he looked at me with worry, his eyebrows turned slightly up, his dark blue eyes kind, and his mouth shaped into the smallest of frowns. A tiny glimpse of his new scar—from where he bit his lip when he was thrown off his horse—revealed itself in his forlorn expression.

He stood next to me during the ceremony, but Nell was busy providing comfort, so he didn't say anything or hold my hand. His presence was enough for me.

I didn't remember much else after that. Father stayed behind at the grave while the rest of us headed back to our homes. At some point, Andresh and Uncle Jolan left us, but not before giving us a basket of bread and cakes. Somehow throughout the day, I managed to do chores and eat food and entertain Nell. I couldn't recall what we did, or how we accomplished anything. The day passed by in a blur.

The weeks did, too. I tried my best to come across as normal and unchanged by Mother's death, but my insistence on avoiding mirrors and obsessively cleaning my hands did not go unnoticed. My fingertips started cracking and stung with every movement, so I moved them slowly. Father tried to talk to me about my behavior, but I managed to excuse it with something that was mostly the truth: "I feel guilty. I can't bear to look at myself. And I still feel dirty from the marshes." Father and Grandma Violet left me to my washing and didn't try to press me further about the mirrors, accepting my explanation with a pitying sigh.

And so things continued on this way for a good while, and it only got worse from there. Two months after Mother died, I was busy cleaning my hands in the kitchen sink when a frantic knocking at our door pulled me away from what I was doing. Grandma was with me in the kitchen pulling feathers from a duck, and she gestured to get the door.

It flung open before I could reach it. Andresh stood there, tears running down his face. His breathing came out shaky, and his voice trembled. "Please help. I think he's dead."

Father was in the middle of coming down the stairs when he heard Andresh speak. "Jolan?"

Andresh gave a quick nod and ran back out the door, Father following him. I trailed them by a few steps, but Father nearly barked at me: "Stay back, Lily. You don't need to see."

I was so shocked by the harshness in his voice that I halted. It could be that he meant I didn't need to see another dead body. He could be worried that doing so would alter my behavior even more. But I listened to him. I looked at Andresh one more time, not knowing what to say, but he didn't see me. He was sprinting towards his house, Father rushing after him.

I retreated to the kitchen. Grandma Violet peered at me, stricken. "Did he say it was Jolan? That Jolan might be dead?"

"Yes." My voice barely came out.

Nell came down the stairs, singing a wordless little song to herself. She froze when she saw us.

"What's wrong?" She looked frightened. "Nothing with Father, right?"

"Uncle Jolan. Something terrible happened. Father's over there with Andresh now," I said.

"We'll wait for the news," Grandma said. "In the meantime, girls, help me in the kitchen."

Grandma Violet continued working on the duck while Nell and I chopped vegetables.

It wasn't long before Father came back, dazed and out of breath, and he stumbled in to see us.

All the color had left his face, except his light brown eyes, which were glossy, the whites colored pink. Tears fell. "Andresh wouldn't let me go to the undertaker for him. He's riding into town himself."

"Uncle Jolan is...gone?" I had trouble saying the words.

"He was lying face down in the backyard, oats scattered all around him, as though he was on his way to the stables. We moved him and covered him with a sheet—" Father sobbed. "Andresh didn't see what happened. He found him like that. His heart gave out, or, or—" Father buried his face in his hands, and his shoulders bobbed from crying.

Andresh lost his last remaining parent. Father lost his best friend. We lost a man so close to us, we called him "Uncle." So much tragedy in such a small amount of time. I couldn't process it. It was as though we were meant to grieve, and only that.

We all stayed quiet for a while.

Grandma Violet's face was frozen in shock. Her eyes were wide, her mouth slightly open. She spoke at last. "He showed no signs of illness, did he? He was fine when we all saw him last!"

"We have no idea what it could be," Father said gravely.

"What about Andresh?" I asked. "He's got no other family here."

"I know." Father wiped his eyes and took a breath. His voice sounded a little sturdier than before. "I know it's abrupt, but I was thinking, if Andresh wished it, I could take him on as a son. He could live with us."

I had no problem with Andresh moving in. But if Father would make Andresh his son, that meant he would become our brother. And something deep within me, something selfish, didn't want that at all. I could never look at him that way. Not after he had kissed me.

I turned the ring on my finger around in a circle, unsure of what to do. But I knew I would say nothing. We needed to do whatever was in Andresh's best interest, and if we could be his family, we would. If we could give him a home, we should.

"Let's feed him at the very least," Grandma said. "Girls."

We all headed back to the kitchen with her, but before we did, I gave Father a hug. "I'm so sorry you lost your friend," I said to him.

"I'm sorry he's gone for you too. For us and for Andresh. This shouldn't have happened."

"What are you going to do while we're working on the food?"

"I'm going to go back to their house. Finish feeding the horses, clean up the mess, and sit with Jolan while waiting for Andresh to come back."

After Andresh returned, the undertaker took Uncle Jolan away in his carriage. Andresh said he was too upset to be alone in his house, so he stayed with us. We fed him, we prepared the settee for him to sleep on, and we waited to listen should he wish to speak, but he said very little. He seemed numb.

The day of the funeral came and went, and it was down to business afterward. It felt wrong—we should have spent more time grieving, but there was the matter of the will and the inheritance to be dealt with. Father had been named executor, and the Zatavier house and everything therein had been left to Andresh. Uncle Jolan had amassed a fortune he spoke little about, due to investing in different schemes in Sindalia, and he left most of it to Andresh, and a chunk of it to us, calling us in the will his "second family." It was a shock to us all, the amounts listed, because the Zataviers lived rather humbly. We had always known that they had more money than we did, and it never bothered us at all. But we had no idea they were wealthy.

It made me think on Mother's death. There was no talk of a will or inheritance when she had passed. Father mentioned nothing at all, and neither did Grandma Violet. It was because Mother married Father against her family's wishes, and there was nothing to inherit because of it. We never saw Mother's family, anyway. I was sure Father sent word to them, but at the funeral, nothing was sent from their side, and no words given.

Funny how families could be so different from one another.

One week passed after Uncle Jolan's death, and we were all seated at the supper table when Father spoke. "Andresh, my boy...I've been thinking about this seriously. If you wish it, you can join our family. You won't have to be alone."

Andresh's eyes glistened for a moment. He swallowed his food and set his fork down. "I've been thinking, too. And...I want to go to back to Sindalia."

I froze.

Nell spoke the words that entered my mind: "Why do you want to go so far away?"

"Now, now, Eleanor. Andresh has his reasons." Father took a sip of his wine. "You still have family there, don't you? Is that why you want to go?"

"That's not the only reason, but yes, I'd like to return to them. There's so much I don't know about them, but I liked every person I met."

"It's only a visit, right?" My voice came out higher than I wanted it to.

"No. It won't be."

I immediately lost my appetite.

"You'll come and see us sometimes, won't you?" Nell asked.

"It may be a while at first, but I know I'll see all of you again." He cut up the beef on his plate into smaller pieces. "I want to sell the house, though. Sell everything. Clear it all out." He nibbled on a piece of meat before speaking again. "Will you help me, Mr. Bellamy?"

"Of course. But...this is all very sudden. Are you certain this is what you want to do?"

"Yes. There are things I must take care of in Sindalia. And I need to see my family there. I hope all of you understand."

"With you selling the house and all, it doesn't seem like you plan to come back." I pushed my plate aside and rose from my chair. Without excusing myself properly, I disappeared up into the bedroom and climbed into bed, sitting upright under the covers against the wall.

I knew I was acting childish. But Andresh—my best friend, and perhaps something more—was leaving us. I couldn't bear to lose another person I cared so deeply about.

He knocked on my door shortly after. "Lily? Can I come in?"

"As you wish."

He entered the room, and looked at me, like he wasn't sure where he should go. I patted a spot on the bed that was empty, and he sat down by my side. "I'm sorry I have to leave."

"You don't have to."

"I don't think I can explain properly why I feel I must go, but I do. You have to trust me. And you have to trust that someday I'll come back and see you again."

"But Sindalia is so far away!" It was a month on a ship to get there.

"I know, I know. But I need to see my family. They can help me. And I want to see them again."

I sniffled. I felt so stupid, acting whiny and immature around him. I tried to hold back my tears but ended up wiping my eyes when they fell anyway.

"You have to write to us, at the very least," I said.

"Sure. Write to me too."

I leaned against his shoulder. "I'm sorry. You have a good reason to leave, and I don't want you to. I know I'm being selfish."

"It's normal for you to feel sad. I feel sad too, but I know in my heart that this is what I should do."

He took my hand and gently kissed my knuckles. He let go of me and headed to the door before giving me a long-lasting look, as though he expected me to say something else. I nodded my head.

The last time I saw him, we were in Mariner, the bustling port city of our country, Brinn, standing at the pier. Andresh had sent word ahead of time that he'd be going to see his family, but by the time the letter would arrive there, Andresh would be a few days behind it. Still, Andresh was confident that his family would welcome him with open arms.

He took very little with him; a bag of clothes and a small satchel he wore at his side. He hid his money on his person, and asked Father to mind the rest of it, as Andresh had promised us, "Someday I will come back."

He went down the line of us, Father, Nell, then me, giving us all hugs.

And I did something that I didn't expect to do but felt like I should. When no one was looking, I kissed him—a small one, on his cheek.

He touched the spot where my lips met his face and gave me the littlest of smiles, a break in the solemnity of us saying farewell.

The bell started ringing on the deck, signifying the ship would soon stop taking passengers.

"I have to go." He smoothed my hair back from my face, eyes lingering on my scar for a second. He smiled again, only this time, wider. "I meant what I said. I'll write."

"I'll write back."

He started making his way toward the ship. "Don't take the ring off, alright?" he called back to me.

I held up my pinkie finger to him so he could see it. "I won't."

He made it to the deck and stood on the prow of the ship,

waving to us. We stayed on the pier, waving back to him, shouting his name. "Goodbye, Andresh," we took turns calling to him. We didn't move until his ship was out of sight.

Father looked around him, taking in the bustling boardwalk, the seafront shops, and the line of ships docked along the pier. He took in a breath and said, "Let's make a home here."

CHAPTER 4

FIVE YEARS LATER

I walked into the shop room, carrying my latest creations in a basket, complete with gorgeous wrapping I had purchased over at Milanie's. Father had given me a place at the checkout counter where I could display my goods, complete with business cards at the ready for Lily's Artisan Soaps. I started making them when I turned fourteen, as a hobby at first, but Nell suggested I make some money off them. Once Bellamy Mercantile got up and running, Father let me sell them in batches. I didn't make much money, but it was enough to buy supplies and have a little extra left over to save for my dream trip to Sindalia...which I hadn't mentioned to anyone yet (except Andresh in one of my letters to him).

I separated the soaps into my top two scents: orange cream and lavender vanilla. I used bits of dried fruit or dried flowers to add texture to the soap, which gave them a pretty, botanical look. I also had washing powders that made a perfumed lather, perfect for bathing, and I put those in fancy jars I also picked up at Milanie's.

My little venture started out as an attempt to remove the

persistent scent of decay from my fingers. No matter how I scented my hands, I could always smell the odor very faintly on my skin. After much experimentation, I was able to come up with a combination of ingredients that masked the scent for several hours before I had to wash my hands with my soaps again. The powders worked wonders, too—I always took bubble baths to drown out the smell, but also to cloud up the bathwater so as not to see my reflection.

Despite avoiding mirrors and glass whenever I could, I gained a reputation in the household for being immaculate in how I treated myself, with constant washing and bathing. My hands remained a chapped-looking pink, but I always put lotion on them to try to regain some of the softness there. The cleansing and grooming became a ritual. And aside from insisting on wearing my hair long and loose all the time, I otherwise was fashionable and presented myself nicely.

Uncle Jolan's money helped a lot with that. It was his gift to us that allowed us to start over in Mariner. It was quite a shock that Father uprooted us from Rookwood for a large, bustling port city, and I think he did it to forget about Mother and the life we lived before she died.

I still didn't understand how Father transitioned from being a carpenter and carver to a merchant. But he invested, and made good deals, and soon had his own ship for trading. He would bring back all sorts of things for us to sell at Bellamy Mercantile, which took up the first floor of the house. We lived on the second and third floors, a place large enough for each of us to have our own rooms. The change in lifestyle was shocking—new clothes, new shoes, new finery—a new life.

Father was presently gone on the *Windchaser* for a trip around Cape Constant to reach the southernmost tip of Celderond, a country in the vast continent of Astacia. The ships could land elsewhere and travel inland to get there without going that far south, but there were three mountain ranges that made travel through them impossible.

Sindalia was the northernmost country in Astacia, and while it took a month to go from Brinn to Sindalia, the path around the Cape was treacherous and added almost another month on top of that. Father had already been gone for a month, and it was winter, an even worse time to be travelling. But our silk stores had run out and Father would be back in early March to replenish them, with two months for everyone to commission clothing from our fabrics for the Season when it began at the start of summer.

While Father was gone, Grandma Violet and I oversaw the shop, and Nell helped from time to time. I was a little rough with her—I wouldn't let her work with customers, as she got too distracted, and so did they—but she proved herself helpful with arranging our supplies.

Nell, now fourteen years old, had been redesigning the bay window display while I was arranging my soaps. The bell to the door jangled and two men let themselves in. I hurried behind the counter, where we stored our bolts of fabric, and smiled at them.

One of them took particular interest in Nell and the way his eyes wandered over her made my stomach drop. All the men who hungered after her thought she was older than what she was—the complete opposite of when she was younger, when she was nine but looked six.

I tried to redirect the men to me. "May I help you, gentlemen?"

The taller man approached me, staring at the large scar that stretched from my forehead down to the top of my eyebrow, with jagged lines that circled outward, like someone had punched glass with their fist. It was odd and ugly, and impossible to conceal, so I didn't bother trying to hide it. But I always bristled when people stared at it for too long.

"We're here for Mr. Bellamy," he said. He was red-faced, with a squat nose and beady eyes that hid their color. Perhaps they matched his mousy brown hair.

"Mr. Bellamy is with his ship," I said. "He's left me to run the accounts in his absence."

The shorter man finally made his way to me. He had skin the color of blank paper and stringy blond hair that looked unwashed. "You're a bit young to—"

I had to tell myself that eighteen was still considered young. "I am young, yes. Is there something I can help you with?"

"I'm Mr. Fitz of Stoneshore Trading," the tall one said. "This is my associate, Mr. Harken. And you are?"

"Miss Lily Bellamy." I reached for the ledger Father kept on a shelf underneath the counting table. "Mr. Harken, Mr. Harken—sounds familiar." I licked the tips of my fingers and flipped through the pages until I spotted his name. "Here it is, Mr. Joshua Harken, Stoneshore. You're here early. We weren't expecting you until next month. I'm glad you've come; we could use the silk a bit ahead of time—"

"You're the only one who's glad," Mr. Harken said grimly. "Bad news brought us your way."

"We lost one of our ships around the Cape," Mr. Fitz said. "And a lot of our product, too. You hear about the *Delacourt* disaster? That was a Stoneshore ship. No survivors."

"That's awful, truly. I'm sorry to hear that." I briefly thought of Father tackling the Cape and couldn't help but worry. If something happened, I didn't know how we'd manage without him. Grandma Violet was seventy and slowing down fast. We couldn't expect her to run the household and the business forever, and time kept moving on—she could pass at any time. I could manage the shop on my own, perhaps, but I didn't know how I'd be able to take care of Nell at the same time. The best I could do whenever Father left was to pray for his safe return, which didn't make me feel any less helpless.

"Do you mean Cape Constant?" Nell had appeared behind the two traders. "Lily, isn't that where Father—"

Another disgusting expression washed over Mr. Harken's face, and I snapped at my sister. "Nell. Grandma Violet needs your help."

"Nell..." Mr. Harken repeated. He licked his lips.

To my surprise, Nell whirled around to him. "*Eleanor.*"

"Forgive me, Eleanor," he said. He held out his hand to her. Nell made to take it, but I repeated, "Go find Grandma. Now."

Nell must've seen the look on my face because she said nothing and hurried through the door behind us and up the stairs to the second floor.

"So, gentlemen," I said hastily, "we're trading silk for wool per your agreement."

My voice did not summon Mr. Harken's attention. "Another Miss Bellamy? Your sister?"

"Yes. We're trading ten twelve-yard bolts of—"

"You don't look a thing like each other!" Mr. Fitz laughed.

"That's very true. Now, we've got you down for ten—"

Mr. Harken's gaze remained fixed on where Nell used to be. "How old is she?"

I frowned. "Too young. Ten bolts silk for fifteen bolts of wool."

"Now, now," Mr. Fitz said, "I'm very sorry, but we can't trade at that amount. And not after the losses our company sustained from the *Delacourt* disaster. It would take thirty bolts of wool to meet our ten silk."

"We don't even have that on hand. We've held fifteen wool for you, and that's all you're going to get."

"We can't trade or sell under cost, understand?"

I tapped Mr. Harken's signature on the ledger page. "Your associate signed a contract. You accepted our terms. It's ten silk for fifteen wool and nothing else."

"I'll take ten for fifteen when I can take your sister," Mr. Harken said, his grin too hard and too wide on his face.

I slammed the book shut. "Get out. Don't come back."

Mr. Fitz blinked in surprise while Mr. Harken shrugged. "Fine by me," he said. "We'd rather not work with a damned harpy, anyway." He and Mr. Fitz exited the shop, slamming the door behind them, the bells on the door jangling.

"What was that all about?" Grandma Violet had appeared at the door behind me, Nell trailing after her.

"When Father gets back, we'll have to discuss the type of people he does business with."

"Who were they?"

"Stoneshore men. They wouldn't honor the terms they agreed to."

"What do they trade again?"

"Silk. They said the cost went up, but I think they were trying to swindle us."

"But you didn't take anything from them at all? What are we going to do about the Season, when all the visitors flood the town? We don't have any silk left, you hotheaded, foolish girl!"

"Father will be bringing back silk, too," I said, though I didn't sound confident as I spoke. "Besides, you should've heard what he said about Nell."

"Me?" Nell shoved her hands in her apron pockets, a new habit that developed when she turned ten, and now that she was fourteen, she showed no sign of stopping it. She always hid them when she felt nervous or excited, to keep herself from fidgeting. "What do you mean? What did I do?"

"You're far too friendly with everyone. You didn't even notice the way he looked at you!"

"I can't help it if—"

"You need to keep your eyes open, Nell, and be on your guard. These men act like they've never seen a beautiful girl before. They come off the ships after they've been long at sea, and they're all stupid and hungry. He thought you were a meal."

Nell stepped backward and balled up the fabric of the apron from inside the pockets. Her face reddened. "Oh."

"Enough of that talk!" Grandma said. "You should've consulted me before you lost your temper with them. If Stoneshore is the only company we contract for silk, we're in trouble."

"They got here early. I still have time to fix things." I pulled off my smock and threw it over the counter.

"What are you doing?"

"Research. You'll be able to mind the shop while I'm gone, right?" I didn't wait for a response. I ran upstairs to put on my winter coat and gloves. It was February, and in a coastal town, that meant the weather was bitingly cold due to the water and the air. I was thankful it wasn't snowing that day, but the wind was sharp and almost unbearable.

As I hurried into my coat, my eyes wandered to my desk in my room. A single letter lay on top of it, with words in cursive scribbled largely, "I have a surprise for you." It was from Andresh, and I'd received it two weeks ago. I couldn't figure out what he meant, because it was only a letter, with nothing attached to it. Instead of shoving his note in my drawer with all his other letters, I kept it out to remind me that something must be coming.

Nell poked her head in my doorway. "I'm going with you." She already had her coat on.

"Fine. But don't get distracted along the way. I'm going straight to Milanie's."

"Ooh! Nice. I love talking to Mr. Milanie!"

We headed down the steps together back into the shop, and Grandma called after us, "You'd better be back within the hour."

"We will." The bells on the door clattered as I opened it, and Nell and I stepped out.

We walked along the boardwalk, where the busiest shops catered to the tourists who came to Mariner, until we found Milanie's Imports at the intersection of Wayfarer Avenue and Quay Street. The shop was even larger than ours and filled with lots of jewelry, tapestries and other hanging art throughout. The shop always smelled sweet and smoky, like incense. It was one of my favorite places to visit in all of Mariner, and it took all my willpower not to buy something every time we stopped by.

I held the door open for Nell, careful to avoid looking at the glass, but all the while, hearing a faint *Save me* in my ear. I ignored it and followed Nell inside. "I don't have a problem with you wandering around in here. But remember what I told you earlier. Don't be too nice. And make sure you take a good look at the people you talk to."

"I'll be fine." She was halfway across the room as she said it, running to a corner covered in small but beautiful embroidered tapestries. By the time I found Mr. Milanie, she had already oohed and aahed over five separate pieces.

"Is that Miss Bellamy?" Mr. Milanie's glasses slid down his long, thin nose. He pushed the frame back up with his pinkie. "I hardly ever see you out and about anymore. This is a treat!"

I removed my gloves and tucked them in my coat pocket before shaking his hand. "It's good to see you too."

"It's an exciting day. We've got something new, never stocked it before, I know you'll love it!" With enthusiasm, Milanie's glasses seemed to jump from the bridge of his nose. He pushed them back up again. "Damn it."

"Those aren't new glasses, are they?"

"No. They're my wife's. I stepped on mine yesterday and smashed them to bits. She had an extra pair lying around for me to use while I wait for the new ones to come in. We put adhesive on them to stay put. Obviously, it's not working."

"Can you see in them?"

"Sort of. It was a bit too strong at first, but I got used to it. Though I have to take them off every once in a while so I don't get a headache. What do you think of them, besides the horrible fit? I think they bring out the color of my eyes."

"They look good with your red hair."

"Well, thank you kindly, Miss Bellamy. Now, let me show you something, you'll be so amazed. Straight from the bright turquoise waters of the Paradis d'Azur. Damn these stupid frames!" Mr. Milanie pinned the glasses to his face with his finger and didn't take them away as he continued. "Yes. The Paradis d'Azur. We have them ready to go, polished and pristine, the fabled blue pearls of the Solomon Mollusca!" In his excitement he ignored the problematic frames. With a big sweeping gesture he shouted, "And they're right over here in a big glass display! They're so beautiful!" The glasses followed his hand and shot off toward the counter.

"I'll get them for you, Mr. Milanie," I said, laughing. "Did I ever tell you you're my favorite person in all of Mariner?"

"Don't forget to tell me again the next time I see you."

I crouched down and found the glasses resting against the foot of the display case. I ignored the dark shadows pooling in the glass of the display and made sure to avoid my reflection in the lens of his glasses. I laid them on the counter. Mr. Milanie reached for his beloved pearls, displayed on a box with black velvet backing, and brought them out of the case for me to see. They were shaped like teardrops, and their blue iridescence shone in the light. "You weren't lying, Mr. Milanie. These are gorgeous."

Nell popped up from behind him, waving a small gold necklace in the air. Four pink roses, fused together to form the shape of a diamond, hung from the chain. "This is only five aums, Lily! Isn't this pretty?"

"Put it back, Nell."

"Aw. Come on!" She groaned but listened to me anyway.

"That was the young Miss Bellamy?" Milanie asked as he put his glasses back on. "She grew another inch or two, I'm certain of it."

"Yes. And she turned fourteen two months ago. I feel old."

"Don't say that. How old are you now anyway? Sixteen?"

"Eighteen. Do I really look that young?"

Mr. Milanie snickered. "No, I'm teasing you. But come back and complain when you're my age about feeling old." He pushed his glasses back up. "So, no shopping today? Just in for a visit?"

"Sorry. I was wondering if you heard any rumors about the price of silk coming from Celderond?"

"Oh yes. That's the sorriest bit of news to reach my ear as of late. It's nearly tripled."

"Are you serious?" I clenched my fists. "Well, it doesn't matter if it's true. They signed a contract. I'm still right."

Nell tapped me on the shoulder, shoving a small silver wire ring in my face. "What about this? This is only two aums. Two!"

"No."

"I can't believe you sometimes." She trotted off to the display, letting out a dramatic sigh as she returned the ring, then journeyed further off to the back of the store.

"We can't spend too much longer here," I said apologetically. "We snuck away from the shop."

"Let me give you something before you go on your way. One moment."

"Nell," I called out toward the back of the shop, "as soon as Mr. Milanie is done, we're leaving."

She didn't answer me. She stood looking at more jewelry, her back facing me, standing closer than my liking to a tall man in a dark fur capelet, beige breeches, and riding boots that came up to his knees. My gaze focused on the man's thick black hair, worn in a loose braid. I couldn't see his face.

"Nell, Nell, Nell," I said, beelining towards her, ready to grab her arm.

She and the man turned towards me, and my mouth dropped open.

"Andresh." The word fell out of my mouth in a funny little murmur, and I blinked at him.

He looked so much older than I last saw him, fully a man now, but he had that familiar smile he always gave me from the corner of his mouth. And the scar there from the accident, too.

"Lily. I was hoping I would see you again."

CHAPTER 5

Hundreds of questions flitted through my mind but all I could do was gape at him. Finally, I blurted out, "Where were you?"

He smiled again. "I've been in the shop for a while. In the back, looking around."

Mr. Milanie reappeared with his right hand cupped, holding something sparkly I couldn't make out. "He asked me where to find Bellamy Mercantile. He'd gotten the gist of its whereabouts but wanted to check. And he felt bad about not buying anything, so I told him to look at some of our items in the back. Did you find anything that caught your eye?"

"Yes, but if I buy it now, it won't be a surprise," Andresh said.

"Ah," Mr. Milanie replied. "Well, ladies, I have a surprise for you. A small one. Hopefully it will entice you to come back again with purse in hand." He held out two pins with gold beads in elaborate shapes hanging down—one for each of us.

"I can get a third one from the back," Mr. Milanie said, "so you all match."

"No, don't trouble yourself on my account," Andresh said.

Nell looked delighted at the little present. She scooped it out of her hands and fiddled with the pin, trying to open it. Once she had, she pinned the jewelry to the lapel of her coat. "This is sweet of you, Mr. Milanie!"

"My pleasure."

I did the same as Nell and put my pin on my coat, too.

"And you, Mr. Zatavier, you promise you'll come back and see me soon?"

"Yes. I know what I'd like. Can you hold onto it for me?"

"Ooh! Sure, show me what you were looking at..." Andresh and Mr. Milanie headed to the back of the shop once more.

"So, did Andresh find you first, or did you find him?" I asked Nell.

"He found me. I almost didn't recognize him. He got so much taller. And his hair." A smile erupted on her face as her cheeks turned rosy. "He's handsome."

That was true.

"Well, he did say he had a surprise for me," I said. "Him being back here shocked me."

"I know! I wonder how long he'll stay!"

"We've got to tell Grandma. We should invite him over for supper."

Andresh came back with Mr. Milanie, who held a basket behind his back so we couldn't see. He quickly tucked it behind the counter.

"I'll see you tomorrow, Mr. Zatavier."

"That's our cue to head out," I said. "Andresh, are you coming along?"

"I was hoping I could."

"Well then, see you later, Miss Bellamy and young Miss Bellamy."

Andresh held the door open for me and Nell. I bobbed my

head in gratitude while Nell stared at Andresh, saying nothing. Her eyes were awfully wide, and she was still blushing.

We strolled down the street, avoiding the iciness of the pier, and I started in with the questions. "When did you get to Mariner?"

"Last night. I'm staying at the Drover's Arms."

"You could've stopped by last night. We wouldn't have minded."

"I was pretty tired, to be honest."

"How do you feel today? Are you ready to see Grandma Violet? Father's away on his ship, so it's just us ladies."

"That's fine. I've been wanting to see you for a while."

I wasn't sure if he meant me or all of us, the way he said it. I was a little flustered by it. "I'm happy to see you too. Me and Nell. And I'm sure Grandma will fall right over when she sees how much you've grown up."

"You've grown up too," Andresh pointed out. His gaze briefly met with the scar on my forehead, then he looked in my eyes.

"Ah, yes." I wasn't sure what else to add to that. I appreciated he didn't linger on the scar, though, as people often did.

"I'm also bigger," Nell was sure to add.

"Yes. You'll catch up to Lily soon, I bet."

We made it to Bellamy Mercantile, where Grandma Violet was holding the door open for the Stoneshore men, who were taking out bolts of wool and cotton and loading them onto a cart.

"Pleasure doing business with you, Mrs. Bellamy," Mr. Harken said, loading up the last of the fabrics. "Can't say the same for your granddaughter," he said, shooting me a glance. The two men wheeled their bolts away onto the boardwalk and headed down the way to one of the ships docked at the pier.

“What did you do, Grandma?”

“I saved the day. Took in all the silk in exchange for fifteen wool and eight cotton. We’ll be fine until Kale comes back.”

“You still gave them more than the contract promised.”

“The stock was important!” She huffed at me. She finally set eyes on Andresh, and her mouth dropped open slightly. “Is that who I think it is?”

Andresh smiled at her. “Hello, Grandma Violet.”

“What did you do to your hair?”

He laughed. “Don’t like it?”

“It’s so long.”

“This is a traditional Sindalian style. They wear it like this in the capital,” he explained. “I like it this way.”

“It looks good,” I blurted. Andresh looked at me, another smile playing on his lips.

“Thank you.”

“Well, I don’t see why we’re all dawdling out here,” Grandma said. “Let’s get inside. Talk about feeding you. You’re staying the night, right?”

“I’m staying at an inn a few blocks off the boardwalk,” Andresh said.

“Oh, tosh. Save your money. You can stay in the guest room for as many days as you need.”

“I’d like that very much.”

“That’s settled, then.”

We all followed Grandma Violet inside the store and Andresh took it all in, peering around in different directions.

“You’ve done well for yourselves,” he said.

“It’s not as exciting as Milanie’s, with all of his imports, but we have some nice things, too,” I said.

“I’d love to give one of your soaps a try.”

“It’s nice you remember them.”

“I remember everything in your letters,” he said.

Nell trudged up behind us, suddenly looking guilty. “I’m sorry I didn’t write that often.” Truth be told, she hardly wrote at all.

“Your sister kept me updated about you, don’t worry.” He reached out to pat her head and stopped. “Ah, you’re probably too old for that now.”

“I don’t mind. If it’s you.”

But Andresh didn’t follow through with the gesture, only nodding.

“So, what brings you here, Andresh?” Grandma asked.

“I wanted to see you again.”

“Will you be returning to Sindalia?”

Andresh grew silent for a moment. “I’m not entirely sure.”

“Oh, don’t go back!” Nell cried. “At least, not for a while.”

“No, I was hoping to stay here for a time. You don’t have to worry. But I don’t want to impose. I still have that room at the inn and can pay for long-term—”

“Enough of that. We have a guest room, as I said,” Grandma said. “You’ll stay with us. Now, what were you thinking about for dinner?”

“I’ll have whatever you’d like,” Andresh said.

“Well, it’s a special occasion. I’ll request a goose.”

“Please get one ready to cook. I hate plucking the feathers off,” Nell said.

“That’s a little more expensive,” Grandma said. “But...oh well, we can make a treat of it. Call it a celebration.” Grandma took her apron off and set it aside. “Lily. Go ahead and turn the sign over. Eleanor, grab your coat. You’ll come with me to the poulterer.”

“I can run to the inn and grab my bags,” Andresh said.

“Would you like me to come with you?” I asked.

“Sure.”

I moved to the front door of the shop and flipped the sign

so it read "Closed." Grandma headed to the back to grab her coat and Nell waited for her while Andresh and I headed out the front door. "You'll lock up, won't you?" I called back to Nell.

"Yes."

"See you soon."

Andresh had held the door open for me and closed it behind us when we stepped out into the cold once more. I turned my back on my reflection in the shop windows and refused to look. "So, the Drover's Arms, you said?" I asked Andresh. "It's a little bit of a walk, but nothing too bad."

"I was worried about finding it again, to be honest. Aside from leaving Brinn for Sindalia, I haven't been to Mariner since I was a little boy. And I mean little. I think I was four the last time Father and I stayed here. I don't even remember why we came."

"Well, I'm glad you're here now. I can show you the sights sometime, if you'd like. I never expected to like the large city, but Mariner has grown on me."

"Sure. Show me whenever you have the time."

Andresh and I crossed the street to the opposite sidewalk closest to the boardwalk. As soon as Andresh saw that I was walking the closest to the street, he maneuvered to change places with me, casually guiding me closer to the wooden walkway. He had always been effortlessly considerate like that, and I couldn't help but smile.

As we walked side by side, I felt compelled to ask him, "So... why are you here? Your letters said nothing of when or why you'd come to us."

"I was hoping for an apprenticeship."

"Really? Merchant trade and sales is something that interests you?"

"I'm not certain, to be honest. But I thought I'd give it a try."

"And you chose us over an apprenticeship in Sindalia? It would've been easier there, I would think."

"But I wouldn't get to see you again. I thought it was high time I journeyed back. I don't want to be a burden on any of you, so I thought I'd work while I was here."

"Normally you'd work under Father, but he's somewhere around Cape Constant by now. If all goes well, you'll see him in March. Grandma technically runs things, but in the meantime, you'd be under my employ."

"And what kind of employer are you?"

"Tough but fair, I would say. I'd put you to work. Although things aren't busy now. They'll pick up in the springtime right before the Season starts. That's when everyone buys silk for their dresses for the dances."

"And do you go to these dances?"

I made a face. "I'm supposed to debut this year. But there have been no invitations."

"That surprises me."

"It is what it is. When Nell turns eighteen, I'm sure it will be madness. She'll have so many suitors lined up I don't think she'll know what to do with herself."

"She is a lovely girl," Andresh said simply. He added, "I think things will still work out for your debut. And I'll be sure to ask you for a dance this Season."

I felt my cheeks grow warmer as he spoke and I couldn't find anything to say to that. Finally, I mumbled a weak "Thanks," and busied myself with looking at the ships docked at the pier.

We were silent for a little while. I decided to break it. "You know, none of your letters were ever very detailed. 'I'm enjoying my time here,' 'I like my cousins a lot,' 'The weather is lovely,' 'I'm glad your family is doing well...' You wrote how you felt a lot, but never what you did. These past five years with you gone have been a mystery."

"I know. To be honest, nothing exciting occurred until just before I turned nineteen, and so many things happened."

"Happy belated birthday, by the way," I said. He had turned nineteen in January, which meant he was probably on the boat to Mariner before he could get my card.

He grinned at me, but only for a second. Then he was quite serious. "I'm a little ashamed of what I've done, which is why I didn't share it in the letters."

"Oh."

"In truth, I was admitted to university in Evandra."

"The capital? Isn't that a four-year university? Why didn't you stay there?"

"It didn't agree with me. I only lasted a few months. I found it stifling."

"What did you do instead?"

"Well..." To my surprise he reddened. "I did some wandering here and there, but mostly I performed in a travelling troupe. The Saint Calico Players. Their mascot was a cat."

I couldn't help but smile. "And what roles did you play?"

He turned a little redder. "Romantic lead."

"Like a prince?" I laughed. "I can see that."

We arrived at the Drover's Arms after a little more talking, and once again Andresh held the door open for me as we made our way inside. There was a young woman minding the front desk, which was a small area before the door next to her led to the main room, an actual pub. Stairs behind her led up to the floors with guest rooms in them, and Andresh acknowledged her with a bob of his head. She returned his look with a sweet smile.

"Nice to see you again, Mr. Zatavier. Will you be supping here tonight?"

"Ah, I've found alternate accommodations. I'll be leaving now. I'm sorry."

The woman couldn't hide her disappointment. "We'll be seeing you."

"Your hospitality was appreciated."

Andresh gestured for me to follow him up the steps to his room. It was a humble space, with a single bed in front of a small fireplace, a settee at the opposite end of the room, and a nook off the bedroom where the bathroom was, complete with a tub. He had three bags on the settee, a large canvas bag, a satchel, and a small bag with handles that looked like he'd been shopping. I could see wrapped boxes in it.

"You packed light for being gone for so long," I said. "And are those presents I see? Nell is going to lose her mind."

"I can't come back from Sindalia empty-handed, you know. I'd like to pass these out after supper, if I may."

"Definitely. It's very kind of you." I wished I would've brought my purse with me to Milanie's. I would've picked up a welcome home present for Andresh, although I wasn't sure how I could've sneaked it out of there. Well, I'd have to do it when he was busy.

I carried the gifts while Andresh handled his two other bags, and we went down the stairs and out onto the street. We made it back to Bellamy Mercantile, and I unlocked the side entrance into the house, avoiding the storefront.

"Let me show you to your room," I said. "Follow me."

The side entrance of the house was a little hallway that led to the kitchen, and a narrow staircase greeted us, situated between the kitchen and its dining area. We had a formal dining room to entertain guests, but that was on the second floor, and we preferred eating in the kitchen like we had in the old house.

I led Andresh up the stairs to the third floor, where the

guest room was located next to the library. The library was not large, but not too small, either. It had several bookcases, a fireplace, and four plush chairs for sitting and reading in the center of the room. Andresh poked his head inside for a moment as we passed it, looking curiously at it.

"The guest room is right next to it," I said. "You can go in the library any time you wish."

I opened the door to Andresh's new room and let him inside. The bed was a large four-poster, and there was a writing desk and wardrobe in there, and a mirror I certainly avoided.

"This is perfect," Andresh said. He laid his bags on the bed and started opening them up as I set the presents on the desk.

"Allow me to take your coat," I said. Andresh let me pull his furs off him and I opened the wardrobe to hang the capelet up. "I'll leave you to unpack. Grandma and Nell should be back any time now with the bird. I'll help them with supper. You can pass your time how you'd like."

"I'll look at your library or at least take a brief nap."

"I'll check on you before dinner. If you need to freshen up, the bathroom is on the second floor."

He nodded and looked at me in that moment, and his dark blue eyes seemed different somehow, like they were shining from the light in the room. "I'm happy to be back here with you." He paused, soon adding, "With all of you."

"I'm glad you're here, too, Andresh. We've missed you."

"Thank you. And...thank you for wearing the ring."

On instinct I raised my hand to him, showing it was still there on my pinkie. "Yes, I've kept it on all this time. I've always liked it."

The clamoring downstairs and Nell's loud voice pulled me from our conversation. "Well, I'd better go help them. See you at supper."

I left him alone in his room to get settled and headed down the stairs to the kitchen, where Grandma was unloading the large goose she'd secured from the poulterer. Lucky for Nell, who was always stuck plucking the birds, the goose was bare and ready to cook.

All of us busied ourselves in the kitchen preparing the meal welcoming Andresh back to Brinn, and when the food was ready, I returned to the third floor. I stepped inside the library, and Andresh wasn't there. I headed to the guest room and found the door slightly ajar, just a crack. After a knock and calling Andresh's name, I pushed it open.

Andresh was sprawled out on top of the bed, his boots off, lying on his back. His hair was undone from its braid, and it spread out beneath him like a blanket. His chest rose and fell with his breathing.

I watched him for a few moments, then crossed the room to wake him. As I passed the mirror, I felt it. Something strange, something different from before. A weird pressure that I couldn't describe. I wouldn't look directly into the glass, but from the corner of my eye I saw a feminine purplish figure in it, watching Andresh, with black ram horns coming from her head.

I blinked. The vision was gone. The mirror started filling up with black, inky smoke, and the voice came to me again, "Save me and open the door." I stepped further away from the mirror to avoid seeing anything inside of it.

But something else had been there, and its eyes were focused on Andresh. What on earth had I seen in the mirror?

CHAPTER 6

After I'd seen the strange images in the glass, I took some breaths to steady my thunderously beating heart and called Andresh's name once more. He didn't stir, so I gently grabbed his shoulder and gave him a little shake. He jerked awake with a start, his eyes wide and open. He sighed when he recognized me.

"You scared me," he said.

"Sorry. I didn't know how else to wake you. Dinner's ready."

He slid off the bed and grabbed his black ribbon from the nightstand to tie his hair back in the thick braid he wore earlier, then followed me down the stairs into the dining room. Nell and Grandma had already set the table, and Grandma gestured for Andresh to sit at the head of it.

The supper was excellent, and Andresh took two platefuls of goose meat, eating as though he was starving. For a lot of the meal, we didn't talk, only ate. When the table was cleared, Andresh said, "Let me get you your souvenirs."

"I'm so excited to see them!" Nell cried out, for a moment sounding like a small child.

Andresh headed up the steps and shortly came back with the gift bag. He passed the wrapped boxes around to each of us, and one remained. "This is for Kale. I bought him a silk banyan for him to wear around the house. What should I do with it?"

"I'll put it on his desk in his room," I said. Father's bedroom was on the third floor on the other side of the library; meanwhile all of us women had our rooms on the second floor.

"Can I open it now, or do I have to wait?" Nell asked.

"Now is fine," Andresh said. He leaned back in his chair and folded his hands on the table, looking at each of us eagerly as we opened our gifts.

Nell had a box of watercolors, although the paints all had a golden sheen mixed in with the standard shades. "You—you knew I liked painting," she stammered, suddenly shy.

"Lily kept me well informed," he said.

Grandma Violet held up a soft, cozy housedress that looked plenty warm enough for winter, and I opened my box to find pressed blossoms and a variety of powders I couldn't recognize. "Are these for my soaps?" The scent coming out of the box was heavenly, all sweet-smelling and flowery, but not overwhelming.

"Yes. A lot of it comes from the amyth blossom, a flower unique to Sindalia. They look like hydrangeas but have a more purple tone to them," Andresh said. "I thought you'd like a new ingredient or two."

"I love it." I scrambled out of my seat and gave him an awkward hug, as he was still in his chair. Nell hurried right over to us and joined in. I thought Grandma was going to jump in, but she put her housedress over her regular clothes and was spinning around, swishing the skirt about.

Nell and I let go of him. "You're always so kind to be thinking of us," I said.

"You're the best," Nell added.

After receiving our gifts and cleaning the dishes from dinner, each of us headed back to our rooms for the night. I poked my head into Nell's room and said, "Nell. We have to sneak out tomorrow and get Andresh some presents in return."

"But he's going back to Milanie's," she said.

"We'll try a different place. Or we can get him his favorite cake?"

"Cake sounds like a good idea."

"We'll go during our break from the shop tomorrow. I'll have to start training Andresh, too."

"I can't believe he'll be working with us!"

"I know. Well, goodnight."

"'Night."

That night I had a dream about the mirror in Andresh's room. The mirror wasn't filled with my haunting, but rather that vague purple figure in the glass with horns that stared at him as he slept. The mirror expanded in size, becoming floor-length, and the creature stepped out of it—a voluptuous woman with panther-like legs and a matching tail, a strange animal-human hybrid. Perhaps the most unnerving were her eyes. They were solid black—no whiteness to them, just an inky void.

She strode over to the sleeping figure of Andresh and smiled, revealing sharp teeth. She looked right at me, and in a seductive, echoey voice, whispered, "You'll need to help him soon. Nigredo. Tell him to open the Gate."

Somehow I managed to speak to her. "The Gate? Is that like...the door?" I was thinking of my mother's bloated figure in the mirror.

She shook her head. "Stir him up inside. Bring him to the brink. He will open the Gate."

I bolted upright in my bed. That was something more than a dream; it had to be. And I needed to tell Andresh. At the same time, I was afraid—I'd seen terrible visions of my dead mother in the mirror every time I looked, and now a new creature revealed herself. Would I see her all the time now, too? What was that strange word she used, and what did she mean by Andresh opening the Gate?

I wrapped my house robe over my nightgown and stepped into my slippers, then made my way up the stairs to check on Andresh.

He was awake, seated in the library, with an open book in hand. I glanced at the title: *A Collection of Verse from Capua Cora.* I knew he liked to read, but didn't know he cared for poetry.

"I'm glad you're awake and dressed," I said. "After breakfast, I'll start you in the shop." I paused. "I have something I need to talk to you about, but the timing... We have to get ready for work now. May I talk to you later about it? How about tonight?"

"Sure. You can talk to me about anything, anytime. Don't worry."

"I'll make breakfast now—if you come down it'll be ready in a few minutes."

We all ate together, and once breakfast was done, Andresh followed me into the store along with Nell.

"This isn't our busy time," I explained, "but we still get the occasional customer wanting to get a head start on the Season. Particularly with the silk we sell. Since I don't expect more than a couple of customers today, what I'm going to have you do is help us move things around, starting with that."

I pointed to a large wooden vanity—Mother's—which was

uncovered except for a tablecloth over the mirror. I had put it there as soon as Father had unloaded it into the shop, mumbling something about protecting the glass, and nobody said anything about it, leaving it on there the entire time.

"It's a lovely piece," Andresh said. "I'm surprised none of you wanted it for yourselves."

"Father carved it," Nell said. "But he wanted to get rid of it when Mother died." Her voice quieted with those words.

"We haven't been able to sell it," I said, "so I thought moving it closer to the front would entice customers more. That, and lowering the price."

The first thing Andresh did was take the cloth off the mirror. "I think part of it, too, is that you keep it covered. The mirror is part of its charm."

He had a point. The edges of the glass were etched like crystal, making a geometric frame around it. Nonetheless, I wanted to avoid it, so I shifted my body away from the glass and stepped to the side, making sure I didn't see anything in it as long as I kept my head turned.

"Lily doesn't like mirrors," Nell said casually. "It's because of her scar."

My shoulders drew up at that. I supposed it was obvious to everyone that I didn't like mirrors, but I never realized they wrote it off so easily due to the mark on my forehead. All of my efforts to hide my ghostly affliction were paying off. Let them think I couldn't bear to look at myself out of pride, not fear.

Andresh gave me a sympathetic look. "I hope the day comes where you care enough to see yourself as you are," he said. "Scars and all." He whispered to me, a little smile on his face, "I always thought you were very pretty, anyway."

Andresh. He always knew how to summon a blush to my face. I felt like my temperature rose five degrees with his compliment.

Nell looked at both of us with a raised eyebrow. "Didn't quite catch that."

Andresh said in a slightly louder voice, "Where would you like this?"

"Let's clear out an area for it first," I said, assuring myself my skin was no longer a heated red.

There was a table that displayed women's evening gloves and reticules in different colors that I thought we could move a little further away, towards the fabrics. I instructed Nell to place the items on the counting desk while Andresh and I grabbed each end of the table and lifted it. I ended up being the one to walk backwards as we headed towards the counter.

"Let's get the vanity now," I said. Andresh and I arranged ourselves to pick up the vanity at each end and lifted. I started walking backward when suddenly the mirror swung on its axis before it detached. I couldn't understand how it happened—it was like an invisible force took it right off its hinges. It crashed to the floor, and I expected shards of glass to scatter everywhere, but it landed face-up and merely cracked. Nothing about the way it happened seemed natural to me.

"That was odd," Nell said. "That should be in hundreds of pieces."

"It will be in pieces when we take it off the floor," Andresh said. He bent down on the ground and carefully lifted the mirror up, and several shards of glass freed themselves from where the crack had appeared.

"Nell, can you get the broom and dustpan?" I asked. Nell nodded and headed off.

"Do you mind helping me with the larger pieces?" Andresh asked me.

I grabbed the waste bin and bent down to assist Andresh, all the while telling myself not to show any reaction to the glass. Nell's comment, and likely my actions, drew attention to myself, and Andresh seemed keen to watch me closely as I picked up the glass and put it in the bin. His gaze focused on me as I first avoided looking into the mirror pieces, but after he eyed me as I did it, I decided to go ahead and peer directly into the glass pieces to try to get his attention off me. I took in a breath as the glass filled with a smoky haze and the voice of something like my mother called out to me, "Open the door. Please."

Andresh picked the mirror up and held it facing me. Only the corner where it cracked had come out in pieces; the rest of the mirror stayed stubbornly put.

Things appeared faster than they had before. Already the figure in the mirror opened her mouth wide and the insects came out of her, swarming the glass and my reflection in it. The winged insects landed on me and started biting, and it took all my willpower not to swat them off.

Andresh was saying something to me, but I couldn't hear him, the buzz of the creatures was so loud, the woman wailing for me to save her just as piercing.

My eyes watered, and tears fell as the insects started crawling in my ears. I rose to my feet and bolted out of the shop, not caring where I was going, as long as I could stop the terrible visions that plagued me.

I made my way to the boardwalk and looked over the ledge into the sea, trying to calm my beating heart. With my knuckles, I rubbed my ears, trying to shake off the feeling of things crawling inside of them. Once I was satisfied nothing was there, I took breaths in and out, matching the rhythm of the tide, thankful I could hear crashing waves and the cry of gulls as they circled overhead. I followed the pattern of sounds until my heart settled, and focused on the thin cloud of white that appeared in the air when I took each breath.

Andresh appeared quickly at my side. I didn't even hear

him come up next to me. He searched his pockets and pulled out a handkerchief for me to use, and I dabbed my cheeks with it.

"Are you alright?" he asked, his voice gentle.

"I'll be fine."

"You don't have a coat."

"Neither do you."

We were silent for a moment, then Andresh spoke. "When you're ready...only when you're ready to...you can tell me what you saw."

I supposed I couldn't truly hide anything from him. I sighed. "It's been going on for years. I'll talk to you about it later. I don't want to get worked up over it again. I need to calm down."

"I understand." Andresh leaned against the railing and looked down into the water. "I almost drowned here. Right at this very spot."

"You never told me this before."

"No, I never have. It was the first time Father took me here as a child, when I was four, and it was a busy summer day. It was the first time I'd ever seen the ocean; the first time I'd ever seen the big ships. The quay was so crowded, it took forever to get through the mass of people on the walkways. I didn't want to wait for Father, and I was small, so I made it through the crowd easily.

"I ran over here for a better look. I thought what I wanted to see, more than anything, were the big ships coming into port. But I couldn't look at them. Not more than a second. I was drawn to the ocean instead.

"The sea is beautiful. And ancient. It has a life and rhythm all its own, and it's been that way for thousands and thousands of years, and it won't ever stop. And no matter how hard you look into the water, as long as it moves, you will never,

ever find yourself staring back at you." He leaned further over the railing, looking down into the greens and grays below. "It's comforting, isn't it?"

"Mmm."

After a moment of us standing there looking into the sea, I had to ask him. "Did you fall in? Or did you jump?"

He kept his eyes on the waves below us, but gave me a tiny, corner-of-the-mouth smile. "In truth, that part I don't remember. I know I went over the railing somehow, and I know Father and some passersby jumped in to pull me out. Everything else is hazy. Father said it's because I knocked my head on the stone barrier before I went under."

I winced. "It hurts just to hear it."

"I had quite the headache afterward, and quite the lump, too. Here, let me show you." He touched the back of his crown and pushed apart his thick black hair, his fingers touching a specific spot. "Put your hand here." He leaned down and moved his hand so mine could rest there.

It wasn't a gash exactly, more like a thin line of indentation, a slight dent in an otherwise smooth skull. "That's definitely a scar." I couldn't help but touch mine on my forehead in reaction, though I tried to play it off by smoothing back a strand of my hair.

"You don't need to do that," he said. "It looks fine. Unique. Almost like a magic sigil."

I raised my eyebrow at him and let out a little laugh. "Magic. As if I could do it."

"You have."

My thoughts flew back to the day we danced and made fire appear from the old pit. "Oh, right. It was fun, wasn't it? Until..." I couldn't finish what I wanted to say because the picture of my mother's dead body entered my mind.

Andresh gave a small nod and changed the subject. "What

are you going to do about the vanity now that the mirror is damaged?"

"I suppose I'll order a new mirror. Something a little more square-shaped this time. That might help make it look newer and more amenable to customers."

"I can put it together for you, if you'd like. So you don't have to..."

"That would be great."

"I hope you're able to sell it. Kale did such lovely work with it. He doesn't carve anymore, does he?"

"He made the sign above the shop. That was the last thing he did."

"Do you think he'll mind that I'm here?"

"Of course not. You know he loves you. You don't have to worry." I shifted. "I hope he makes it back home safely."

Nell raced across the street to us at the pier. She looked stricken, her face pale and her eyes watery. "Help! Help! It's Grandma!"

"Oh God." I immediately assumed the worst. Once you lose someone, there's always a fear in the back of your mind that more will be lost.

Andresh and I rushed with Nell back to the shop. It was marked "Closed," so we switched directions and came in through the side door.

Grandma lay on the floor on her back, her face looking strange and out of sorts, as if it were drooping. Her eyes were closed.

"Is she breathing?" I knelt at her side, checking to see the rise and fall of her chest. To my relief, she was.

"We need to get her to her room," Nell said.

Andresh nodded. "I think I know what this is," he said softly. "Let me see." He cupped her forehead for a moment, as if he were checking for a fever. "She's had a stroke. The fire—"

He quickly stopped himself. "I can carry her if one of you wants to go fetch the doctor."

"I'll go," I said. "Nell, stay with Andresh and Grandma." With care, he and I got Grandma upright, enough that Andresh could scoop her up off the floor. "Where's her room?"

"I'll show you." Nell led Andresh up the stairs and I called out that I was headed for Dr. Basseter's.

I rushed out the door, once more without my coat, not thinking about anything except finding the doctor. He was located next to the apothecary on a higher-level street of the city.

That was the thing about Mariner...it was a vertical city. Closer to the water, the buildings were all multi-level and painted in bright colors, but once you headed upward, you made it to the wealthy district at the top of the hill—Highgate, where the dances of the Season were held in pale brick mansions with stone streets the color of cream.

Dr. Basseter was located right at the center level of Mariner, servicing a wide variety of patients. We never needed his services except when Nell caught the children's fever early on when we moved to the city. He was the only doctor I knew of by name.

I raced up the hill crossing streets haphazardly, not watching where I was going, until I made it to his home. He didn't keep an office, making house calls instead, but the first floor of his abode was open for people to come and request his services. I prayed that he wasn't busy when I crossed through the door, slightly out of breath.

A servant greeted me, a man in a black suit and a white wig. "May I help you, miss?"

"Is Dr. Basseter available? My grandmother collapsed in our home." I trusted Andresh's assessment. "It's a stroke."

"I will summon him immediately for you." The servant

disappeared, and it only took a few moments for Dr. Basseter, an older gentleman with snow-white hair, a matching trimmed mustache, and dark copper-colored skin, to meet me. He carried a large black bag with him, along with a smaller one he held out to me. "Miss Bellamy. It's been a long time. Can you help me carry this? The contents are fragile."

"Yes, doctor." I accepted the bag, and the sound of glass clinking came from inside. I held the bag carefully, keeping it at my chest in front of me as opposed to slinging it under my arm, and I followed him out the door.

"Thank you for coming with me under such short notice," I said. He walked by my side as we hurried down the criss-crossing streets of Mariner towards the waterfront. I led him through the side door of our house and told him, "She's in bed," and we went to her room on the second floor.

Andresh and Nell were at her bedside, Nell holding Grandma's hand. They had brought extra chairs for me and Dr. Basseter ahead of time, pulling them from the other rooms.

"Allow me to examine her," he said. He focused on her face, the side of it that drooped down. It looked like it didn't even belong to her.

"Her hemispheres are imbalanced," Dr. Basseter said. "Too many fluids pooling to one side. That's why her face looks the way it does." He held his hand out to me. "Miss Bellamy, if you could hand me that bag."

I did, and he set it on her nightstand table. He removed a jar with leeches. "To restore balance, we'll have to bleed her. But that's not the only fluid." He reached into the bag once more and took out a jar with a small amount of liquid in it. "When she wakes, you must have her drink this cinnamome-calomel mixture, and it will rid her of bile and phlegm. Thus, the excess fluids should be removed, and the hemispheres will be in balance once again."

Andresh rose to his feet and shot me a look I couldn't interpret, but I sensed its urgency. "Can I talk to you?" he asked me. "In private?"

"One moment, doctor," I said. Andresh and I walked into the hallway, but Andresh said, "Even more private."

We went into my bedroom. "What's the matter?" I asked him.

"That doctor—I know he's trying to be helpful, but he has no idea what he's talking about. Dr. Basseter was on the right track about balance, and it does involve blood, but you can't let him bleed Violet. It has no beneficial effect. It either does nothing or hastens death."

"What is it? Do you know something, like how to cure her?"

"I can't cure a stroke, but I can help. I don't know how to explain this very well...but we're full of doors and gates and pathways. And...everything is also Fire."

"What?"

"There's too much Fire in Violet's blood. And it's sealed the door; welded it shut. So, the blood can't pass through like it should. When the blood can't cross the threshold, it kills the mind, and the body quickly follows."

There was a weird sort of logic to his explanation. I didn't understand most of it, but I recognized the important part. "She's not getting enough blood, so taking even more blood from her solves nothing."

"Right."

"How do you know all of this?"

"My Aunt Roxahna in Sindalia. She had one, and my family —well, there's not enough time to explain now."

"So what are you going to do?"

"I can try to help with her blood. With the Fire."

It hit me with stunning clarity. "Magic. You're going to use magic."

I remembered the clearing in the forest, and the exuberance of our dance, and the sheer joy and power of it all as the flames exploded out of the earth.

"The Fire. You're going to call it out."

CHAPTER 7

There was no polite way to drive out Dr. Basseter. Andresh and I made it back to the room and the doctor held a leech with a metal tong over Grandma's body. He was aiming for Grandma's arm, as her sleeve was already pushed back, and Nell wore a look of disgust.

"That's enough, Dr. Basseter. You can stop," I said, gesturing for him to put the leech away.

"This will only take a moment, Miss Bellamy."

"I'd like to do it myself," Andresh cut in.

"Why would you want to do that? This isn't an enjoyable task."

"I'm a student of medicine. The University of Evandra."

"Ah, I thought you were Sindalian. And from so far away! Goodness. You want to give it a try? I'm happy to supervise."

Andresh looked at me and gave me a small frown. "That would make me nervous," he said.

"How am I supposed to know you'd do it properly?"

Andresh stood over Grandma, then he pointed and said,

"Here, here, and another one here. Just to start, to see if she wakes."

"Well. That's correct. Very good, Mister—"

"Zatavier."

"If you wish to do it yourself, Mr. Zatavier, I won't stop you." He passed the leech to Andresh. "When she wakes, please give her the mixture for purging, and summon me once more. I'll come straightaway."

"Here you go, doctor," I said, handing him his small bag as he took his larger one. He left a jar and tongs with us for the leeching, and I led him downstairs to our door. "We'll call on you again, hopefully with good news," I said as he turned and left.

I made it back up the stairs as Andresh stood there, still holding the leech over Grandma.

He mouthed at me once I came into the room, *What about your sister?*

"Nell, you're looking a little green," I said. "You don't have to be here for this."

"I want to help. I don't know what to do," she said.

"If you'd like to help out, we need this household to function. I can have you run errands in the city, if you'd like."

"I don't want to leave Grandma. What if she wakes up and asks for me?"

"She very well could." I thought about it. "Fine, I won't send you out. But we can't stop everything here. You can either prepare a simple lunch for later today or do the laundry." She'd probably stick me with laundry. We had everyone's bedding to do on top of nightclothes and undergarments, so it would take a while.

"I'll do the food," Nell said. "I know how much you hate to prepare it, Lily." She made like she was ready to go downstairs and then paused. "Are you and Andresh going to be up here alone with Grandma?"

"For a little bit, yes. When it's time for me to do the laundry, you can take over watching Grandma."

Nell eyed Andresh curiously. "And you know how to take care of her? Because of university?"

Andresh nodded, and I added truthfully, "I think out of all of us, he would be the best one to stay with Grandma."

"I'll call if I need any help or notice any changes," Andresh said.

Nell looked hesitant, but still, she headed to the door. "Make sure she gets better," she said, her voice hardly above a whisper.

Andresh and I waited until we heard the sounds of her feet disappear down the stairs, and when we knew she was out of sight, I hit him with questions.

"What are you going to do? No dancing, are you? How long is this going to take?"

"I'm calling the Fire out, like I said, and I'm powerful enough I can do it by Will. It should only take a few minutes."

I paused. "Did you really study medicine at university?"

"Literature," he said.

"How do you know what to do?"

"I told you, my aunt. It's not going to be easy, though. And...because I'm removing her Fire...she will lose some of her life force."

"What? Do you mean she's going to die?"

"Not if it works. It just means her life will be a little shorter than it was before. Could be days, could be months. If it's really bad, she might lose a year. I'll try to take out as little as possible, but it needs to come out."

"How long will it take you? If you're pulling Fire out?"

"I have to go very slowly, but even so, it shouldn't take more than fifteen minutes."

"If Nell throws herself into her chores—and she very well might, as a distraction—she shouldn't interrupt us."

"You don't plan on telling her about me. About magic."

"No. I thought you wanted as few people to know as possible."

"Yes, that's true. But I do feel a little guilty about it."

"...Did you feel guilty telling me?"

He paused. "For some reason, no. I've trusted you in the past, when we were children, and you've kept my secrets. I'm grateful for that." He paused. "You can sit with me, if you wish."

"Thanks." I pulled Nell's chair closer to the bedside, opposite Andresh. "I'll start housework in a little bit."

Andresh put his hand on Grandma's forehead, looking at her intently. After a few moments of his sitting with her like that, I glimpsed a change in the light. It shone beneath Andresh's fingertips, barely escaping, a deep violet color like Grandma's namesake. He pulled his hand away, and the tiniest speck of a purple flame, smaller than a button, glowed in his palm. He folded his fingers over it, extinguishing the fire in his hands. No—extinguishing Fire. This was something different from an ordinary flame.

"That's Grandma's life? I mean, her life force?"

"Yes. Fire is the energy that permeates all living things. It's not exactly a soul, but something close to it. It's personal to each and every one of us. I learned the true name for Fire back when I first visited Sindalia as a boy, not understanding I was dealing with life. I thought I was reanimating a fire that went out. In truth, whenever I pulled Fire out of the ground, I was taking it from the grass and plants that grew nearby, slowly draining them of the energy to live."

"That's...terrible, actually."

"Once I learned the truth of it, I did feel terrible. I don't do that anymore, knowing the cost."

"Is this what you spent time learning about in Sindalia with your family? This type of magic, of Fire and life?"

"And why wouldn't I? We've had so much death hanging around us. My mother, when she gave birth to me. My father. Your mother. We shouldn't have to lose the ones we love. I won't let your grandmother slip away from us."

His voice sounded thicker and heavier, suddenly filled with emotion. I didn't know how to respond, so I let a moment pass between us until I thought of what to say. "You know, you've shared a big secret with me. It's time I told you mine. My family has gotten hints of it, but no one knows what's been happening to me after all these years."

"Years?" His voice was filled with concern.

"It started when my mother died, when we found her body. She was in the water, reaching for me. It was more than how her body happened to be posed. She was literally *reaching out* to touch me. Ever since, I've seen her corpse in every reflection, and she begs me to open the door and save her. I don't know what it means, but she's been relentless. The visions get worse the longer I stay in front of the glass. I've tried to avoid looking at myself, so I don't see her there, but it happens whenever I do."

Andresh sat there quietly for a moment, looking deep in thought. "She asked you to 'open the door?'"

"Yes."

"And have you tried?"

"A few things, when this affliction was still fresh. Nothing worked. Not that I knew where the door was leading to, anyway. I just wanted to get her to stop."

"What did you do?"

"I held a mirror up to an actual door, and in the reflection, opened the door. Nothing changed. I went to a priest at Saint Oliman's Church, that big one on the hill near the cliffs, and I prayed with him, and he gave me an amulet that didn't do anything. Finally, I went to Dusty Corners to meet with the soothsayer there, who said, 'Give it lots of fire and it will go away.'"

Andresh raised his eyebrow at that, but only for a second. I almost didn't notice it.

"Anyway, I took a small hand mirror and tried to burn it," I said. "That was my last attempt at breaking the curse, and I've played this game of dancing around the reflections for years."

He gave me such a look of concern that it almost made me feel ashamed of what I was telling him. "Do you know something about this?" I asked.

"I have a few ideas, but I don't know for certain. The first thing—that creature in the mirror isn't your mother. I think it's a demon known as Aineiron. He is bound to mirrors and likes to feed on fear. He haunts people who are already vulnerable and brings them closer to death."

"People who are already vulnerable... Well, my mother had been acting strange for some time. She was always staring in the mirror."

"She could have been sensitive enough for Aineiron to prey on her."

"She killed herself in that marsh. Drowned herself with stones in her pockets. I knew back then, and Father told Nell when she was twelve, but we never told anyone else."

"I'm so sorry. I didn't know."

"I kept wondering if she truly wanted to die... I was always convinced it was because she was sick, or because somewhere deep inside of her, she didn't want a family. But what if... What if it was the demon pushing her all this time?"

"That's very possible."

"And Aineiron is after me now because I'm vulnerable, too?" I didn't see myself that way immediately, but I thought about it. I was a mess after Mother died, after seeing her body so bloated and disfigured-looking. After all of that horror, wouldn't something terrible want to latch on to me?

"I think Aineiron is focused on you because you might be a Key. Remember how I said things were doors and pathways? Well, the mirror, which is where Aineiron is stuck, is a kind of door. Think of it like a door with a window to look through. Demons crave the living realms but can't get to them without difficulty, so they use mirrors to watch us and talk to us. Aineiron has been begging you to let him out because he knows you can free him, and he has appeared as your mother this whole time because that's what makes you vulnerable. He's underestimated how strong you can be, how much you can endure all this time."

There was a lot in his statement I wanted to ask about. Living realms? Realms, plural? Demons? But the one that pressed me was, "How am I a Key? What does that mean, exactly?"

"I'm not sure how someone becomes a Key. It could be something you're born as, or it's something you grow into naturally. No one knows how one is chosen or how it comes to be, it's just one of those things that is."

"And you said I can open all doors? Literally?"

"It's more, how do I say, ethereal?" He put his hand back on Grandma's forehead, and the light beneath his fingers reappeared, stronger and larger this time. He drew the purple flame out and extinguished it with his fingers as sweat appeared on Grandma's brow. "Gates often appear in fours, and they repeat in a pattern. You can find them in nature, in the human body, and in even darker places. You could open those if you learned how to see them. You can travel to different places, different planes, different worlds."

I gaped at him. "Why would I do that, though? Is there any benefit to it?"

"That's complicated. I could try to show you if you like, but not now."

"I'm very curious about all of it."

"If you are truly a Key, you could also do something similar to what I'm doing with Violet now. I'm calling her Fire out by using its name, but you could simply put your hand on her forehead, open the door there, and let the flames out."

"Should I try it?"

"It doesn't hurt unless you draw out too much fire. You can try, but I'm worried about you burning yourself, or your grandmother."

"Oh. I don't want to do that."

"If you want to know if you're a key, you can open your own door. There are four within the human body. The head, the heart, the hands, and..." He lowered his palm down his waist to where his legs met. "Here." His hand returned to his side as he shifted in his seat. "Each gate has a name, and they correspond with other gates: Nigredo, Albedo, Citrinitas, Rubedo."

"What are those words? Sindalian?"

"They're alchemical terms."

"Alchemy? And Fire and demons and doors? I'm not understanding any of this. It's overwhelming. I don't understand how they all relate to each other."

"I see that it's a lot, and their connections, even more so." He put his hand back on Grandma's forehead. "You can try one of the gates in your hands to see what I'm talking about. I want you to try to open your door and reveal your Fire. A quick in and out." He lifted another violet-colored flame from Grandma, and his fingers closed over it, snuffing it out.

"What do I do? Is there something I should say?"

"It's Magic by Will that opens gates. This is going to sound overly simple, but you have to concentrate and put all of your intention behind opening the door. Despite how easy it may sound, it takes a lot of work. If you can't get it this time, don't worry about it. I think it's worth a try."

"I don't understand exactly what I should do. Should I close my eyes?" I did, then thought "open" in my mind over and over again as I held out my hand, *OPEN OPEN OPEN OPEN*. I furrowed my brow and squinched my eyes shut even harder, and gritted my teeth, repeating the words in my mind.

Nothing happened.

"Am I supposed to feel something while I'm concentrating?"

"If you remember how it felt when we called on the Fire with the dance, it should be something similar. Magic feels, well, like a shifting. A change in the air, a buzz or a hum of sorts."

I tried again, although I couldn't figure out how to try harder than what I was already doing. I even stopped breathing for a moment. But I couldn't make any change, no opening or transformation in my hand, nothing.

"It looks like it will take some practice," Andresh said, not unkindly.

"I can't imagine myself doing magic."

"We all have the capability to. If you want to learn, I could teach you."

"How much do you know? What on earth did you learn in Sindalia?"

He was silent for a moment, then said simply, "A lot."

He pulled more violet flames from Grandma's forehead,

slowly and carefully, then extinguished them. He took a handkerchief from his pocket and blotted Grandma's forehead, where beads of sweat had trickled down. "Two more of these, and I'll stop, and we'll wait and see if she comes out of it."

We sat in silence, and I watched him again separate Fire from Grandma after he waited a few minutes. At last I spoke. "Andresh, about Aineiron—do you know how to stop him?"

"Maybe. Tell me, when you see the demon in the mirror, can you feel what he's doing?"

"When I saw the reflection in the marshes, I could. And ever since, I feel everything that happens in the mirror."

"It sounds like the gate to Aineiron is already partly open, but not enough for him to slip through. What we would have to do is close the gate all the way. I can do that. Although it might be better if I just kill him."

"*Kill?* You know how?" After a beat I added, "There's so much about you that I don't know."

"A lot has happened since I left Brinn."

He pulled the flames from Grandma's brow one last time, stuffed the handkerchief in his pocket, then clapped his hands together in finality. "Now we need to leave her to rest. I think I've pulled enough; if so, she should wake within a day, though I can't say what state she'll be in."

"Andresh...you've always been such a giving person, looking out for us all the time."

To my surprise, a little bit of blush filled Andresh's cheeks. "I would do anything for you. I love this family." He rose to his feet. "I'll do what I can to break Aineiron's spell over you. I promise. Aineiron is attached to you, so only you can see him, but I want a look at him before I end things. I'll need to borrow your Fire in order to do so—to trick him into thinking I'm you. Demons' eyes can only see Fire. So he will see your color within me, and I'll give you some of mine to confuse him."

"We're exchanging Fire? Is it like...a soul exchange?"

He gave me a small, somehow sweet smile. "That's a romantic way of putting it."

The heat pooled in my cheeks. "You said Fire was something like a soul."

"Yes. And yes, we will briefly exchange some of each other's Fire."

"What if we get too much of each other's Fire in our blood? Will we end up like Grandma?"

"I'll be careful. I've handled Fire for years now and can work with it well. I'll do enough to see Aineiron and how his gate works, and aside from getting warm and perhaps a dusting of sweat, you won't feel anything when we exchange Fire. I'll put it back inside of you as soon as I'm done taking a good look at him."

"I don't know, Andresh. This sounds risky, more so for you than for me. I've endured this for years. I've always stopped it before it's gotten too much for me. I can bear it a little longer."

"No, it's no good to have a demon at your back, especially for so long. I'm surprised he hasn't exacted more curses since he latched on to you. You haven't seen anything else, have you?"

I thought about it. "I suppose I should share what I wanted to tell you tonight. Yes, I've seen another creature. A panther-like woman with purplish skin and jet-black eyes. And black ram's horns, too. I saw her in a mirror first, but last night she spoke to me in a dream."

He surprised me with, "You don't need to worry about that."

"But it's another demon, isn't it?"

"Isabelle won't harm you. She won't harm me, either. She just...watches over me from time to time."

"Don't you want to know what she said to me?"

"It doesn't matter. She sometimes speaks incoherently and throws in random words. But she's also very helpful."

"She told me to help you."

His eyes widened, and he tried to play his reaction off with a small flick of the corner of his mouth, a smile, but not completely. "Yes, I suppose she would." He raised his hand, palm out to me, then tucked it away. "Say no more. I'll talk to her. She won't bother you again."

"But what about you? Doesn't she bother you? How long has this been going on?"

"For several months. Don't worry, I have control over her. Trust me."

I stared at him. "What did you do in Sindalia?"

"I became very powerful. And it's all building towards my dream, one where we will never have to lose the ones we love. It's been a lot of work, and more work is to come, but I promise you, it will all be worth it in the end. And I'll be fine. Please, trust me, and let me help you." He held his hand out to me in offering.

I hesitated, looking at the earnest expression on his face. Everything he said to me, from Fire to Aineiron to his own demon Isabelle, frightened me. I knew he wasn't lying, but it was all testing the boundaries of belief. But I couldn't ignore the look he wore, and I accepted his hand.

"It's a lot to think about," I said. "I don't know if I can manage all of it, but I trust you. However, Grandma is the priority. I want to give her my full attention the next few days, and then we can try for Aineiron."

"Thank you for letting me help." His thumb grazed the tops of my fingers before he pulled away from me. "So...what do we do now? Besides let her rest?"

"You're going to help me with laundry."

CHAPTER 8

For the next couple of hours Andresh helped me with the clothes and bedding. This was always a time-consuming task, and most of it was done outside, where there was more room. We'd start with dumping the bedding into basins where they first soaked, and then we heated them to a boil while adding lye, and after stirring them for a while, we'd take out the washboards and get to work scrubbing.

Nell had made soup and sandwiches—something I usually relied upon making on the regular—so she could run back up to Grandma's bedside. We all ate together, mostly in silence, before I returned to work.

"Can you...come up and sit with me, Andresh?" Nell asked him, suddenly shy.

He looked at me. "Did you still need help, or is this fine?"

I still needed help, but Nell looked like she could use the company. She seemed so anxious about Grandma's health.

"She hasn't woken up yet, and I need someone to talk to," Nell added.

"I think it would be good for Nell to have you keep her company," I said to Andresh. "You already did so much with the laundry. Thank you."

The only time the three of us reunited was for the next batch of food at supper. Nell and Andresh had been together for hours, watching over Grandma. I wondered how they'd passed the time with each other.

"Have you noticed any change in her?" I asked.

"She hasn't woken up," Nell said. "I don't think I have the energy to stay by her side the rest of the night. Lily, you'll take over, won't you?"

"I certainly will. But tomorrow we have to reopen the shop. We've got to get some of that new silk stock out. I'm torn—Father's got to be here by March, but we can't just sit on the merchandise while waiting for him. At the same time, we can't afford to sell all of it, either, in case something has happened."

"Understood."

After dinner I crept into Grandma's room to freshen her up, bringing with me a cloth, a towel, and a bowl of water to wipe her down. She looked peaceful, and I wondered how much Andresh helped her. It seemed like he knew what he was doing, but the longer Grandma remained unconscious, the more nervous I became. How much life had slipped away from her?

I dried Grandma off with the towel and set everything on the night table beside her bed. I sat in one of the chairs we left at her bedside. I held her hand. She felt warm.

I didn't remember falling asleep. All I knew was that I woke up with a blanket around my shoulders in the morning, and then Andresh knocked on the door.

"It's after breakfast," he said, bringing me a plate of sliced apples, buttered toast, and a mug of tea. I thanked him as soon as it was all in my hands.

"The shop's been open for an hour and a half. Eleanor is handling it fine. She sold some lace trim and one of the beaded reticules you had lying around."

"Oh, that's good," I said. "We brought those bags in from Silva, and they were popular last year, but the interest tapered off. What have you been doing?"

"Your sister took over your project and is having me move things around the shop. I got one of the display cases cleared out and stationed closer to the front of the store, then reorganized everything that was in it. That didn't take too long."

"Thank you for your hard work," I said with a grin.

"It was nothing, really."

I finished eating the small breakfast he had brought to me and stood up from the chair at Grandma's side. "I'm going to go bathe and I'll be dressed and with you two shortly."

"See you downstairs," Andresh said, taking my plate and teacup from me.

Once I was cleaned up, I made it to the shop and spotted Andresh chatting with a customer. "Of course, this is the finest silk in Mariner. And you can dye it if you wish," he said.

The customer, a pretty young woman with ebony skin and spiraling curly black hair pinned in a bun, smiled at him. She was wearing a lovely gown in red with a capelet of silver fox fur. She was clearly from Highgate based on her dress.

"I am looking for a custom color," she said. "It has to be a dark blue, but something more than that. It's expected I'm to be the grandest at the ball."

"A dark blue that is more than just blue..." Andresh paused. He caught me watching him. "Lily, Milanie's sells imported dyes, yes?"

"We recommend the shop a lot," I said. "They have very unique colors."

"That's settled. You can get your silk here, and I'll escort you to Milanie's and help you choose the perfect shade," Andresh said.

The woman's face turned rosy with pleasure. "Such excellent service," she said. "Of course I can't turn you down." She let out a merry laugh. "I'll proceed with the silk."

Andresh had an easy charm, and I knew that if he continued to work with us, he would disarm every customer that came our way and they would happily buy from him. It didn't surprise me that he got the sale. But I couldn't help but feel a little twinge at how easily he won her over, and how he offered to spend more of his time with her. And then I felt another twinge, this one of guilt, because Andresh had spent so much time with us, with me, and what he was doing wasn't hurting anyone—he simply did what he did for the sale.

I headed to the counter and grabbed the bolt of white silk. I also pulled out our sizing booklet. "For someone of your height, I'd say...four yards. Will you be purchasing muslin to line the dress?"

The woman looked to Andresh, who gave her a nod of assurance. "Yes, I am," she said.

I set to work cutting the silk and three yards of muslin for the lining. I folded each fabric as neatly as possible and wrapped them in tissue paper with a blue ribbon around each.

"Would you be interested in any of our artisan soaps?" I asked, gesturing to my little display at the counter.

"No thank you," she responded.

"I'm a fan of the lavender vanilla myself," Andresh said. "Subtly sweet and fresh. My favorite scent."

The woman looked at him for a moment, studying his face, then relented. "Fine. Add that to the bag, please."

"It's seventy-seven aums for the silk, thirty aums for the muslin, and four for the soap, to total one hundred and eleven aums."

She opened up her purse and searched for coins. She laid the pile of them on the counter. "And you'll accompany me to the other shop?" she asked Andresh.

"I'll be happy to walk with you," he said.

The woman accepted her fabric from me and linked her arm with Andresh's. The two exited the shop together. Nell, who had been closer to the front of the store, held the door open for them as they left. But she turned and rolled her eyes at me as the door shut behind them.

"What is it?" I asked her as she approached.

"She likes him. And you let him go with her, just like that!"

"I'm not *that* worried. After all, Andresh likes—" I stopped myself. The last I knew, Andresh liked me, but that was years ago, and even though we shared letters, he never said or wrote the words, "I like you." And with the years passing us by, it was very possible Andresh's feelings cooled, and he only saw me as a friend.

"Who does Andresh like?" Nell demanded.

"Never mind. I might be wrong." I raised my eyebrow at her. "Why does it bother you so much? Do you like him?"

"I do. He's handsome, and he's nice."

"That is true."

She looked at me, a pout spreading across her features. "Don't tell me you like him."

I hesitated for a moment, wondering what Nell's reaction would be, but I went ahead and said it: "I do."

"Oh great. So now we're in competition with each other." She let out a dramatic sigh.

"I don't know, Nell. What matters is who Andresh likes."

"Yeah, yeah." She went over to the shelf that advertised satin from the nation of Kimeria and took the boxes of gloves out. A mountainous country on the continent to our west, Sartōly, Kimeria was famous for its satin made from the horsehair of its unique breed, the Starsheen. Not a very subtle name for how the horses looked. The fabric that came from them was incredible, though, and very durable.

Nell opened each box to examine the pairs of gloves, and when she was satisfied, rearranged the boxes back on the shelf when she decided to change the subject. “Most of our cloth goods and fashion pieces are in solid shape, but we need to dust a lot of the other things. And we should lower the price of these gloves.”

“Kimerian satin is still hard to come by,” I said. “The sanctions Brinn put on Kimeria are still in effect.”

“But nobody’s buying them. Nobody wants to be caught dead in a pair of these gloves, considering the politics of it all.”

“...I’ll consider your point.”

“While we have a break, I’m going to check on Grandma.”

“That’s fine.”

Nell headed out the back entrance and up the stairs to the second floor, and I stood at the counter, wondering what to do next.

Andresh had done a lot of physical labor for us, and Nell was right, some of our products needed to be wiped down. There was still the mirror for the wardrobe to consider, too. And at some point, I’d need to show Andresh the contracts, price book, and our ordering and shipping schedules.

But I wasn’t in the mood to go over any of that with him. I kept thinking about Grandma, and soon after that, all the things Andresh told me about magic and demons and Gates. I simultaneously wanted his help and feared it. Feared what it meant for him to see Aineiron. Because, truth be told, I didn’t think Andresh was planning on only looking at him.

Nell came back downstairs and interrupted my thoughts. “She’s still out. I’m nervous. How long is it going to take for her to wake up? Should Andresh put the leeches on again?”

"When he comes back, we can ask him if he should try again. Dr. Basseter didn't come out and say how long it would take for Grandma to wake up, though. We should be patient." I didn't believe what I was saying. The longer Grandma was unconscious, the more scared I got, too.

It took almost an hour for Andresh to get back to us. I had no idea what had taken him and the lady so long, as Milanie's was a short walk away. But Andresh came back without her and instead, with a bag in his hand.

"That took forever!" Nell cried as the bells rattled and Andresh came in through the storefront door.

"She insisted on looking at nearly everything in Milanie's shop before settling on the dye. She doesn't come down to the Lower Quarter often, she said, because she's so busy at the hospital. Here, I brought you both something."

He reached into the bag and pulled out two small boxes for Nell and me. In them were stationery sets, one with lilies for me and another with marigolds for Nell. "How lovely," I said.

"So did you two talk about anything special?" Nell asked, brushing off her gift.

"She very persistently asked me questions about myself. I played charming and aloof." He smiled.

"I guess whatever it takes to get the sale," Nell said with a sigh. "I'm going to check on Grandma. Want to come with me, Andresh? You can carry up the supplies while I wash her down."

"Do you need me in the store right now, Lily?"

"I'll give you ten minutes, but someone needs to come back down and help me. Doesn't matter who. We are getting busier, after all."

The two of them nodded at me and headed back into the kitchen, where I heard some clanking of dishware and mugs hitting each other, the pouring of water, then the sound of steps up stairs.

Andresh and I didn't want Nell to learn about magic, but it seemed like magic was all Andresh could do to help. He wouldn't try anything with Nell there, would he? And he took a decent amount of Fire from Grandma—did he need to shave off more of her life in order for her to live?

While no one else was around, I gave it a try. I held my hand out, palm up and fingers spread, and thought to myself: *Unlock. Open the Gate. Let the Fire out.* For a second I thought my hand buzzed, but other than that, nothing happened. I sighed. Andresh was really the only person we could rely on for help, but even his help seemed to have limits.

I headed over to the counting desk and pulled out the world map, where Father had drawn in a neat red line the route from Brinn to Celderond. Near the Cape, cherubs with fat cheeks blew circles of wind out of their faces, and there was a picture of a ship broken on a set of rocks. *Travel with care,* Father had written, as if he couldn't help stating the obvious.

It was February twelfth, and Father was supposed to come back by the first week of March with silk in tow. Technically, he was still on schedule, but the problem was, we should have heard from him by now, and we hadn't. He always made certain to send word to us that he was fine whenever Cape Constant had been cleared, and when his ship had arrived in Celderond. The Stoneshore silk wouldn't last us long if Father's ship was delayed, or worse, never arrived. But...we had to sell it anyway.

A jangle above the door interrupted my thoughts, and a middle-aged man wearing a waistcoat and jacket slightly out of fashion—perhaps a decade old—entered the shop.

"Please," he said, his eyes watery and a look of desperation on his pink face. "I need more silk. Word is it Stoneshore brought you some. Do you have six bolts minimum?"

I paused. That was seventy-two yards of silk—enough for about eighteen dresses. We'd get over thirteen hundred aums, for certain, but...could we part with that much stock? It was half of what we had.

"Who are you purchasing this for?"

"I'm a representative from Dauphine's, a dressmaker's shop over in Ville-du-lac."

That was the city next over from Mariner. It was about twenty miles away. "How did you hear we had silk?"

"The Stoneshore men. We were supposed to get some too, but they were all out. The orders have started coming in. Please. We can't afford to turn away customers while we wait for the shipments to come in. They told me I can't come back empty-handed, or I'll be without a job." He was getting out of breath as he spoke, and for a moment I thought he would cry.

That moved me. I couldn't help it. We'd be selling half our stock, but...we could still sell our own set of eighteen dresses from it until March rolled in. But if Father's ship didn't come back on time...would I be dooming us to a failed Season?

Oh well. "I cannot sell you more than six bolts. And it'll be thirteen hundred and eighty-six aums."

The man grabbed my hands and clasped them in his own, shaking me with gratitude. "Oh, thank you, thank you!"

"Um...please don't advertise where you found the silk. We can't fill more orders like this until our own stock is refilled."

"You've done me a great service," he exclaimed. He pulled out a chequebook and wrote the total amount before tearing it out of his book and handing it to me.

"I have a coach secured out front," he said.

"Ah. I'm...unable to leave the store to help you," I said. I didn't want to abandon the front, or abandon Grandma if something were to suddenly happen.

"Understood. I should be able to handle all of them from here."

I went to the shelves and roughly pulled down six bolts of silk for him and piled them in his arms. The least I could do was hold the door open for him on his way out, and I did so.

Six bolts. Not bad...but then again, I hoped Grandma wouldn't wake up and kill me over it.

I slipped out of the store into the hallway and hollered, "Andresh? Nell? Can someone mind the store? It's my turn to start lunch," I said.

I thought for certain Nell would come down, but instead, it was Andresh.

"Oh. Are you ready to man the shop on your own?"

"I will try to make as much money as possible," he said with a grin.

"I, uh...I just sold a lot of our silk. Half of it. I hope I did the right thing."

"Don't you *want* to sell your product, though?"

"Yes, but if Father's silk shipment doesn't come in on time, or doesn't come at all, I might've ruined things for us. True, whether I sold half now or half later, the money incoming would be the same, but if Father doesn't return with more silk, we won't be able to fulfill future orders." I turned Andresh's ring around on my finger, suddenly quite nervous.

"If you want, I'll try to sell other things in the shop and hold off on silk unless someone directly requests it."

"You could really sell anything, I have no doubt about it," I said. "Just in case someone is coming in for fabric, let me show you."

Andresh followed me back into the shop to the counting desk and I pulled out the price book. "Everything is catalogued in here. Fabric is pre-calculated by yard up to twenty yards—anything more than that and you'll have to do the numbers on your own. The most common yardage requested is about four; each bolt holds twelve yards. You see there on the table, that slit? That's to help guide the scissors as you cut. And you saw where we keep the tissue paper and ribbon, right?"

"Yes. You don't have to worry about me. Although if I have questions, I can duck into the kitchen and ask for help, right?"

"Yes. I'll come out and check on you from time to time, though. See you soon!"

I left him alone in the shop and headed back into the kitchen. Honestly, I didn't feel like cooking at all. I surveyed our food, and we were out of fresh meat. Grandma was normally the one who kept track of all our food and did the shopping and preparation; she insisted on doing the work herself as she was thoroughly against hiring cooking staff for the house. "It's a waste of money," she had always said. Father had listened to her, and we were one of the rare merchant houses that didn't keep a staff or servants.

Now that Grandma was ill, I assumed her duties, even though Nell was a better cook than I was. I sighed. I was going to have to make a quick run to the butcher's shop. I went upstairs to my room to grab my coat. The butcher sold ham that was already boiled, and I could roast that in the lidded cast-iron pot for two hours, so lunch would only be a little bit later than scheduled. I decided that's what I would do for the meal, and I could boil some of the potatoes we already had in the house.

I put my coat on and grabbed my handbag to take with me, then got the urge to pop my head into Grandma's room to see how she was doing.

Nell was there, too, fast asleep in her chair, a blanket draped over her all the way up to her chin. She snored lightly.

Meanwhile Grandma was lying on her back, her eyes still closed, looking as comfortable as she had before. The drooping of her face seemed to have disappeared altogether. I took her hand in my own and squeezed it. "Hold on, Grandma," I said.

I placed my hand on her forehead. I felt her warmth there, and remembered what Andresh said about opening gates, that the forehead was one of them.

I don't know what made me do it. I suddenly wondered if I could open Grandma's gate by keeping my hand there. I felt this tingling sensation envelop my hand, and the next thing I knew, a small plume of purple shot out of Grandma's head. *No, no, no!* I didn't mean for that to happen! I hurriedly thought the word *CLOSE* and pulled my hand away, and as I did so, Grandma's eyes opened.

"Lily," she whispered.

CHAPTER 9

"Grandma," I said, and I teared up. "I'm glad you're awake."

I none too gently shook Nell until she roused. Her eyes widened, and her mouth dropped open. "Grandma!"

"Water," she said. Her voice sounded funny, as though she were far away. She drew the "r" sound longer than normal, making the word sound slightly slurred.

I ran downstairs to grab a glass from the kitchen and filled it. I ducked my head into the store where Andresh diligently dusted some porcelain figurines we imported from Lynette and nearly shouted at him, "Close the shop. Grandma's awake."

He let out a breath and moved to the front door, turning the sign over to "Closed" and locking it down. He followed me back up the stairs as I sat with Grandma and gave her some water to drink.

Nell, in the meantime, had started crying, as she held onto Grandma's hand.

She finished the cup and slowly pushed herself upright in the bed.

"Dr. Basseter said once she woke to give her the purgative," I said to Andresh in a soft voice, "but do you think that will help?"

"It would have the same effect as the leeching, I would think," Andresh said. "It would make her feel sick, as she would vomit."

"I thought so. Grandma, do you want more water?"

"I'm fine for now," she said, her voice still sounding off.

"You had a stroke," I explained. "You're going to be taking it easy for a while."

I looked at Andresh. "We should still contact Dr. Basseter now that she's awake, to see if there's anything else to be done. He wanted us to, anyway." I stood. "Andresh, come with me into the hallway for a moment."

He gave me a curious look but obeyed. "What's the matter?" he asked once we were there.

"I was—well, I wasn't playing around, but I was touching her forehead—and I brought Fire out of her. And she woke up."

"And you don't know the name of Fire, so you must have opened her gate."

"That's the only thing I can think of. I didn't mean to. It was a fleeting thought; I wasn't even concentrating. I didn't take another year off her life, did I?"

"You might have. I don't know because I didn't see it. But whatever you did helped her out of unconsciousness immediately." He squeezed my shoulder. "So, you saved her."

I couldn't believe it had happened. "I'll leave now for Dr. Basseter's. You won't mind staying with her, will you? I'm sure Nell would also appreciate it."

"Of course."

We both went back to Grandma's room, and I told her I was going to fetch the doctor. She nodded and said to Andresh in a slightly slurred voice, "I think I'll have more water after all."

He followed me down the stairs to refill her glass and I left him alone to head outside. I rushed to Dr. Basseter's hoping he was home. He was glad to hear that Grandma was awake. He and I returned to the house and made our way back upstairs to Grandma's room.

She and Andresh were talking, the conversation slow, but her voice sounded more like it used to. Nell interspersed with repetitive phrases: "I'm so glad you're up," and "I'm so relieved you're talking to us."

"I'm pleased to see you, Mrs. Bellamy," Dr. Basseter said to Grandma. He listened to her breathe, and checked her pulse, and asked her a few questions as to how she was feeling. "She seems to be in great shape despite what happened," the doctor said, "but I'm still putting her on bedrest for the week. Let her sleep whenever she wishes. No heavy meals—think broth and toast. She may need assistance moving around at first, too."

"That won't be a problem, doctor," I said.

He moved to the table where we'd left his things—the jar of leeches, the tongs, and the bottle of purgative. "There's still a lot of this left," he said.

"She didn't need that much," I said.

"Very well." He started packing his things up in his physician's bag and I walked him downstairs to our door to let him go. "Call on me in one week's time and I'll check her again."

"Thank you," I said. I headed back up the steps. "Grandma, Andresh and Nell are going to keep you company—I need to head to the butcher's to get our lunch. I'll be back soon."

I left them alone and made my way outside. I hurried along the street, excited that Grandma was awake, but fearful of what I'd done, wondering if I'd drained too much of her life force when I opened her gate. It was a little burst of flame—

maybe a few weeks' worth? Andresh didn't seem too bothered by what had happened, happier that she was awake now than anything else. Perhaps I shouldn't have worried so.

I picked up the meat from the butcher's, and once I returned home, I set to heating it up. It would take two hours, so lunch would be later than all of us were used to, but I thought with Grandma waking up, no one would mind. In the meantime, I made some toast and brought it upstairs to Grandma.

"She's back to sleep," Andresh said as I entered.

"Where's Nell?"

"She also went to sleep, but in her room this time. She's exhausted."

"Oh. I guess I'll eat this now. Do you want some? Lunch will take a little while to put together."

"Sure, I'll have a piece." He and I finished the toast, and he asked me, "What do you want to do about the shop? Should we reopen again now that she's feeling better?"

"I suppose we should. But I'll be running in and out of the kitchen again."

I took his empty plate, and Andresh followed me down the stairs. We readied the store and Andresh moved behind the sales counter, eyeing the shipping map that I'd left there earlier.

"Andresh. Do you honestly think Grandma is fine? That we didn't shorten her life too much?"

"I tried to take as little as possible, but with this magic, you can never be sure the exact amount of time. The worst of it would be a year, I think."

I grew silent. Andresh turned to me. "Listen. We did what we had to do to save her life. She's alive. That's what matters. And when the time comes for her to pass, well...I'll have figured things out by then."

I wasn't sure what he meant by that. I would've asked, but he turned his back to me once more and went back to work, and I took that as a sign that he didn't want to talk anymore.

Except I couldn't stand the silence. I went back to the kitchen to check on the ham and came back into the shop ready to talk about something, anything. "It seems we're not so busy right now."

"It doesn't trouble me. I'm ready for when it picks back up."

"You've been so helpful. I know you haven't been with us for long, but every day you've done something for us."

"You know I don't mind though, right? Put me to work as you see fit."

"Well, perhaps tomorrow I'll start showing you the trade routes—you seem pretty interested in that map—and how we put orders together. We have to do everything on a clockwork schedule."

"Sounds good to me."

I left him to go check on the ham, and the next hour was like that, where I would make small conversations with him about the shop, or what else he wanted to do now that he was in Mariner. He obliged me with answers, and then Nell returned to us from her room, looking groggy.

"Did you peek in to see Grandma? She's fast asleep," I said.

"I was wondering if I should stay up there with her some more."

"If you wish to. Andresh has the shop, and I have the meal. It should be ready in fifty minutes. I can call you down then."

When lunch was ready, we were all so hungry that we barely spoke during the meal, and after that, Nell said she wanted to stay with Grandma more, so I let her, as Andresh and I manned the shop.

The days continued similarly. I taught as much as I could to

Andresh about shipping and making deals; at the same time, we helped random customers who made their way into the store. When we weren't busy, it was back to cleaning things and rearranging them. I also switched between Nell and Andresh making deliveries for us when we picked up small orders here and there. It did make me nervous, as we soon were on our last bolt, and Father had sent no word of his arrival in Celderond.

Meanwhile, in between everything, I would check on Grandma, who grew stronger and more talkative every day, her words returning cleanly and clearly to her. She needed assistance moving around, and even though she got better, she still seemed a little wobbly. I picked up a cane, a curving piece of imported wood, from Milanie's for her to use. She was put-upon at first, but once she realized she could move without my help if she used it, she warmed to it. Although she was on bedrest still, she was able to take herself to the bathroom without issue, or she would practice walking circles in her room for a little bit each day. We were worried about stairs, though, so we always brought things to her, including her meals, which she ate in bed.

Dr. Basseter visited one more time and cleared Grandma for less bedrest, marveling at how well her health seemed back on track. "Of course, any time she wants to rest, let her," he said.

One day, when Grandma was well enough to take over her house chores, with Nell dutifully assisting her, a delivery came to our door—the new mirror for Mother's vanity I had ordered when we weren't busy. It was covered in sheer cloth, so I could still make out the outlines of shapes in the glass. I avoided it when the delivery man brought it to us at the counter.

Andresh noticed my discomfort and took the glass from me as I paid the delivery fee. He placed the mirror on the vanity table and grabbed some tools and took to installing it. He covered the glass with the cloth that used to cover it before.

"We've waited too long," he said in a hushed tone. "We need to work on Aineiron soon. I don't like seeing you work so hard against whatever visions you see. I want to help you."

"What do we need to do?"

"Tonight, come down here... When is everyone asleep? Midnight?"

"Sometimes Nell likes to stay up late. Better make it two."

"So two o'clock, come down here. I'll be waiting. We'll use the new mirror, I'll borrow your Fire, and I'll see what you see. Then I'll know more about Aineiron and his door. And how to kill him."

That didn't reassure me. I could overlook everything he said except for the demon-killing. That seemed incredibly dangerous. But he seemed so determined, so I did not speak up about it.

The nighttime came and as soon as it turned the hour we were to meet, I headed silently down the steps from my room into the kitchen, then the shop.

I was in my nightgown and bed jacket since it was chilly, and Andresh in his own gown and robe. Even in sleepwear, he looked like a prince, his bedclothes giving him a regal look. But what I noticed the most was his hair—freed from its braid, it cascaded around him like a velvet cloak, nearly down to his waist. I halted when I saw him, taking him in.

I snapped out of it. I folded my arms across my chest for warmth, and all sorts of thoughts entered my mind. What was it going to feel like? When I pulled Grandma's Fire, I didn't feel anything except a slight change in the air and some heat when the flames burst out, but nothing touched me, and nothing burned me. But this time, Fire was going to go out of my body, and Andresh's would flow in. Was it possible I would feel that, too? That type of connection between us?

As if Andresh knew my thoughts, he said, "I'm not going to hurt you; I won't let that happen. I'm not going to tell you not to be afraid, because you'll be seeing Aineiron again, but I'll be with you."

He gestured to me to approach him. "I'm going to stand close to you, right behind you. And the gate I'm going to open is the one above your heart. Because Aineiron is haunting you as someone you loved, and there are so many emotions tied to that haunting, Citrinitas would be the right one to open." He gestured to me, his voice gentle. "Here. Come closer."

The cover was off the mirror and Andresh took me by my shoulders and positioned me in front of him. "May I?" he asked, gesturing to my jacket.

"Sure," I responded. He drew my jacket open, revealing the low collar to my nightgown. "I'm going to place my hand here now."

"That's fine," I said. But I held my breath anyway as the stark-white skin of his palm met with the cool skin of my chest. I jerked my shoulders when he touched me, ever so slightly.

"What is it?"

"Oh. Your hand is warmer than I thought it would be."

"It's going to get much warmer as I start the magic," he said.

"Hurry," I said to him. While Andresh was getting in position to work his spell, inky tendrils started forming around the corners of the mirror, and mist appeared along the bottom of it, inside the glass.

Heat pooled in my chest, like a flower bursting into its first bloom, and I felt lightheaded as something pulsed within me underneath Andresh's hand. I felt it melt away, brimming upward and out, pouring into Andresh.

While I couldn't see the actual flames, light shone in the lines between Andresh's fingers to reveal a lilac-colored hue. "So that's what it looks like. My Fire."

"They say everyone has their own color," he said. "You'll see mine in a second."

A tendril of brilliant turquoise intermingled with the lilac, and it brushed along my skin like a feather, before settling deep into my heart. I still felt a slight tickle there where his blue flames entered my body. And for every bit of Fire that left me, Andresh's filled me up, and a dizziness grew within me, along with the heat, and a bizarre feeling of elation...until the thing that looked like my mother appeared in the glass. A bloated corpse with eyes missing, lips and eyelids chewed away, and hair floating around in the air, as if underwater, a pulse and rhythm moving the tendrils on their own.

Andresh kept pulling heat from me and I continued to warm up, sweat starting to form at my brow. "Do you see her?" I asked him, my voice hardly above a whisper.

"Yes, I do," he said, and to my surprise, his words came out a little shaky. "But remember who it is. It's not your mother."

"Save me, please. Open the door," the figure begged.

I shook my head. A bead of sweat trickled down my face, and as Andresh continued to pull Fire from me, I felt myself growing dizzier. "How much longer will this take?"

"I need to see if Aineiron will either show himself, or the door—"

The woman in the mirror opened her mouth in a silent scream and thousands of flies escaped her lips, swarming the mirror.

"If we take any more time, we'll feel it," I said.

The scene in the mirror changed. All the flies had disappeared, and Aineiron was nowhere to be seen. It was a smoky background that had opened up, like a room with no walls to be seen, going on forever and ever. A large black gate appeared, circular, like a moon gate, and an eerie green light permeated the smoky, dark atmosphere.

A new figure emerged from the gate—something white and marble, like a statue, the shape of a man, carrying a huge golden staff in its hands. It would have been beautiful if it weren't for its solid black eyes and the pale scorpion tail attached to its body, giving it a menacing aura. The tail was raised to strike. The figure advanced towards us, raising its staff and pointing it at us.

"No," Andresh whispered. "Not yet."

Heat flooded my chest in a rapid burst—it almost hurt—as Andresh pushed and pulled at the Fire in my body. In one fell swoop he broke away from me and threw the cover back on the mirror. I didn't think it was possible, but his alabaster skin had turned two shades whiter, and he looked frightened.

"Was that Aineiron? His true form?"

"No," he said, his voice breathy, "that was something else."

"What was it?"

"I don't know what it is," he said quickly. The color started returning to his face and he sounded a little calmer. "I had no idea it was that bad for you, what you've endured for all these years."

"I'm glad you didn't think I was crazy, that you didn't think any of this wasn't real."

He clutched my shoulders. "Of course I'd believe you." He smoothed the hair back from my face, his fingers gently touching my scar as he glided his hands over my reddish-brown strands. "What strength you have, to endure such a thing."

"I admit, I'm tired of being strong," I said. I still felt a little faint, but I was coming back to myself.

"It won't be much longer now," he said. "I promised to help you, and I will."

I nodded, then felt my face. "Ugh. I feel so clammy."

"I wasn't gentle when I returned your Fire to you," Andresh admitted. "I'm sorry. I should have been more careful." He offered his hand to me. "Let's get you back to bed."

I grabbed my jacket and accepted his hand, letting him lead me up the stairs to my room, where I lit a taper. Andresh disappeared as the light filled my room, and he came back with a small bowl of water and a washcloth.

"Here," he said. "I thought you might want to cool down." He dipped the cloth and wrung it out, eyeing me closely. His brilliant blue eyes looked black in the dim light, but there was a sheen to them, a glossiness there.

He gently brought the cool cloth to my forehead and slowly wiped around my hairline, my cheeks, my chin. I stood there, hardly breathing, as he smoothed the skin at my neck and collarbone with the fabric. After the slightest of pauses—he had stopped breathing, too—he reached with the cloth at the collar of my nightgown, gently wiping the beads of sweat from the very top of my breasts at the cleavage.

I did not cool down when he did that.

The tips of two fingers grazed me as he washed me down, and it felt like a shock between us. I flinched. He stopped and set the bowl and cloth on my dresser. "...In case you get warm in the night again," he said, a trace of huskiness in his voice.

I crawled into my bed as my heart beat fast in my chest where he had touched me. I couldn't take my eyes off of him as he made it to my doorway, his beautiful black hair a long veil against his sturdy back.

Andresh stood there for a moment in silence. The fingers of

his left hand flicked ever so subtly, and he said without looking at me, “I’ll see you tomorrow.”

“Wait.”

That turned his head. He peered at me with his brows slightly raised in curiosity.

I pulled the covers of my bed aside. “Stay with me.”

“...You want me to...”

“Stay. Keep me safe.”

He returned to my room, slowly and silently. He removed his robe, revealing his white nightgown, and walked to the side of my bed.

“Are you sure?” he whispered.

“Yes. Please come to bed.”

Andresh slid onto the mattress, leaving the comforter pushed off, and tugged the bedsheet up over him. He turned to his side, and his breathing tickled the back of my hair.

I reached for his hand and held it for a moment, before pulling it to wrap his arm around my waist.

Andresh let out a little breath and repositioned himself, and his arm circled me tighter as he drew me into him.

After a moment of silence, Andresh whispered, “Good-night, Lily.”

We fell asleep like that, together in each other’s arms.

CHAPTER 10

In the morning, I woke to Nell's voice in the hallway: "How could you!" I rolled out of an empty bed and rose to my feet. Andresh was standing in the hall in his nightclothes, his robe in his hands, as Nell turned on her heels and left in a huff.

"Did she see you leave my room?" I asked him.

"Yes."

"Well, that's going to be fun to explain."

"Perhaps we shouldn't have—"

"It made me feel better, being with you. I don't regret it."

To my surprise, Andresh turned a little red at that. "I liked being with you, too," he said.

"Don't worry about Nell. I'll talk to her now and try to calm her down. Go ahead and get ready for the day."

Andresh nodded and headed back upstairs to his room while I took a breath and knocked on Nell's door. "I'm coming in," I told her.

"Fine," she said, sounding abrupt.

To my surprise, her face was puffy and red, and her eyes pink and watery. I had no idea she would be so upset.

"Nell..." I gestured to her bed. "May I sit down?"

She didn't protest, so I scooted by her side next to her, my back leaning against the headboard.

"What was he doing leaving your room?"

"I was frightened, and he stayed with me, that's all."

"It better not have been in bed."

I paused. "Well, yes."

She let out a gasp. "Lily! You know that's not proper!"

"I know. But I didn't want to be alone. And Andresh wanted to be there for me."

"I don't stand a chance, do I?" she said miserably.

I knew I had to be careful with my words, but I also wanted to tell her the truth. "There's been something between me and Andresh for a long time. I wasn't sure if it would continue after all these years apart, but...I think our feelings are the same as before."

"Does he love you?"

"I don't know if I'd call it love, exactly—he's never said as much—but we've shared moments together where I know he likes me. It's his actions more than his words," I said.

"Have you kissed him?"

"We have. Years ago, though. It was more like he kissed me, though."

She let out the most dramatic sigh. "I wanted to be the one to kiss him. I wanted to be the one he liked."

"I don't know if Andresh can see you beyond a friend, though. And sometimes like a sister, too."

"If only I was older. Then he'd see me as more of an equal."

"I'm sorry. I want to be as honest with you as possible. This might not turn out the way you wish it."

"But I love him so much."

"You feel that strongly about it?" I had to admit she surprised me a little, using a word like "love."

"Don't try to tell me I don't love him. I know my heart. My feelings are true! I love him! He's so handsome, and he's always been a gentleman! He's perfect!"

"I don't want to tell you not to feel your feelings. But you should know, Andresh and I might become even closer than we are now. And...I'm not going to stop that."

She looked at me, saying nothing for a moment, as my words seemed to churn in her brain. She clenched her hands into fists and swallowed. "...He hasn't said he loves you yet. So I'm going to do my best to make him notice me. If that doesn't work, I'll stop. But I don't plan on giving up just yet." She sounded newly determined, different from the misery she expressed before.

I wasn't sure what to say to her. I didn't want to discourage her, but I wanted her to be realistic. "It's whoever Andresh chooses," I said. "Fair?"

Nell nodded. "Fair."

The understanding we came to made me feel a little bit better. I didn't want to be in competition with Nell at all. Truthfully, if it were anyone but Andresh, there'd be no contest—anyone would fall in love with Nell, and easily, too. And I didn't want to look at Andresh like he was a possession, believing that he was mine and no one else's. But I knew that I also needed to be honest with Nell about where he and I might be going with our relationship. I wondered if perhaps I should ask him pointedly what he felt about me to stop this potential rivalry between Nell and I in its tracks. Plus, it was better for me to know how he felt so I could steer myself accordingly. The more time I spent with him, the deeper I found myself falling for him.

I headed back to my room and noticed the bowl of water

and washcloth resting on my dresser. Andresh was so gentle with me...and I wanted him to touch me again.

I brought my palm to my cheek to feel the skin there, and sure enough, I was warming up from the memory—embarrassment, lust, whatever—and I knew I needed to calm down. I took my morning bath, the water a little cooler than usual this time, and headed to my room to dress and start the day.

Nell was already downstairs in the kitchen talking to Andresh, who, to my surprise, was making breakfast for us.

"This is a nice treat," I said. "We appreciate it."

"I figured I should contribute a bit more," Andresh said. "It's a simple meal, but I hope it's filling."

I could smell the eggs and sausage links cooking, and Andresh took a moment to briefly slice up some tomatoes. It didn't take long before three plates were at the dining table, ready for all of us to dive in.

Truth be told, I never cared for tomatoes, so I drank a lot of water to wash my slice of it down and hoped Andresh didn't notice my struggle with it. He did not, until Nell pointed it out.

"Lily, you still hate tomatoes, I see." She laughed and turned her attention to Andresh. "Father tried to get us into vegetables ever since we were little, and for whatever reason, tomatoes would make her gag. She can't even chew them. She has to wash them down in pieces with a drink."

I wiped my mouth and said, "Some habits can't be broken."

Andresh smiled. "If I would have known that, I wouldn't have served you any."

"It's quite alright. They remind me of Father. He wanted me to like tomatoes very badly, as they are his favorite. He even bites into them like apples when he has the chance."

"I love it when he cuts them up into small pieces with tomato sauce, beef balls, and noodles," Nell said. "He said he learned that dish in Celderond. It's delicious."

"I'll have to ask him to make it when he returns," Andresh said. "I've never had a meal from Celderond before."

"What's strange is I could stomach the sauce, just not the tomato pieces," I added. "It is *almost* a perfect dish."

Andresh gave me an amused look, the corners of his mouth turning up into a slight smile. "I never realized you were such a picky eater."

"You were never around when we ate tomatoes," I said simply. "You should see me when I try to eat broccoli."

Nell cleared her throat to make an announcement: "Andresh, I'm going to paint a portrait of you."

His eyes widened. "Really? I'm flattered."

"I'll be using the watercolors you got me from Sindalia. I've been thinking about this for a while and I wanted to give you something special. So you can remember me every time you look at it."

"I'll always remember you, Eleanor. There's nothing for you to worry about."

The glow that spread across Nell's features almost didn't seem real. Her cheeks turned pinker and her eyes had a gloss to them that made them shine. She burst into a brilliant smile, and I could see the love for Andresh oozing out of her. The face she made would win anyone's heart.

But Andresh was looking at me instead. "Would it interfere with work, sitting for a portrait?"

"Well...things are still not busy. I'll give you an extra forty minutes after lunch to work on it. I don't want this taking weeks, though."

"It won't take weeks," Nell said, sounding slightly offended. "I'll have it done in three days."

"That's good," I replied.

"You're very kind for letting us do this, Lily," Andresh said.

"And Eleanor, this is a generous gift. I look forward to posing for you."

The sound of Grandma Violet's cane thumping down the stairs drew our attention away from the conversation. She had made it to the kitchen slowly, but without needing help, which was a great improvement. "Smells good," she said. "Any left for me?"

"I'll make it fresh," Andresh said, rising out of his chair.

Grandma Violet moved to sit at the end of the table, and she folded her hands and perched her chin on the top of her hooked cane.

A pounding on the door, so loud it shook the bells attached to it, startled us. "Who could that be, knocking so violently?" Grandma Violet asked, her voice a mixture of fear and annoyance.

I stood up. "Let me look." I darted into the shop to the front, and a man in a black tricorn hat and black jacket stood there, holding something in his hand. I unlocked the door.

"Mrs. Bellamy?"

"Miss Bellamy. But I can answer for her."

He gave me a quick nod. "I apologize for the noise, but this is urgent." He passed to me what turned out to be a letter:

> *It is with great regret I inform you that the merchant vessel Windchaser was beset upon by brigands off Cape Constant who opened fire on the ship; the Windchaser returned blows but was lost. There are no known survivors of the attack, and while the brigands seized some items, the rest of the goods transported sank with the ship. It is a total loss of merchandise, and more tragically, life. We encourage you to contact the Maritime Indemnity Company to begin the claims process. You have our deepest condolences. Sincerely, Robert Thrasher, President, MIC.*

The letter fluttered out of my hand and my knees buckled; the messenger kindly caught me and pulled me up until I was sturdy again. The tears flooded my eyes and streamed down my cheeks.

"I am so sorry to deliver this news to you," the messenger said.

"When did this happen?" I managed to ask.

"The letter should be dated, miss."

I glanced at the top of the note and saw it was from the end of January, a little less than a month ago. The Maritime Indemnity Company must have spent more than a bit to rush this letter to us.

I wiped my eyes. "Thank you for coming all this way. I'll share this with the family." My voice trembled as I spoke.

"My deepest condolences," the messenger said, sounding like his letter. He gripped the tip of his tricorn, turned, and left.

I inhaled, then let out the shakiest of breaths as I relocked the shop door and stumbled back toward the kitchen.

Nell's jaw lowered when she saw me, and her eyebrows turned up with worry; Andresh, however, spoke first. "Lily. You look like you've seen something."

I swallowed and passed the letter to Grandma Violet. "I've read it. I don't think I can bear to read it out loud."

Grandma nodded and took the paper from me. She read it for all of us, her voice starting out strong and authoritative, but dwindling down as she got toward the end of the note. She placed it face down on the table. "My son," she whispered.

Nell started sobbing, and she buried her face in Andresh's ribs. With one hand he clutched one of her shoulders, and the other hand patted her back. The rhythm of it was awkward, and Andresh looked uncomfortable and unsure of himself as Nell bawled.

I cried, too, albeit silently, and soon Andresh's eyes grew

wet and pink, although he shed no tears. Grandma Violet remained visibly stoic compared to the rest of us as she stated, "We're ruined for the Season. Even if Maritime Indemnity compensates us for our loss, it'll be too late to import what we need." She gripped her cane so hard her knuckles turned white, and she rose to her feet. "The shop will be closed. I don't know how long. But I can't help plan another funeral." She trundled to the doorway and called back to us, "I'll see to the accounts and file the claims. Don't disturb me."

I sank into one of the dining table's chairs. "I suppose we're going to take care of the funeral and headstone...he should rest next to Mother, shouldn't he?"

Nell pulled herself away from Andresh and wiped her eyes roughly. "I don't want to talk about that right now."

"Fair enough." But I knew there was a lot we had to do. We hadn't gone into mourning since Mother died, and none of our old clothing would fit any of us. I could commission new dresses for me and Nell, but an immediate concern now was saving money. Although Grandma threw herself into the paperwork, we didn't know how long it would take for Maritime Indemnity to get funds to us.

"Nell...we don't have to talk about this more, but when you have a moment, give me your white dresses and lay them on my bed. I'll dye them."

She nodded. "I'm going to my room. I want to be alone." She shakily made it up the stairs and out of sight.

I rubbed at my eyes. "I have so much to prepare..." I said with a sigh.

Andresh took the seat next to mine. "I don't understand how this could have happened," he said, his voice wavering. "How he could just be...gone?"

"Death seems to follow us, doesn't it?" I gave him a pitiful half smile. I didn't know why, because nothing I had to say was worth a smile. "Both our families. No more mothers or fathers." I started sobbing.

Andresh pulled me to him in his chair, lifting me slightly so I would fit in his lap. I buried my face in the space between his neck and shoulder and wrapped my arms around him tightly. He cradled my head in his hand, and his other rested on my back.

We stayed like that in silence for a few moments as I struggled to contain my emotions. My body shook but I was able to stop the pathetic sounds I made when I was crying harder. I took in a breath, and at last I stilled.

"There must be something I can do," Andresh said. "There has to be. To have all this power, all this magic, and yet not be able to—"

"It's alright, Andresh. The best thing you can do for us is to be here."

His voice softened. "And what can I do for you?"

"...You can hold me like this for a while."

He did.

A WEEK HAD PASSED, and some days it seemed to have flown by without any of us comprehending what happened over the course of hours; other days slowed painfully to the point that time seemed to stop.

Father's death hurt so much more than Mother's did, because he had been such a sturdy presence in our lives. Even though he'd leave us for adventures on the *Windchaser,* he always came back. In Mother's absence, he raised us the best he could, and he was always there with a kind word, a hearty laugh, and soft embrace. And in our grief, we didn't talk about any fond memories like that.

Grandma saw us at meals but kept to herself. Nell threw herself into her art, although she wanted to wait until she was out of her gloom before painting Andresh. I busied myself with menial tasks, doing laundry far more often than was necessary, and impulsively reorganizing the books on the shelves in the third-floor library.

Andresh helped me with the books. They had been properly alphabetized, but now I wanted to shelve them by size so there would be some visual uniformity and less madness in the stacks. As we worked, he listened to me list all the things we needed to do for Father's funeral, and he listened to my worries, and he listened to my fears. He wouldn't give advice. He simply said, "Tell me what you need me to do, and I'll do it."

By the second week, I had dyed all of our mourning gowns in a deep, rich black. Andresh didn't have such clothing at the ready, so he went to Regal & Smith, the most talented tailors in Mariner, for his suits.

The most expensive thing was the headstone. To save money, we opted for slate instead of marble, but the engraving and intricately carved borders in stone drove up the price. Nell wanted to see the stone first before settling it in Rookwood's cemetery, so we commissioned it from a mason in Mariner and brought it with us on the lengthy carriage ride to Rookwood. Grandma did not come with us.

Nell wanted to carry the tombstone but it was on the heavier side, so Andresh gently asked her for it, and she gave it to him. When we all piled into the carriage, he clutched the tombstone on his lap beside her hard enough that his knuckles had turned white, as though by his sheer grip the stone would be fully protected. While clutching the stone, he busied himself looking outside the carriage window, taking in the view of the coastal city retreating from his gaze.

I sat opposite them and took a cue from Andresh, watching the landscape change. Stone roads gave way to wide, muddy paths. The environment grew grassier, hillier, and wilder.

"Should we...drive by our old homes?" I asked the question cautiously. It popped into my head, and I immediately regretted asking it when Nell and Andresh both said in overlapping voices, "I'll pass."

"I understand," I said. Too many bad memories for all of us.

We remained silent until we reached Saint Briscol's Cemetery, the major resting place for generations of Rookwood villagers. The coach stopped once at the outer gate, and we stepped outside.

I remembered where Mother was buried, even after all these years. I could trace the route like the lines on the palm of my hand. I led our tiny procession to the far back of the graveyard toward the weeping willows that formed a barrier at the end of the cemetery. Mother's resting place was in front of one of those trees, looking lonely.

Even though Father's tombstone might keep her company at last, his body never would.

I swallowed. That thought brought tears immediately. I wiped them away in silence.

Nell stepped forward, her hand resting on Andresh's arm, as if to guide him with the tombstone. "What do we do now?"

Andresh eyed the area around Mother's grave. "The foundation hasn't been added yet. We can't put the stone up."

"So what do we do?" Nell's voice started to rise. "Just leave the stone on the ground face-up? It'll look like a pauper's grave."

"I've got to put it down, though," Andresh said. He laid it where a body would go. "I'll find the groundskeeper or someone else who can help us," Andresh said. "Possibly the church?" He turned away from us. "You can have the funeral without me." He didn't sound cross, but there was something short in his voice, and a little pained.

Nell and I didn't stop him. She and I stood there in silence for a while.

"I don't know what to say."

Nell sighed. "I don't know, either. We should have gone ahead and hired the priest."

"It seemed strange to have a ceremony when Grandma wouldn't stand for one," I said. "It's enough that we say something to Father, I think."

"I don't want to say it out loud. I'll pray." Nell stepped forward to the spot where Father's stone was. "Guess this will have to do for now." She folded her hands and closed her eyes. After a moment, she whispered, "Humble Father, Heavenly Mother, bless us," then her usual posture returned. She looked to me.

"Um..." I shut my eyes but decided to speak aloud. "Kale Bellamy, our beloved father, thank you for being such a warm and wonderful person who never hesitated to let us know how much he loved us. May you be reunited with the ones you love and wait for us to return to you in the time of our death. We'll see you again." In my mind I added, *I hope that what you always wanted for Andresh will come true: that he will finally be a part of this family.*

"That was nice," Nell said.

"Thanks. You think we're done here?"

She nodded. "Let's go get Andresh."

We walked back along the pathway through what seemed like a forest of headstones until we were back to the entryway to the cemetery. The Church of Saint Briscol stood imposingly off to the right of the graveyard, and Andresh exited out of a side door with a sign marked "Administrative Office." He clutched a paper in his hand and waved at us with it, hurrying over.

"It's done. The foundation will be ready in two days, and they'll fix the stone. They said I could leave it at the site so it would be easy to find."

I leaned over to him and said in a low voice, "How much did it cost?"

He dismissed me with a wave. "It's done," he repeated. "You don't need to worry about it."

I couldn't help how loud my voice came out: "You took care of it? You paid for it?"

He gave me a solemn look; something in his sapphire eyes communicated a vow. "I'll take care of you."

I blushed and immediately looked to Nell. Her eyes widened.

"I'll take care of all of you," Andresh said. "I promise."

CHAPTER 11

I poked my head into the third-floor library. Andresh was seated in one of the plush chairs, keeping perfectly still and looking straight ahead, while Nell sat across from him and finished sketching him onto her canvas.

I couldn't keep myself from peeking, and I strode over to her. She had just finished the final details of Andresh's long, plaited hair.

"Nell, that's a solid likeness!" She had nailed his appearance, of course, but the tiny details were there, too, like the secret smile he wore at the corner of his mouth sometimes. She captured it perfectly.

Andresh strained in his chair and Nell said, "You're not allowed to look until it's done."

"I'm going to have a hard time waiting, Nell," Andresh said.

Nell's hand stilled, and the stylus she used for her silverpoint sketch fell from her fingers.

Her cheeks flushed with a feverish red color, and her eyes instantly watered. She took in a breath and said, her voice shaking, "Andresh, are you to be my brother? Because only then can you call me that."

Andresh's eyebrows raised up slightly. "Eleanor. I'm sorry. I know that's your preferred address."

"Can you answer me, though? Will you be my brother?"

"I've always hoped you'd consider me a brother," he said carefully. "I've not only thought of you as my little sister, but as a dear friend."

Nell rubbed at her eyes. "Ah, I understand." Her voice sounded breathier than normal, flimsy and feathery. "I'm going to go to my room for a while." She rose from her seat and quickly draped a cover over the canvas.

Andresh rose to his feet, too, and to my surprise, Nell went up to him and gestured for him to lean in to her. She murmured something in his ear—all I caught was *declare*—and she squeezed his shoulder before disappearing downstairs to the second floor.

"I should go after her," Andresh said. "I've hurt her feelings."

"It's a bit tricky with her," I said. "Sometimes she wants to be chased, and sometimes she doesn't."

"I'll give it a try."

"You understand why she's so upset, yes?"

He nodded. "She's felt something for me for years. If I gave her any sign—if I suggested anything to her—"

"You haven't, Andresh. You've just been your friendly, kind self as always."

"I'm relieved, thank you." He had made his way to the doorframe. He paused to look at me.

"It's you, Lily. It always has been." A pale pink dusted his alabaster cheeks when he said it.

My lips parted and I thought I would say something, but

nothing came out. He darted from the library, leaving me alone with my thoughts.

That was certainly a confession. And with Andresh's actions as of late, and how physically close we had gotten (tiptoeing the lines of propriety), all of that could only mean one thing: He loved me. And I loved him, too.

It was unfortunate how his declaration came about, and even more unfortunate that Nell was a casualty in all this, but I couldn't help feeling a dizzying elation at the thought that my feelings for Andresh would be reciprocated.

The bells to the storefront door jangled so loudly from the banging knocks that I heard it clearly all the way up on the third floor.

I hurried down the stairs. When I made it to the second floor I casually shouted, "I got it!" and rushed down to the bottom, through the kitchen, and into the shop.

Grandma was already there, undoing the lock and opening the door to an older gentleman in a gray suit and white stockings.

"Mrs. Bellamy of Bellamy Mercantile?" he asked her.

She nodded.

"Delivery for you. Please look over this document."

As he handed Grandma a paper, I sidled up beside her and spotted a large, two-horse-drawn wagon parked in front of our shop whose painted sides read: *Pendric's Fabric Emporium, established 1806, Capua Cora.*

"Did we order something, Grandma?"

Grandma Violet looked bewildered. "Is this care of Maritime Indemnity?" she asked the gentleman.

He shook his head. "It's on the document I gave you. Full accounting of the silk, size, weight, colors, and quantity. From your benefactor. That's all I can tell you, Mrs. Bellamy."

"Silk?" My mouth fell open. "Do we have a benefactor, Grandma?"

She seemed just as stunned as I was. "Not that I know of."

"Please sign the line at the bottom of that note and I'll take it back with me to confirm you have received your stock. My workers and I will unload. Tell us where you want it."

The gentleman handed a pen to Grandma, who signed the paper as asked. The man tore the bottom of the sheet off so she could keep the inventory list, and he tucked that piece of paper into his satchel. "Pendric's Fabric Emporium thanks you for your patronage," he said, and gave a little bow.

Grandma directed three men, who had been riding in the back of the wagon with the stock, to place the bolts of fabric on the counter, but that was quickly filled up, so we had to resort to stacking things on the floor in addition to the shelves. Thick tissue paper was wrapped around each bolt to protect the silk from getting marred in any way, but we could still see the colors through the paper. White and cream. Pastels. Jewel tones. We had never had such a variety of silk in our shop before.

All in all it totaled fifty bolts. I was so shocked I couldn't have even possibly figured how much that would have cost our "benefactor." And to have it hand-delivered to us all the way from Capua Cora, a three-day ride from Mariner? The numbers wouldn't stay in my head because all my thoughts kept dwelling on a single conclusion: *Andresh did this for us.* The Zataviers had always been wealthy but lived humbly. This was no humble gesture, but incredibly kind.

As we profusely thanked all the men from Capua Cora and gave them some cold food to take back with them, I noticed Nell and Andresh staring at us curiously from the kitchen and hallway.

"Come out here! Come and see!" I waved wildly at them as

Grandma shut the storefront door behind her. She stood there, leaning on her cane, but looked at all of us. She burst into a smile, one I hadn't seen in a very long time.

"We're saved this Season, and possibly more."

"Look at all the colors we have!" I said, gesturing to the piled bolts of fabric everywhere.

"They're beautiful," Nell said, tiptoeing around all of them.

Grandma walked with her cane right toward Andresh. She gestured for him to lower himself to her, as if she wanted to whisper in his ear like Nell did earlier. She gave him a kiss on the cheek, the sound of the air and her lips making an exaggerated smacking sound. "Thank you, Andresh, my boy."

Andresh paled. "What?"

Nell, who seemed emotionally healed from the day's earlier events with him, wrapped her arms around his waist, and Grandma hugged him by the shoulders. "Thank you, Andresh," Nell said.

"No, it's your benefactor—"

I added myself to the group's embrace, my arms circling everyone else. "Thank you, Andresh."

He let out a sigh. Then came the corner-of-the-mouth smile, but he said nothing.

Word spread through Mariner that Bellamy Mercantile got a massive shipment of silk in, and we were the only shop to stock such variety for miles. We quickly became busy, almost *too* busy, fulfilling single orders and making special deals with the local seamstresses and tailors to have silk sent to them directly for their commissions. Even Mr. Milanie stopped by to give us both condolences for Father and congratulations on such a turnaround in business. And our busyness continued through March and into April and May—right before the Season officially began in Highgate.

When people wandered into the shop, they greeted us kindly, as all of us were still in our mourning clothes. They'd no doubt heard of the *Windchaser* disaster, and as we would package up their fabrics in tissue paper and ribbon, they'd offer a simple, "Sorry for your loss."

Soon it was the first Thursday in May. We closed our store Thursdays and Sundays, and Nell had packed up our mourning dresses to take to Phoebe's shop for alterations. The black dye I had used months before on our gowns worked well, but was a little harsh on the more delicate fabrics—the lace that trimmed our bodices and sleeves had started to shred.

Nell didn't mind heading out to Phoebe's on her own, or doing other chores for us. And with the shop closed, Andresh asked if he and I could be alone somewhere for a good while.

Nell *did* hear that part. "Oh, you two," she muttered, but for once, she did not look unhappy that Andresh sought to be with me. Whatever he had said to her on the day of the name slip must've calmed her down. "Make it a picnic," she said. "It's supposed to be a beautiful day."

"And you'll be fine busying yourself after dropping our clothes off?" I asked her.

"I think I'll finally finish that painting," she said. She meant the one of Andresh. Her silverpoint of him looked so beautiful that it alone would have sufficed as the art, but her specialty was watercolor. She had paused everything in order to help get the store set up, and although I said nothing of this, I thought a tiny part of her was still upset with Andresh and halted the project until she decided she felt better. No matter what, it was good she had chosen to resume her work. She was talented, and I wanted to see how the portrait would come out.

Meanwhile, there was Grandma Violet. I was surprised she

would let me go with Andresh unattended, as the rules of polite society dictated I be chaperoned or with a third person during excursions with a handsome young man...and perhaps the even bigger rule, there was to be no courtship or social activity while in mourning.

She didn't seem to care at all. "Be back before supper. Behave yourselves."

Soon I had a small basket of fruit and cakes in hand, and Andresh, looking like a prince of the night with his black suit and braided black hair, held the side door open for me as we stepped out.

He carried a black satchel with him, something that looked new, but I couldn't recall seeing when he'd picked it up. As we went along the narrow alley in between our shop and the other buildings, he took my arm in his, and we walked together.

I was certain I blushed. My face grew warm and the heat pooled in my freckled cheeks. But I wouldn't unlink myself from him.

"How secluded do you want us to be?" I asked.

"A place where people won't see us," he said, "but, not so far that we'd not be able to come back here easily in case something should happen."

Ah. There it was. "This isn't only going to be a picnic, is it?"

"I promised you I would take care of you. I let months go by without helping you."

"You've done so much! How could you say something like that? You saved us, our livelihoods—"

"I'm going to save you, Lily."

"I'm happy with the way things are now. I don't want you rushing off into mirrors and darkness when we...when we've gotten so close. I've endured these visions all these months, all these years. Let's just have a picnic today?"

He stopped and unhooked his arm from mine. He gave me

such a pitiful look, like a puppy whose tail had been stepped on. "I finally figured out how to kill him, though."

"Aineiron?"

"All of them. Anyone that dares to hurt you. The answer was in front of me the whole time, so simple, so straightforward, and I *know* I can do it."

"I don't think I want you to kill anything, though."

"Even something that's hurt you for years and won't stop?"

"You can't stop him without killing him?"

He paused. "It's the least dangerous method." He must have noticed how quickly the excitement for our trip disappeared from my eyes, because he added, "We don't have to do it today, Lily. I'm sorry."

"You don't have to apologize. I want to have fun with you, after all the tumult and trials we've been through. We can delve into the supernatural some other time."

"So you *will* let me help."

"I don't want to keep you from doing what's important to you."

He gave me a small smile. He didn't offer his arm to me again, but he stayed by my side as we kept walking along the street. After some moments, he asked, "Where are we headed to?"

"Rinnea Abbey."

"The ruins? Wouldn't that be a popular spot?"

"Surprisingly, no. It's been picked apart. Some of the walls still stand, but it's mostly grass and rubble. The stained glass and anything that used to have gold in it is gone. And a few years ago, robbers chipped away the saint's face from her statue, too, so you can't see her beauty anymore. Well, that's not true—the statue is still beautiful. It makes you imagine what Our Lady would have looked like centuries ago."

"There aren't a lot of Our Ladies left in the world," Andresh remarked. "There's Our Lady of Willows, Our Lady of Nightshade, Our Lady of Feldspar, Our Lady of Eternal Rest—she's popular in Sindalia, and she has a huge cathedral in Evandra. Which one is this one?"

"Saint Rinnea, Our Lady of Knives," I said. "I always liked her story. Patron saint of righteous anger."

Andresh smiled. "You've never struck me as an angry person."

"I think I'm capable. But nothing has pushed me far into anger; only grief."

To my surprise, he leaned over and kissed the crown of my head, something soft and light.

I tried to catch him with a kiss back, but he moved away quickly and my upper lip dragged across his cheek, revealing my teeth on his skin, and a faint trace of slobber. I covered my mouth, horrified, as he started laughing. He wiped off his cheek with his hand.

"We'll get it right next time," he said.

I couldn't help but laugh with him, too.

"Is it far away, the abbey? I'd heard of it but have never been there," Andresh said as we resumed walking.

"We'll have to head up through Highgate and into the field until the hills start to appear. It doesn't take all that long. It's sitting lonely on top of one of them. Can't miss it. I'm surprised you didn't see it when we took the ride out to Rookwood—we passed it along the way."

"I wasn't paying much attention to anything that day, to be honest," he said.

"Understandable."

We continued to chat as we made our way up the crisscrossing streets to Highgate's stately homes of cream and rose-colored stone, then behind them to where the yards turned to a great field with a pebbly dirt path leading up the hill to the overlooking Rinnea Abbey.

I was out of breath making the climb up the hill, as I hadn't been out walking as much as I should have, and I tried to take in little bursts of air to hide from Andresh my impulse to breathe with heaving gasps.

He noticed. "Let's stop here. The grass looks soft and comfortable, and we have a perfect view of the abbey." We were only twenty feet below it and could see it plainly.

"I agree, it's a lovely spot," I managed. While he busied himself with his satchel I took in a big gulp of air and steadied my breathing.

He had a thin, soft blanket with him. I hadn't realized he even packed one in his bag. He pulled the satchel off and tossed it aside. He shook the blanket out of its folds and raised it up, letting the air catch it and straighten it out before spreading it on the ground.

"This is nice," I said to him. I sat on the blanket with my legs folded in my lap, and I got into the picnic basket. Andresh sat beside me, a little closer than I expected, mimicking my posture. His knee was nearly up against mine.

"What are you feeling like? Strawberries? An apple? How about a piece of banana cake?"

"I'm not very hungry right now, to be honest." He unhooked his long legs and stretched them out in front of him.

"We don't have to eat anything now," I said. I set the food aside and realized I had copied his posture back without knowing it—suddenly my legs were out in front of me, too, following the line of the blanket.

We sat there in silence for a few moments. Andresh's fingers clenched and unclenched strands of grass as he stared at the decaying abbey.

"I want you to," I said, breaking the silence.

"Want me to what?"

"Kiss me."

His eyebrows raised, only for a second. He gave me the most dazzling smile I'd ever seen from him, showing his teeth and part of the scar on his bottom lip. His eyes seemed to glisten as he gave me a little nod, and he leaned forward to me. One of his hands cradled my back, and the other grasped my cheek as he drew me into him.

His mouth was as soft as I remembered it, but there was no clumsiness from childhood. His lips eclipsed my own, and it was our most intimate embrace yet, where buried desires had finally started to reach full bloom.

His breath brushed against my skin, and my own slightly hitched when his tongue slid in between my lips, seeking mine out.

It was my first real kiss, and I wasn't sure what I was doing, but I cautiously touched my tongue to his, and he took that as a sign of welcome to do more. He drew circles around my own, he flicked in and out, teasing me—

His hand cupped my breast, and I gasped. "Andresh!"

His voice came out lower, huskier than normal. "I want to touch you." He gave me a softer, gentler kiss on the mouth and asked, "May I touch you?"

I stared at the fever in his eyes and the flush on his face, and a tickling feeling shot up from my stomach into my chest, a surge of pleasure and nerves and who knew what else—my emotions were a storm, but in that moment, some clarity: "Put your hands on me," I whispered.

He let out a soft moan and climbed over me, and I fell back against the blanketed grass floor. He kissed my lips again, then my neck, then the tops of my breasts. His hand found his way there again, only this time he tugged at the top of my bodice, trying to free me from my dress.

I wanted to explore him, too. I placed my hand on his heart. My fingers drew a line down his chest, down his stomach, and found the spot between his legs. My hand trembled at the length of him, at the hardness there, and he gasped. "Lily, you—"

His face changed. All of the healthy rosiness to his skin vanished in a second, and he turned an unnatural shade of white, something ghostly and otherworldly. He let out a groan, nothing heated this time, but instead an audible sound of pain.

He backed away from me, away from the blanket and our food, and into the grass. A massive amount of flames escaped his body, through his mouth, his hands, the top of his head, and his most intimate place, and he screamed. The fire was a brilliant turquoise blue—his Fire—and it overtook him rapidly.

"No! No! I'm not ready yet!" he screamed. "I can't do it!"

"Andresh!"

Once the flames covered his whole body, he vanished, leaving nothing behind but the ashy remains of his clothing and boots.

CHAPTER 12

"Andresh!" I cried out again, and my tears fell freely as the panic rose in my chest. He wasn't dead—he *couldn't* be. I refused to believe it. He was gone somewhere, and that was that.

I sifted through his burned clothes and shoes, ran my hands over the scorch marks in the grass until the blackness of ash colored my fingertips.

I shook the blanket out and tossed it aside in a pile as it revealed nothing to me. I spotted his satchel and dumped out the contents. He was planning on killing a demon, so there could be a magical clue there to help explain what had happened.

A hand mirror glinted in the sunlight, and I grabbed it, staring at my reflection. The blackness came, along with the smoky tendrils in the air, and the familiar figure of my dead mother appeared. "Please. Open the door."

"Aineiron," I said, mustering the most commanding tone I had.

That stopped it. The figure tilted its head to the side and

said in a beautiful, haunting, masculine voice, "You know my name."

A flash of light filled the mirror, and in the next instant, a man in a short, white sleeveless tunic, like the robes of the ancient world, stood before me.

"Are you...an angel?" I was so confused. The man was stunning—long, blonde curling hair, a slim but chiseled form, marble-white skin, and six pairs of white wings sprouted from his body. Four from his back, two from the back of his head, which were folded over his eyes to cover them, and then two more from his calf muscles.

He grinned at me, which showed an unnerving set of fangs in his mouth, and then the wings over his eyes burst open and flapped to the side, revealing jet-black eyes with no whites to them at all. "'*Angel fallen, angel fell. Down from Heaven, now in Hell*,'" he said, in a sweet, low tenor. "It's true. You could call where I am a hell. That's why I want out. I've suffered far too long."

"You've made me suffer, and countless others you've haunted." I nearly spat the words at him. "If you wanted me to let you out, you would have done a better job if you stayed as you are now."

He laughed. "Fear is far greater a motivation than beauty. And it tastes *so delicious*... But you have a delicacy all your own, my dear. A pretty lilac color."

He must have been speaking of my Fire.

"I need you to do something for me," I said, trying not to let myself become afraid of him. "I know your true name, so you're supposed to listen to me, right?"

"I'm listening."

"I need you to find him. Find Andresh, and bring him back."

"Andresh?"

"You've seen him before, haven't you?" I remembered the night that Andresh and I switched Fire, but the dominant color would've been my flames, not Andresh's. But when Aineiron haunted me, there had to have been a time when the demon saw other people standing in front of the glass near me. "He's turquoise," I offered.

"Oh, that one. You wish to make a pact?"

"What is the nature of the pact?"

"I'll get you Andresh. You let me out."

"You've told me to let you out for years. Remember when I tried to? What do I have to do?"

"Draw my sigil. Put your hand through the center of it, then twist and pull back. The door to me will open."

"How would I have known what your sigil was to let you out?" My voice grew angrier. "I tried to let you out forever ago, and you never told me what to do."

"Demons cannot lie, but...we omit things. The full tale of it only comes out when you speak the True Name."

I grit my teeth, trying to relax myself. "Fine. What is your sigil?"

His clawed finger drew a complicated series of lines on the mirror, and through some magic, the pattern stayed, the lines giving off a faint green glow in the glass.

"Right. Keep it there—it's too difficult for me to memorize." A scary thought entered my mind. "If I let you go, you're not going to...*kill* people, are you? You don't eat mortals, do you?"

"I love humans. All demons do." He gave me another grin, this one looking a little too wide for his face. "But it's part of your price, to always wonder, isn't it?"

"Are you sure you can get him out, since you couldn't get yourself out?"

He pouted and folded his arms across his chest. "Fine. Give me some clues about him so I know where to look. Tell me about him."

"You don't know?"

"B, the sixth general of Hell, that's her domain—hidden things. Secrets. I'm not privy to that."

"What is your domain?"

"I haven't had one since I was cast into the glass." He looked *mournful* for a second. "It used to be music. Alas."

I was growing impatient by the second. "Andresh is a magician. He's from Sindalia."

"A Sindalian magician, yes... What type of magic does he do?"

I tried to remember our conversations from before. "He does stuff with Fire. And he said some words from alchemy."

Aineiron's face lit up. "Alchemy? I know where he is. I'll be back."

There was another flash of light, and the mirror emptied, leaving my own reflection there staring back at me, for the first time in years. In the glass I saw my giant scar, my startled, tear-stained face, the freckles across the bridge of my nose and upper cheeks. I saw the green of the grass on the hill higher up, and part of the abandoned abbey.

A weight lifted off of my shoulders in those few minutes, experiencing for the first time the relief from not seeing a bloated corpse with my reflection.

I waited. And waited. I started to think I was tricked, that Andresh hadn't disappeared, but that he had burned to death; that Aineiron wanted a reason to play with me as he had over the years; that all of this was a fool's dream.

Around twenty minutes had passed. I had set the mirror face-up on the grass beside me and almost missed the flash of light that reappeared within it. I grabbed it and brought it close to my face.

In the glass, Aineiron stood holding a naked, bleeding Andresh in his arms.

"Andresh!" I half-screamed, half-sobbed.

"Draw the sigil. They're going to come after me," Aineiron said, with a trace of panic in his voice.

I pushed my finger against the glass and traced the figure into it. I tightened my fingers into my palm and reached forward, and to my shock, *kept going.* Silver cascaded like water over my hand as it plunged through the glass. I turned my hand to the right, as if unlocking a door, and pulled back, freeing my hand.

The glass shattered. I shouted and covered my face, but one of the pieces nicked my cheek. When I put my hands away, another flash of light appeared and revealed Aineiron's angelic-looking form, still holding an unconscious, bloodied Andresh.

I rushed to both of them. Aineiron let Andresh fall into my arms, and he stepped aside.

"If she gets enough Fire in her, she'll be strong enough to follow me here," he said. "I've made her angry."

I didn't take in much of what he was saying—I caught the giant puncture wound in Andresh's thigh that blood poured out of. I took off my Spencer jacket and wrapped it around his leg, tying the sleeves into a knot, to help staunch the bleeding.

"Can you save him?"

"No," Aineiron said. "I have not the power within me, and you have not enough to give me." His eyes suddenly clouded up, like milk being poured into a black coffee, and the whites had returned, along with a lovely violet color. He shook his shoulders and head, kicked his legs out slightly, and the feathered wings fell off onto the ground, then disappeared into it like they were never there.

I blinked. Aineiron now looked entirely human, complete with the fashion of the era on his body. "Glamour," he explained. "One of the oldest magicks there is, and most effective."

He grabbed the brim of his hat and tipped it to me. "Thank you, Lily." He headed down the hill to the dirt path.

"Wait! What do I do?" I called after him.

"I'm sure you'll think of something!" he shouted back.

Blood had drenched the jacket I had tied around Andresh's thigh. *He's going to bleed to death.*

The wound needed to be closed. The blood needed to be stopped. And the only thing I could think of was, *I need fire.*

There was nothing there for me to make one. The frenzied thought came to me: I would simply use mine. I was a key, and my hands were doors, so I would open myself to use my Fire to burn him, to save him. I didn't care about my lifespan shortening, so long as it extended his.

I opened my palms and spread my fingers wide, both hands hovering above his enormous puncture. What on earth had caused that? I took a deep breath and called out through my mind, *Humble Father, Holy Mother, all the Saints, everyone... let me save him!!!*

My lilac Fire exploded out of my hands. At first I felt nothing, but when the flames grew in power and vitality, I pushed my burning palms against Andresh's gash to cauterize the wound. The smell of burning blood and flesh filled my nostrils, but I kept my hands there.

Andresh woke and started screaming in pain. As soon as I heard his nightmarish cries, I pulled away from him. My hands made fists, and the light purple flames disappeared.

"Bleed it out," he sobbed. "Let me bleed it out."

"You'll die!"

"*But it's inside me now.*" He fainted.

"Andresh? Andresh!" He wouldn't respond to me. He had turned a sickly grayish-white and was still vulnerable. I wrapped the blanket around him to give him modesty and realized I needed to get him out of there, and that there was no one on the hill who could help. Aineiron's form had disappeared out of sight.

I took in a breath, trying not to think about his terrifying words, then reached for Andresh by the waist. With difficulty, I slung him over my shoulder and, trembling, rose to my feet. I couldn't grab all of our things, and honestly, I didn't care about them any longer—I knew I had to get Andresh away and in front of a doctor.

I knew that if I ran down the hill I would trip and fall, so as soon as I made it to the dirt path, I started a speed-walk while balancing Andresh on me. I tried to quicken my pace and nearly dropped him. I reshuffled him onto me and started up my brisk walk again.

As soon as we made it to Highgate, we made it to people, and I shouted to the passersby there, "I need help! He's hurt!" Immediately four gentlemen came to my side, all looking stricken, and one of them took Andresh from me. "To Dr. Caliday's," he said. "Follow us."

I'd never been to a Highgate doctor, but I couldn't object about the cost because Andresh was all I could think about. I'd do anything to help him. I nodded and went after the men who led me to the office of Dr. Caliday, which, in fact, took up an entire building—living quarters and patient quarters shared the whitewashed brick structure.

"What happened?" one of the other men asked me.

I wasn't sure what lie to tell, so I said, "I found him like that. I have no idea what's going on or why he has that wound on his leg. I burnt it with a...with a hot spoon. I didn't know what else to do to stop him bleeding."

"That's quick thinking, Miss—"

"Miss Bellamy." We had made it to the entryway of Dr. Caliday's and one of the men held the door open for all of us and we hurried inside.

"We need a bed for him right away," said the man who carried Andresh. A middle-aged woman dressed in nurse's clothing nodded and led us down the hallway to a large room with three male patients resting in bed, with curtains surrounding the sides of them to offer privacy. One of them napped; the other read a book; and the third was nibbling on a plate of sliced oranges.

The fourth bed was free. The man and the nurse worked together to gently unwrap Andresh's naked form from the blanket and laid him down on the bed. The nurse covered up most of his body but exposed his wounded thigh so she could get a closer look at it. The area around the blackish crusty burn was a bright red, and he was swelling; meanwhile a hideous yellow fluid had started oozing from his leg.

"Do you know what happened?" the nurse asked.

I shook my head. "We were picnicking and he went into the woods to fetch me something, he didn't tell me what, and when he took too long I went after him and found him like that."

It sounded stupid to hear it out loud, but I didn't want to have to give too many details because I couldn't come up with them fast enough. I had no idea if I was consistent or coherent with my excuses.

Luckily they all seemed to accept what I said.

"What did the wound look like before your burned him?" the nurse continued.

"It looked like something gored him. Like something stabbed him or struck him and took a piece out of him."

The men looked at each other knowingly. One of them squeezed my arm and said delicately, "It might have been the stag. We call him Old Devil because he is wild and violent and has evaded the hunters so far. Perhaps your friend got too close."

"That makes sense to me," I managed. I would go with it.

"But that doesn't explain the singular wound," one of the other men chimed in. "He should have multiple stab marks on his body, not one big hole."

"We'll have to investigate further, but when he is conscious again," the nurse said. "In the meantime, I'm clearing all of you out of here. I will fetch Dr. Caliday who will bring the surgeon. What is your companion's name?"

"Andresh Zatavier," I responded.

"Thank you for bringing Mr. Zatavier in." She waved her arms at us and ushered us out of the room.

We all filed out into the hallway and I took each man's hand and squeezed them tight in appreciation. "All of you helped me in a great time of need. I don't know how to thank you enough."

The man who carried Andresh gave me a small smile. "We couldn't let you or him suffer, Miss Bellamy. Here in Highgate, we never turn away someone in need."

I couldn't help but flinch slightly at that. Highgate, as it was named, had high gates around it, seemingly to bar the riffraff out. I had never heard anything awful about Highgate, but there was a level of exclusivity there, and parts of it closed off to the lower quarters of Mariner. I didn't think a place like that would extend help to just anyone, but these men had surprised me today.

"I'm so grateful to all of you."

We headed down the maze of hallways together to the reception area where we first came in. The men bowed or tipped their hats to me and left. I stood and eyed my location, feeling helpless.

A gorgeous young woman with deep, dark black skin, with tight braids arranged in a bun on the top of her head, greeted me. "Miss Bellamy." Her plum muslin gown looked stunning—too nice for a hospital, I thought.

"Yes, I'm Miss Bellamy." I bowed my head to her. When I raised it, I realized—I had seen her before, at the shop. She was the one who took Andresh on the trip to Milanie's.

She gave me the sweetest smile. "The soap Andresh recommended to me is divine. And with your silk, and Milanie's dyes, I can honestly say that your work is astounding. I am going to be the belle of the ball." She took my hand. "Dear, come with me to Dr. Caliday's office and tell me what happened. I have some questions for you."

I squeezed her palm but felt uncomfortable clutching on to her hand as we moved through the hallways. To my relief, my letting go of her didn't faze her.

"My name is Adanya Caliday. I assist Dr. Caliday with the administration of our hospital. I also serve as the almoner and calculate payment." She gestured for me to stand by her side. "I'm Dr. Caliday's daughter, if you were wondering."

"Nice to meet you. Again."

"The pleasure is mine, but the circumstances are unfortunate."

We entered a small room with tall, thin windows with a

diamond pattern running across them. A mahogany desk served as the centerpiece, and there were bookcases taking up the walls on both sides of the room.

Adanya took a seat at the desk and gestured for me to use one of the chairs that had been pulled up to it. She grabbed a pen and ink and opened a rather large ledger.

"I'd like to get some information on the patient, and we can discuss payment."

"Um... I usually see Dr. Basseter... I've never been to a Highgate doctor...so I'm not sure if we can afford you."

"We'll discuss that, don't worry. So, what's the patient's name?"

"Andresh Zatavier."

Her eyes widened and she swallowed. "Andresh? You mean—"

"Yes, the one who helped you at the shop and at Milanie's. He... It was awful." I wiped at my eyes. I didn't want to cry for what felt like the hundredth time in a week.

"We'll give him the best of care," she assured me, though her voice came out more somber than before. "How old is he?"

"Nineteen."

"Does he have any physical ailments or known impediments that existed before you came here today?"

"He's never mentioned any. He's typically healthy and fit."

"Can you tell me what happened?"

"Something in the woods took out a chunk of his leg. He wouldn't stop bleeding. I...used a spoon and heated it to burn his wound shut."

Adanya's eyes widened. "That was very brave of you."

"I appreciate that," I said, my voice wavering.

"He'll stay overnight with us for a few days. We will need to clean and redress his wounds daily with supervision until he is stable enough for us to teach you how to do it, if you're the one who'll provide him care."

"Yes, I'll be the one caring for him." I said it without hesitation.

"Please tell me your financial situation," she said.

I explained the loss of the *Windchaser* and that we were waiting on insurance funds, but had done well with silk sales thanks to a benefactor providing stock for us. I didn't mention it was Andresh.

"Can you afford two hundred aums a night? This includes all medical treatment and meals."

I swallowed. That was pretty steep. But I didn't think transferring Andresh to Dr. Basseter would be a good idea, and everyone at the Caliday Hospital seemed nice and understanding. "We'll make it work," I said, sounding more confident than I felt.

"Payment is due at the end of treatment," Adanya said, "And we can take it in installments if you feel more comfortable doing so. We do not charge interest."

"I understand. We can proceed with care."

"Glad to hear it. Mr. Zatavier is in safe hands."

"What should I do now? Can I stay with him until he wakes?"

"Dr. Caliday is examining him. They're trying to determine if he'll need autologous skin translocation. We'll be working on him the whole of today. I recommend stopping in tomorrow in between noon and three. Those are our hours for visitors." She rose from her chair and extended her hand to me. "Please don't worry for Mr. Zatavier. We will do everything we can for his health and comfort. I make this as a personal vow to you."

I took her hand in my own and couldn't help but blurt it out: "He said something was inside him. What could that mean?"

"People say strange things while under duress—I would try not to worry about it."

Except he said, "Bleed it out." Of course I would worry anyway. But instead I just told her, "I appreciate your help so much. I'll stop by tomorrow."

I left the hospital and headed down the overlapping streets that led to the lower quarters of Mariner and down to the oceanfront.

As I made my way back home, the thought plagued me: *What on earth do I tell the family?*

CHAPTER 13

When I got home, Nell was the first to greet me, and her face whitened when she saw my dress covered in Andresh's blood. "What happened?" she practically screeched at me. "Where's Andresh?"

"It was a terrible accident. We were at Rinnea Abbey and he went into the woods and...they think he was gored by a stag."

Nell looked confused, like the words wouldn't permeate her brain. "That sounds—"

"Insane. I know. Whatever creature he happened upon, it took out a chunk of his leg. He nearly bled to death. He's at a hospital in Highgate with Dr. Caliday supervising him."

"Can we see him?"

"Not now. Dr. Caliday's daughter said we could come back tomorrow during specific hours. Can you tell Grandma? I want to take a bath, get this blood off of me." I took a breath, as if I hadn't been breathing since Aineiron brought Andresh back. "He's in good hands, Nell. And the worst of it is over. They're basically keeping him cleaned up and watching for any infection."

Some color returned to her face when I told her that. "I'll let Grandma know while you get cleaned up."

When I got to my room, I tore my clothes off my body and slipped into my robe before heading outside to take the several trips needed at the cistern to draw enough water to bathe. I knew I wasn't dressed, but I didn't care who saw me. I just wanted to be free of the blood.

I didn't waste time heating the water. I felt like I needed to be purified by the cold, both in body and mind. As I dumped the water in the tub, I realized I felt no strange buzz or hum in the air, no presence behind me. To make sure, I headed to the mirror above the sink and stared at myself.

My reddish-brown hair looked slightly amiss, but it remained straight and untangled. My face was drained of color due to the day's harrowing events, making the freckles on the bridge of my nose and cheeks stand out more. The pastel wallpaper, decorated with flowers and looping lines, appeared behind me. And of course, dominating it all, was the scar on my forehead—a reminder of when everything terrible in my life had started.

Absolutely no shades or shadows or spirits or demons appeared in my view. Nothing.

I started crying. At first, I cried in relief for myself, and then I felt selfish for crying for myself when Andresh was in the hospital with a chunk of his leg gone, so I started crying for him.

It wasn't until I stepped into the shocking cold water of the tub that my tears stopped. Goosebumps covered my arms, but I ignored them, and submerged myself in the freezing water. Red mixed in with its clearness as I hurriedly washed myself.

When I was done, I didn't feel pure or clean at all. By

freeing Aineiron, I wondered at what horrible thing I'd unleashed upon the world.

~

That night, I slept in Andresh's room, yearning for a hint of him, a scent or a random strand of long, black hair to comfort me in his absence. He was impeccable in how he cared for himself, and to my disappointment, left no trace of himself behind in the plush comfort of his bed.

I lit a candle and set it on the nightstand next to the bed and decided to read the book Andresh borrowed from the library: *Nine Poets of Capua Cora.* The first poet featured was a woman named Sofia Tarlemane, and she wrote of fantastic, celestial things, and of worlds that layered on top of our own.

Other worlds. I learned there was more than one—there had to be. A world for demons, and a world for people, and the two must somehow intertwine. If Aineiron was my demon, but without a proper pact, what was Andresh's demon to him? She had to know something about what happened.

The most desperate thought entered my mind—*you could always ask her.* After all, she somehow had appeared to me before. I couldn't control my dreams and ask her to come to me, but what about the mirror?

A mirror was a door, but I wasn't going to open it. I refused. But couldn't it also be a window of sorts? Would that be safe enough?

I must be mad. But the whole day had been madness. This would be nothing different.

I crawled out of bed and stood before the mirror on the wall. I tapped the glass with one of my knuckles and spoke softly. "Isabelle." I didn't want to speak too loudly, for fear of drawing outside attention. But it wasn't enough to bring her the first time I called, so I knocked once, harder, and raised my voice slightly. "Isabelle."

She appeared. I didn't even see how it happened—she wasn't there and then she was, and I saw almost no difference between the two. Perhaps I blinked.

"You do not know my name, yet you called me out. I did not think anything else could surprise me after all these years, yet here we are." Isabelle smiled at me, revealing her sharp fangs. She was gorgeous and horrific all at once; human and animal, angel and devil.

"Isabelle's not your name?"

"A name. Not *the* name." She cocked her head to the side, and it felt like her solid black eyes bored a hole into me. "You wish to know something, do you not?"

"What happened to Andresh today?"

"I'll tell you, true and simple. The Magnum Opus requires completion. Nigredo Gate called him in, the sacrifice overdue. He fought the Guardian and lost. Aineiron saved him just in time, but Andresh will continue to be punished until he crosses Nigredo."

"I don't understand most of that," I said.

"I've told you exactly what happened. You can accept it or not."

"Fine. Will Andresh survive?"

"Andresh will live a long life, as he wishes." She drew out the word *long* in a slow, syrupy fashion, making the word almost sound seductive.

I wanted to feel relief at her words, but there was something about the way she said them that made me not want to trust them.

"How do I know you speak the truth?"

She laughed. "I *love* humans. I do not lie to them." She paused. "I love you too, Lily. If you made a pact with me, I could share so many things with you...and I'm getting hungry."

That shocked me enough that I took a step back from the mirror. "No thank you. I appreciate the help thus far, but I'm done talking to you now."

She gave me a smile again, but followed it up with a bored look, her face instantly slack. "Very well." Just as she had appeared—in a way I could not see—she disappeared from the glass.

Whatever it was Isabelle was referring to, I knew I needed to bring it up with Andresh somehow. I didn't think I could blurt it out upon his awakening, but I was very concerned with Isabelle's mention of a punishment. Was his wound from the fight with whoever the Guardian was, or was the wound his punishment? What if the punishment was something else? I couldn't quite dismiss the feeling that Andresh was still in danger.

Three days passed and Andresh remained unconscious. I visited him during open hours at the hospital along with Nell and Grandma, and whenever we got to his room, we did nothing but stare at his sleeping form. He had always been pale, but the sheen on him now was deathly white. Other than that otherworldly pallor, though, he seemed more like his old self.

On the fourth day, we walked in on Dr. Caliday and one of his nurses finishing the redressing of Andresh's bandages. There was still some blood on them, and Nell made a disgusted face when she saw them. "Ew, gross."

Dr. Caliday laughed warmly. "It was worse before. There was an infection. But truth be told, he's healing nicely." His expression changed, though, and he added, "My concern is the fact that he is not awake. His injury does not explain away his lack of consciousness. I would attribute it to a mental affliction, an enduring panic or trauma of sorts, but that is not my specialty, and I can only guess. Even more baffling, he sleeps peacefully. He does not call out or make any pained expression, so my theory of trauma might be misguided."

I wasn't sure how Andresh was sleeping easy, either, considering how traumatic our day together had been. I kept having nightmares about it, mixed in with visions of Isabelle telling me that she was hungry. But it was true that, every time we came to see Andresh, he looked undisturbed.

"How long is it before his lack of consciousness is considered a danger?" I asked. Isabelle told me he would live a long life, but what if that life was entirely in sleep?

"We're going to give him two more days to wake up naturally. If he doesn't, we must discuss care of a longer term. My daughter Adanya would be the one to speak to about that. But please don't worry for now." The doctor and nurse excused themselves from the room.

At the doctor's words, my mind went to institutionalization. I had never heard anything good about that. People were left in places like that to die. There was no way I would let Andresh be taken or shelved away in some dubious hospital. I would take care of him at home if it led to that.

"I know we all just got here," I said, "but could you both let me be alone with him today? I want to talk to him. In private."

Nell looked a little disappointed, but nodded her head.

"We'll come again tomorrow," Grandma said, and she and Nell headed out.

I took Andresh's hand. I expected it to be freezing, but it was so warm. Almost unnaturally so. It was like he had been standing in front of the fireplace heating it.

I squeezed his palm. "Andresh. You have to wake up." I took in a steadying breath. "I don't understand what happened that day. I'm sure you were scared for your life. I'm sure sleep is easier than being awake when there are demons out there. But you have to fight to wake up. You can't let the world pass you by in a state of slumber.

"It's only been days, but I miss you so much. You make every day of mine worth living. I... I love you."

His hand squeezed back.

"Andresh?" I let go of him and hopped out of my chair. I leaned over him, inspecting him. His eyes stayed shut; he did not speak. I grabbed his hand again and waited, but it stayed limp in my own.

The next day, he woke up.

ANDRESH WAS STILL WEAK when he left the hospital with us. I escorted him down the steeper streets from Highgate to the Lower Quarter, walking slowly with our arms linked together. Grandma and Nell accompanied us, with Nell leading the way down, and Grandma following a few steps after her, the bottom of her cane clinking on the cobbled streets.

Andresh had seemed so dazed when we met him at his hospital bed. He stared off into nothingness. His eyes would refocus and he'd return our gazes, and give us a limp, lazy smile. It was almost as though he was in a stupor that carried over from his time asleep. He moved slowly and mechanically, and his face would go slack until he caught one of us looking at him, and he'd give a weird little grin again.

I don't know how Nell or Grandma felt about it, but it unnerved me. Was a piece of him left behind in that demon realm? He didn't seem fully himself when he came back to us, that was certain.

He politely let me lead him down the crisscrossing roads and didn't speak until we got to the flat area that comprised the boardwalk and sea-facing streets. "Thank you, Lily," he said, his voice soft. He unhooked his arm from mine, and as we headed to Bellamy Mercantile, he walked in a relatively slow gait. Slow for Andresh, anyway. I wondered if his leg pained him.

We entered the store and made our way to the back compartment that comprised the kitchen.

"Hungry, Andresh?" Grandma asked.

"Not really," he answered, sounding far away.

Grandma reached into the pantry and grabbed a loaf of bread, slicing off a piece of it and handing it to Andresh. "At the very least, nibble on this. You need something in your belly."

Andresh took her very literally, using tiny bites to consume the bread, and he chewed slowly.

He winced and put his hand to his mouth, dropping his piece of food. He spit something out of his mouth, and saliva mixed with a touch of red dripped down his chin. He wiped his face, his gaze searching the floor.

I was still standing by the doorframe, but I caught something white shooting off in my direction. I bent down and picked it up.

It was his tooth. I held it up to him. It was an important one, one that was easily visible if he smiled or opened his mouth—his eye tooth, the sharp cuspid that looked like a dog's fang.

"Ohhhh," he remarked. He seemed fazed and unfazed at the same time, a feat I did not know could be accomplished.

Nell and Grandma stared at Andresh, stunned.

"Was it loose?" Nell asked.

Andresh shook his head.

"Here, Lily, give it to me. I'll put it in a small jar." Grandma held out her hand and I dropped the tooth in her palm. She did as she said she would, and when the tooth was secure, she screwed a lid on the glass.

"The only dental surgeon in Mariner is back up in Highgate," I said. More money gone, even though the sales of our fabric had done us a bit of good.

"Could they reattach the tooth?" Nell asked.

"They can try, or get a donor tooth to fill it," I said. "Andresh, are you up for going back to Highgate tomorrow? I don't know how comfortable you are with...with your mouth looking that way."

"That's fine," he said simply.

"Does it hurt now?" Nell asked, her voice sounding more desperate.

"No."

"We'll leave in the morning, so we can get there right when they open," I said.

"I'd like to sleep now."

His request startled me. I thought for a moment, *what if he sleeps and doesn't wake?* But I stammered out, "As—as you wish."

Grandma, Nell, and I watched Andresh slowly and methodically make his way up the stairs until he disappeared from our sight.

We immediately plopped down at the dining table.

"Something is seriously wrong with him," Nell blurted out.

"He does seem out of sorts," Grandma conceded.

"Do you think he remembers what happened?" I asked. "He's not mentioned it at all. In fact, he hasn't even talked about the injury. He's...distant. And his smiles bother me."

"It is a bit unsettling," Grandma said.

"I think he's putting something on for us," Nell said, "to make us feel better and not worry."

"It's not working," I said. "I need to talk to him, to see if he remembers what happened. I'll see him once he wakes up, and I'll redress his wound."

Nell and Grandma had heard me volunteer myself in the hospital to be Andresh's caretaker, and that meant I was excused from store duties for a while. But it also meant I had to take over household chores, like cooking and laundering the clothes.

I busied myself with such things while Nell and Grandma opened up the shop and got to work. Every hour or so, I impatiently headed up the stairs to Andresh's room to see if he was awake yet.

On my fifth check, I almost jumped backward from the door once I had cracked it open. Andresh was sitting upright in bed, his braid gone, his hair loose and wild about him. He was looking ahead at...something. Just staring at it. He didn't move at all.

I swallowed, my throat suddenly dry. "Andresh?" My voice cracked as it came out.

He broke his gaze and turned his head toward me. He gave me a lopsided, childlike smile, with the gaping hole in his grin. "Lily."

For some reason, I had no desire to go in there and see him. There was something about him that seemed deeply broken, and it scared me. I knew I had to though, so I forced myself through the door. "I need to talk to you."

"That's fine."

If he was his usual self, I would have joined him in bed, sitting at the foot of it. But I felt like I had to keep some distance, which was silly, given I would soon be taking care of his leg. Nonetheless, I sat on the chair at the writing desk.

"Andresh. Do you remember what happened to you?"

He turned his head up toward the ceiling, as if there would be answers there for him. He thought for a moment. "We went to the abbey. We kissed." He smiled again, this time, mouth closed. "It was a lovely kiss."

My face warmed a little bit, and some of my nervousness went away. "It was." I shifted in my seat. "Do you remember what happened after that?"

"I woke up in bed at the hospital. My leg was bandaged but felt strange, like prickling all over it. I wanted to scratch at it, but they told me not to."

"Do you know how you hurt your leg?"

"No."

I tried a different approach. "Do you know you tried to save me that day? From years of hardship and madness?"

He looked at me curiously, raising an eyebrow. "What do you mean?"

"I can do it now. I can look at myself, and there is nothing else there in the mirror with me." I didn't want to tell him I freed Aineiron in order to do it.

He still looked confused. I rose from my chair and strode over to the mirror on the wall. I stood in front of it silently, for almost a full minute.

"What's going to happen?" His voice sounded full of wonder. I would've laughed if it wasn't so creepy.

"Nothing is happening. That is the point."

"Ohhhh." He sounded as if I'd let him down somehow.

This time I did sit at the edge of his bed. "Andresh. It's clear you don't remember what happened to you, but you also lost a lot of what happened before. The mirror is so significant, but it triggers nothing from you." I sat there in thought. "What about Isabelle?"

"Isabelle?" He squinched his forehead up, concentrating very hard. "I don't think I know her."

"...I suppose I could show you. If she'll help." I wondered

what she could possibly want from me in return. Could I do anything with her without it requiring a pact?

I went to the mirror and knocked loudly on it. "Isabelle. We need your help."

She smiled at me, her fangs looking sharper than usual. "Hello, Lily."

Andresh's eyes widened in fright. He flew back against the headboard of the bed, scrunching his body up. It was the most vivid I'd ever seen him since he woke. I did not like that he was scared, but it was a real, primal reaction—proof of his former self.

"She's not going to hurt you, Andresh." I held out my arms to him, with my palms facing out. "See. I'm not hurt."

He looked at me, blinked once, then timidly gazed in the glass.

"Andresh. My darling. Look at what's happened to you," Isabelle said, simultaneously sounding seductive and motherly, a combination that somewhat disturbed me. She started to sing to him. Her low, beautiful voice echoed with a hint of other voices whispering, and the sounds came together as one to form a language I could not understand or recognize. It seemed like a lullaby of sorts, and I felt myself grow drowsy as I listened.

For Andresh, it was something else. He calmed, and the tension left his body. His eyes glossed over, and the familiar corner-of-the-mouth smile appeared so that he looked like his old self again. He got out of bed and walked to the mirror.

I stepped aside—it seemed like Isabelle was calling him to her, and that she wanted his full attention. I didn't move very far, though, in case something were to happen.

Her song finished. "Touch your head to the glass, Andresh," she said gently. "I'll show you what you've hidden."

CHAPTER 14

Andresh placed his palms on the wall, one arm on each side of the mirror, and pressed his forehead against the glass.

It didn't look like anything was happening, but Andresh closed his eyes, and his shoulders started shaking. It wasn't a substantial quake, but it looked like trembling out of fear.

When Isabelle was done with whatever she was doing to him, Andresh pulled his head away, and his arms returned to his sides. Tears streamed down his face. His voice came out low and somber. "I understand."

"Think well on it, Andresh," Isabelle said. "Nigredo awaits. You must finish the Opus." She was gone.

Andresh turned to me, crying silently.

"Are you back, Andresh? Are you with me?"

He nodded. "I am so sorry, Lily."

"Why are you sorry? You've done nothing wrong. You've been through a terrible ordeal."

"I was ready to do the unthinkable. I might still have to do it. My choice will hurt you." He wiped his eyes with his fists and sank back onto the bed.

I sat by his side, closer than before, feeling comfortable enough to narrow the distance between us. "What do you mean?"

"I tried to do it once before. Make the great sacrifice to pass through Nigredo Gate. I failed the first time because my desire wasn't true. I had abandoned it already. But with you... I love you. I want you. I desire you."

My cheeks felt flush at his words.

"That's what the Guardian wants before he lets me pass through the Gate," Andresh continued. "He consumes desire. That's the key to crossing over—make the sacrifice, and you can traverse the Gate. And I'm only at the beginning of the Magnum Opus. There are three more Gates after that. I don't think I can do it. I don't think I can give up so much of myself. But once you start the Opus, you have to continue it."

"What is the Magnum Opus?"

"It comes from a type of magic known as alchemy. It's the Great Work. A refining process that leads to immortality."

That sent a shiver through me. "You would put yourself in so much danger so you won't die?"

"It's more like this: I don't want *you* to die. I don't want any more of your family to die. Our fathers and mothers never should have died. Isabelle showed me the way, the true way of the Magnum Opus. It's not locking yourself in your room refining chemicals and recomposing materials to make a stone that grants eternal life; you are refining and recomposing yourself to become *the thing* that bestows eternal life: a god."

My heart thumped harder in my chest. "Is such a thing possible?" I whispered.

"If there's no difference between above and below, and all and one are exactly the same, then anything is possible."

"...Do you truly want to become a god?"

"Gods live forever and they can do anything. My one task was to bring about the end of death, and everything I had done as a magician was leading me up to that point. But now I'm not so sure."

"Right. Because what if you're not Andresh anymore? You said you had to make sacrifices—what if you lose everything about yourself?"

Another tear fell from his eyes. "My first loss would be my desire, one of the basest and most innate parts of being human. And that means I couldn't love you anymore, Lily. Not like this. But if I became godlike, I could bring that part of me back, because the power of a god is endless. After I changed, I planned on reuniting with you and being with you forever."

I tried to say it as delicately as possible. "Andresh. I love you. But I don't want to live forever. I'm scared to die, but I know that the cost of living is death. I've seen so much of it. And it is inevitable. Your cause is noble, to save people who don't want death, but...it doesn't feel right to me."

His voice trembled. "You wouldn't spend forever with me?"

I was so scared he'd take what I said personally, and he had. "I would spend all of my life with you, Andresh. Every single day. Every single night. I'm yours."

After some moments of silence, he held my hand. "See... this is why I don't think I can continue my journey. I want you *now*. I love you *now*. I don't have it in me to stop, even if I could start it again in the future. And that's why I'm in danger. Once you start the Opus, it's like a pact—you must follow it through to the end, or the consequences are dire."

"What will happen to you?"

"I don't exactly know. When my Fire consumed me, it made me temporarily ethereal, able to cross planes and worlds. But it took me right to Nigredo Gate. That's because of Isabelle.

When I tried to give up desire before, it failed because it wasn't true. She told me when the moment of sacrifice was at hand, she would send me to the Gate to help me continue the alchemical path. She meant to help me because the Opus was the only thing on my mind, and she encouraged me. But once we...once you and I gave in to our desire for each other, I no longer wanted to walk away from you. The Guardian was angry when I told him I wasn't going to give him the sacrifice he wanted, and we fought. He got me with his scorpion tail." He pointed to his thigh.

"And there's poison in me. I don't know how fast it will work. Maybe I'll lose more teeth. Maybe my bones will rot while I live. Maybe I'll slowly fade, or keel over one day. But poison is poison. And if there is any hope of a cure, I have to go back to Nigredo Gate and give up my desire for you, then cross on through. I... If I want to live, I have no choice."

My eyes grew watery as I considered everything he had been through, and how, at some point, he was ready to give me up. But I couldn't be mad at him for it. He had taken on an incredible burden to try to save everyone, if not the very least his loved ones, and he was willing to reshape and reform himself into something unfathomable to do so. Instead of anger, I felt an incredible sorrow for him. No matter what action he would take, it would end in a deep loss.

"We can't give up, Andresh. There has to be some way out of this; something we haven't thought of. Poisons have antidotes, right? I could do some research..."

"This poison is supernatural. I don't know if a mortal cure will help. I... I don't want to think about it anymore. I'd like to live out these next days with you and your family with ease. And...I want to sleep."

I leaned over and kissed his cheek, which was still wet from his tears. I brushed them away with my fingers. "I'm not going to give up on you. I'll figure something out. You can rest. Rest as often as you need to. Take care of yourself and heal. And we'll end this, all of it."

His nod felt hollow and unsure to me, but I didn't press him further.

I rose from his bed. "I'll come back in a couple hours and redress your wound. Goodnight."

Andresh scooted forward, his head back on the pillows. The minute he made contact, he exhaled the slow breaths that came from deep sleep.

I left him alone and headed down the steps to the kitchen and to finish the chores of the day, while Nell and Grandma made good sales at the shop.

Meanwhile, Andresh slept and slept. I visited him again to change his dressings, but he didn't stir, and I didn't think I could start the process while he was lost in slumber. I imagined him waking in fright at the sensation of me pulling off the wrap, tugging at his sensitive skin. He had already been frightened so much today, and I didn't want to add to it. It would have to wait until tonight, perhaps after supper.

Supper. Gah, I didn't want to think about it. I hated cooking so much. So much effort for only a few minutes of joy, followed by endless dishes to wash. But I wracked my brain, anyway, trying to think of something simple yet filling for everyone tonight. I had delayed preparation so much that I only had an hour to cook, anyway.

Nell screamed. Not a sound of horror, but as though something enormous had startled her. I made out the word: "FATHER!!!"

What? I rushed out of the kitchen to the shop, which was five minutes away from closing for the day.

Sure enough, Nell's arms were wrapped around the tall figure of my father, only new things about him caught my eyes immediately: His right leg was missing at the knee, and his pants were knotted right below the stump, and he balanced himself with a crutch. And his hair had grayed considerably.

Grandma practically threw herself at him, and she and Nell threatened his balance. Nell started sobbing uncontrollably, her wails filling up the room, crying as though she were a small child again.

I was like Grandma. Tears fell instantly, but she and I were more silent about it.

"Father!" The word trembled when it left my throat. I approached him, but didn't embrace him, afraid I'd knock him over.

Father joined in with the tears. He eyed each one of us and said in a voice that sounded older and more gravelly than before, "Girls, my girls, my darling girls. I never thought I'd see you again."

"What happened to you?" Nell cried. "They told us you were dead. Lost at sea!"

"The *Windchaser* is lost. The crew is lost. I am the sole survivor. I... There are some things I still cannot bring myself to talk about. I'm sorry. All you need to know is that I was found on shore, with a piece of wood from the ship lodged in my leg. They couldn't save it, so that's why they took it. It was a long time for the rest of me to get better, all the while...I was in a stupor. I thought of your mother when I was like that...how she would look at things, but not really *see* them. How she sort of...drifted off. It was like that for me. I was awake without seeing. I wanted to speak, but I couldn't find words. I wanted to write to you, but I couldn't bring myself to make the effort. I took so long to heal. But as soon as I was able to, I got on the first ship available to come back to you. I believe that it will be my last."

Father must have experienced an indescribable trauma if

he no longer wanted to set foot on a ship. He loved the sea. He loved the wind in the sails and the freedom of the open water. He loved the adventure of setting off to places few dared explore and coming back richly rewarded for his efforts.

I assumed none of us knew what to say to that, as we all kept silent, occasionally letting out a garbled sob or a loud sniff. When Grandma and Nell let go of Father, I gave him a quick hug. "Are you hungry after all this travel?" It felt like a stupid question with an obvious answer, but I wanted to break the sob-filled silence.

"Desperately so. The last meal I had was on the ship."

"I'm in charge of supper," I said, "but I don't feel like doing anything. Do you want a fresh meal? I can run to the market stalls and get us all some chicken, and warm potatoes, and freshly baked bread..."

"That sounds good," Nell said.

"I would like that," Father said.

I paused. "Someone else will be joining us for dinner. Andresh."

"Andresh!" Father's eyes glistened again. "Our dear boy. He finally made it back to us from Sindalia." He sounded more overwhelmed than overjoyed, but it was still a positive reaction to the news.

"He's been living with us for a few months now," I said. "He's staying in the guest room. But...he's in a bad way. He was in the hospital in Highgate for almost a week."

"They say he was gored by a stag," Nell added. "Lily was there but didn't see it." Without taking a breath she added, "Somehow he was naked."

Oh no. I had forgotten to come up with an excuse for that. "Uh...I was the one who took his clothes off. I needed to see if he was hurt elsewhere. There was so much blood, I couldn't tell what was happening." I felt the heat pool in my cheeks, somewhat embarrassed all of a sudden. "Forgive me, Father. It was improper, but I thought he would die."

Father's voice was quiet. "There is too much death around us," he said. "And too much near-death. Ever since your mother passed, I always wondered if we were under some sort of curse. Our family, our friends—alive, but perhaps barely after all this time."

I was so shocked to hear Father voice the thoughts I'd occasionally had. Though I never thought of our family and Andresh's as being barely alive. We'd had near misses, but everyone was still spirited and full of life. Father, of course, was only able to be that way because he had the ocean, the shop, this family. Now that the ocean took practically everything from him, I worried he'd succumb to melancholy or madness, just like Mother likely had.

"Andresh did well at the hospital," I offered, "though his leg looks awful. I've been in charge of his home care and have been cleaning his wounds. Although he is tired all the time, he's on the way to recovery."

Father let out a sigh—I hoped one of relief. "Will he be well enough to join us for supper? I would like to see how he's faring. I've missed him. As you know, he's like a son."

"He's been sleeping almost all day, but I'm sure he'll want food and want to see you. He never admitted it to me, but he was deeply hurt by your...your absence."

Father swallowed. "I should have written before coming. I know I should have done something to let you all know I was on my way. But I wasted no time after I was awake and cleared from the surgery. I had to get out of there as soon as I could. I'm sorry I was gone so long."

He sounded brokenhearted, his voice heavy but trembling. I started crying again.

"No one blames you, Father. A terrible thing happened, but

something precious came out of it: your return. You're back home to us. That's all that matters."

"We love you," Nell added, wrapping her arms around him again. Her hug was a quick one, as she asked me, "Will you need help at the market?"

I thought about it. "Yes. I don't think I can carry everything."

Grandma and Father walked with their supports into the kitchen, where Father sat down at the dining table, and Grandma sat across from him, holding his hand. Nell and I waited until they were comfortable before we rushed in and headed toward the pantry. Two large baskets hung on the wall on hooks. Nell and I helped ourselves to them.

"Love you!" Nell called out, and I echoed her, as we went out the door and out onto the street.

Because it was May and a nice, comfortable warmth filled the air around us, more people were out walking through the streets and along the boardwalk. Children were racing each other. Couples young and old linked their arms together and walked side by side. The sun was hazy but still bright despite it being close to supper.

As we walked to the market, Nell touched my arm to get my attention. It startled me. "Lily. Do you think...something is going on?"

My heart beat a little faster in my chest. "What do you mean?"

"Andresh getting hurt. Father getting hurt. I know they are both with us and still alive, but something has changed in them."

"They each have been through terrible ordeals."

"...I wonder who will be next. What the next accident will be. I have an awful feeling that I can't get rid of. I've had it since you first came home covered in Andresh's blood. And now, with Father home, I don't feel better. I feel worse."

"You know...I feel the same way," I said. I didn't think about Father—for what happened to him, he seemed surprisingly composed and aware—but Andresh and the entire mess of the Magnum Opus hung over me like a dark cloud, and if I couldn't figure out how to treat the poison in him, well...darker things were ahead, that was certain.

The thought hit me: *I wonder if I should share what's going on.* If Andresh's situation worsened, the family would want to know something. On the other hand, Andresh had been evasive with me and held off on telling me the truth until his situation forced it out of him. He would probably prefer to keep his secrets as long as possible, and it wasn't my place to share them, but I had the feeling that the truth would come out sooner rather than later.

Nell and I continued down the streets of Mariner's lower quarter until we made it to the market square—literally called Market Square—which served as the centerpiece of a five-point street crossing. Stalls lined each side, but in the middle the largest stall was situated below the old Guildhall and clock: the butcher's.

Mr. Davies, the kind, well-muscled man who was in his forties, but looked no older than thirty, wore a bloody apron, and when he turned to us, he wiped his soiled hands on it. "Miss Bellamy! Young Miss Bellamy! I hardly see you two out together anymore."

"One of us is usually at the shop," I said. I smiled at him. He was always very friendly to us.

"What will it be? The pork cutlets are on sale today."

"We're looking for something already cooked and hot. How's the chicken?"

"Roasted and coated in garlic butter. Half chickens are all we have left."

I didn't know how hungry Father or Andresh would be. It would be better to overcompensate for their appetites than leave them wanting more. "Do you have five of them?"

Nell side-eyed me. "That's a lot."

"Then we'll have leftovers."

"You're clearing our stock, my lady," Mr. Davies said with a grin. "It's five aums per chicken."

I opened my reticule and searched for my coin purse, then paid him for our meal.

"Much obliged." Mr. Davies dipped behind the counter to wrap the meat and placed it in a box, stacking the chickens carefully. He passed the parcel to me. It took up almost my entire basket.

We headed to the other stalls to purchase freshly cooked potatoes and a luxurious stick of butter. We ended it all with a sizeable loaf of wheaten bread.

"Dessert?" Nell asked. I eyed each of our baskets, which were full.

"That would be nice, but how would we carry it?"

"Good point." She didn't hide the disappointment in her voice, though.

We made our way back home, and Nell and I set the food on the countertop. Father was sitting in the same spot, exactly as we had left him, but Grandma was on her feet. She came over and took the boxes out of the baskets. "I can't deny that it smells good," she said. Her eyes widened when she saw the stacks of chicken halves. "Girls! How many did you get?"

"There's one chicken for each of us," I said. "I thought everyone would be hungry." I looked over to the table. "Are you hungry, Father?"

He nodded. "As soon as you said 'chicken,' I was ready for dinner."

"Eleanor, help me set the table," Grandma said.

"I'll see if Andresh is up for some food," I said, and took the steps to his room.

I knocked on the door. "Andresh?"

To my surprise, he opened it immediately, but he hunched over and spoke in hushed tones, as if he was trying to hide something. "Lily."

I noticed a dribble of blood on his lower lip, and he opened his mouth wide.

His other tooth was gone. The cuspid. The gaps in his mouth were symmetrical—one dog's tooth for each side. He looked like a jack o' lantern.

"Do you have the tooth? We can put it with the other one and bring them with us when we go to the dental surgeon tomorrow."

He nodded. He opened the door wider for me and let me in. He gestured to a bloody ivory shape on his night table, where it rested on a handkerchief. I wrapped the tooth and held it carefully in my hand.

"We're having supper," I said. "And you won't believe what happened. Father is here. He came back to us."

Andresh's eyes widened at the news. "What? How?"

"He is not...unharmed from the journey. He lost his leg as a result of the attack on the ship."

Andresh's eyes glistened, and his face crumpled with emotion. "I'm so glad he's returned. He's been like a second father to me. I didn't want to lose anyone else."

I pulled him into me to give him a hug. His hands gently clutched my back.

"I know Father will want to see you. But...with your teeth...

do you think you can eat? It's chicken, potatoes, and wheaten bread."

He let go of me. "I don't know. I don't know what will happen. The food sounds too good to pass up, though."

I thought about it. "I'll cut your meat off the bone. Slice it into little pieces for you. And I'll smash the potato until it's soft. I don't think you can eat the bread though—too hard."

"I appreciate you, Lily." He looked off to the side, and some color came to his face, filling his cheeks. "My mouth. I don't know if I can show myself like this. I know I look strange."

"Do you want me to bring your supper here? I can tell the others you are not feeling well enough to come down." I held up the handkerchief. "Don't know if I can hide this, though."

"You can tell them about the tooth. But please, let me eat up here."

"I understand. See you in a little bit."

I made my way down the stairs, and sure enough, my little bundle caught people's eyes.

"What do you have there?" Nell asked.

"Unfortunately, Andresh lost another tooth." I found the jar with the other one and deposited the fresh one inside it.

Nell let out an audible gasp. "What's wrong with him?"

"Is there a deficiency of some sort?" Father asked. He could recognize some problems, having been at sea and witnessing what came of the men who had trouble with their diets.

"We're going to the dental surgeon tomorrow with haste. He's worried, no doubt. And he's embarrassed. He doesn't want to come down. So I'll prepare his meal and bring it to him in his room."

Before I settled down with my food, I cut as much meat off as I could, and transferred the pieces of white and gray chicken to a separate plate. I quickly peeled one of the potatoes and set about mashing it until I could get it as light as possible, although there were some chunks of roast potato in there that I couldn't manage. It looked soft enough, though. I transferred the potatoes to the plate of sliced chicken and poured Andresh a small glass of red wine to help calm his troubled heart, then grabbed the silverware before returning up the steps to his room.

I had somehow balanced everything well enough, but had an awkward time trying to knock on his door, so I called his name.

He came to the door again and took the food from me, thanking me for preparing and bringing it.

"Let's go to the surgeon in the morning, right when they open, and see if they can help you as soon as possible."

"I appreciate it."

THE NEXT MORNING, we were at Dr. Remedy's (that was his real name) in Highgate, Andresh walking with his mouth shut, not speaking at all, and me holding his teeth in the little glass jar.

He was clearly nervous, fretting his bottom lip or occasionally swallowing.

"I can go into the room with you, if you'd like."

He nodded.

Once we got him sorted, he and I followed the doctor into the patient's examination room. Andresh climbed into the recliner chair and opened his mouth wide.

Dr. Remedy gently gripped Andresh's chin and turned his head side to side as the doctor observed the interior of Andresh's mouth.

"This is quite peculiar," he said. "But those teeth—they're already starting to grow back."

CHAPTER 15

"What?" Andresh and I managed to speak at the same time.

"Here son, tilt your head back a little more. Miss Bellamy, you can come over and look."

I stood by Dr. Remedy's side.

"It's far up in there, but each hole has a trace of white bone. A new tooth coming in." He took one of his tools, a thin metal scraper, and reached in to tap the spots where Andresh had lost his cuspids. There was the slightest sound of a "clink" when the surgeon made contact.

I could see them, barely, but there were white spots starting to fill the holes.

"I've never seen anything like this before," Dr. Remedy admitted. "You just lost the teeth yesterday, while new ones have broken the surface. A medical mystery to be sure."

"Is there...anything wrong with me, doctor?" Andresh asked.

"Not that I can tell. I want you to keep me posted on this,

though. New teeth can take six months to grow in, but...I feel as though something strange is at work here. An anomaly. Can you visit me again in a month so I may see its progression? Pro bono. Consider it scientific research."

"That's fine." Andresh gave me an unsure look, though. The doctor was right to assume something strange was going on, but it was supernatural. Andresh and I might be thinking the same thing—that he couldn't help with any research when this was a result of what happened at Nigredo Gate. We left the dental surgeon's office feeling unsatisfied.

Andresh did not need months for a new development to occur. It took one week; although, truth be told, it seemed like it happened in one random day.

He hadn't been leaving his room very often because he still felt bad about the holes in his smile, until the day he surprised me at my bedroom door.

"Andresh? Do you need me?"

He spoke with his voice lowered, but I could see it already.

He had fangs.

"Lily," he said, sounding desperate as he barged into my room. "What am I going to do? No one can see me like this!"

His canine teeth were longer than normal, only by a few centimeters, but they ended in what looked to be incredibly sharp points. These were not the teeth of a human. The image of a vampire or demon immediately came to mind. And yet... somehow...he remained handsome. Otherworldly. Dark.

"Did they come in now? Do they hurt?" I asked.

"They were like this when I woke up."

I took in a deep breath and let out an exhalation louder than I meant—it was supposed to calm us both down, but it sounded dramatic. "Andresh, I don't think we can keep hiding you. Father has wanted to talk to you for a while now. Nell thinks you're practically dying. You're going to have to let them see. You should tell them *something*."

That notion clearly frightened him. His eyes had grown wide, his brows raised, and a deathly pallor overtook him. "How could they suddenly understand that the world they know is merely a fraction of the worlds out there; that as long as there are gods and saints, there are demons, too; and that magic is in fact real? What will they think when they learn that I'm a magician, an alchemist? Alchemists aren't even supposed to be real; they died out with the quacks when the true chemists took over."

"You don't have to tell them everything," I said, gently. "The bare minimum to get them to understand. You were trying to help the world. You risked yourself for that kind of magic. And you were poisoned by a demon."

His lower lip trembled, and suddenly he looked so forlorn, my heart seemed to sink in my chest. "Will you help me? Tell them? Stay by my side?"

I kissed his forehead. "Of course."

We headed downstairs together.

Father was busy in the store—word had gotten out that he was home, and that meant people wanted to visit him and welcome him back. They were there more to socialize than shop, but nobody seemed to mind.

Nell was at the fabric counter, and Grandma was in the kitchen.

Grandma was the first to react to Andresh's appearance. "What on earth happened to you? Look at those teeth! When did those come in?" She paused. "There's something not right about this."

Andresh frowned. "I know. I think I'll have to go back to Dr. Remedy's to get them filed down."

"I know you told us they were growing back in," Grandma said, "but how is it possible they came in so fast and so full? And what is with their shape?"

I looked at Andresh, and back to Grandma. "Um, we need a family meeting. With everyone. When the store closes, we'll all pile in here."

Grandma squinted at us. "Sounds serious."

Andresh said, a slight tremor in his voice, "It is."

"We'll be back here at five, if you can tell Father and Nell," I said. I turned to Andresh. "I have to help out, but you can stay in your room or the library if you wish."

He nodded, and without saying anything else, disappeared up the steps.

I spent my time outside with the large basins, hand-laundering clothes. I always wanted to see what it would be like to wash the fabrics with my homemade soaps, to see if the fragrance would stay on the clothes, but I was also afraid that perhaps my soap wouldn't wash out all the way and leave a residue of some kind.

Clothes. I thought about them for a moment. With Father home, our mourning period was over. No more black.

And the other thought struck me—what about the cemetery? Father's headstone was there! Could we write to the staff of the church and have them take it away? It wasn't cheap, but I didn't think we should keep it as a souvenir, either.

I thought about things as soon as they popped in my head, with no real link between them—only random ideas and observations. My brain whirred like that until I realized the Guildhall clock, all the way down at Market Square, was chiming five. You could hear it through almost all of Mariner, although the bells were far more gentle-sounding in our neighborhood.

I rushed to hang everything on the clothesline and darted inside.

Father and Grandma were seated at the dining table. Nell was there, too, and Andresh was kneeling on the floor in front of her, looking like he was ready to propose. Instead, he held his mouth slightly open, lips curled back, while Nell said from her chair, hunched over him in wonder, "Are those even real? They can't be real!"

Huh. She seemed to be taking it rather well.

I glanced over at Grandma and Father to compare. They seemed somewhat grave.

"I'm sorry I'm late, everyone," I said, swooping into the kitchen. Instead of taking a seat, I stood aside as Andresh rose to his feet and brushed his pant legs off.

"Do you want me to speak first, or are you good to take the lead?" I whispered to him.

"I'll do it." He squeezed my hand, out of love, kindness, or in need of reassurance, I wasn't sure.

"Um..." He sounded nervous. "So...centuries ago there was a family, the Xaviers, who were known for their pursuit of all things esoteric and magical. At one point, they were advisors to the kings of Sindalia, reading the stars and offering counsel. But they had their own magic that they kept to themselves, in secret—magic that involved the energy of every living being, what we call, Fire."

Andresh opened his palm to my family, and a turquoise blue flame slowly rose from his hand.

Nell's eyes widened, and Father and Grandma exchanged baffled looks with each other.

Andresh passed his other hand over the flame, and it grew in size and length. He molded it as if it were clay, and with a small smile, extended it to me. He had formed a lily out of his own flame.

"This is my Fire. The color is unique to me. This is the energy that pervades every living creature in this world, from humans to animals to plants. Every being has it, and every flame has its unique shade, even colors the naked eye has never glimpsed before."

Andresh closed his fingers over the lily, and the Fire sank back into his flesh and disappeared, almost as if it passed through a frame, and a door shut behind it.

"My God," Father whispered. Grandma and Nell only stared.

"The Xaviers could use Fire magic to heal or purify; to change the body so it would pass through barriers between realms; and even to shorten the span of a life. This was a secret only shared within the ancestors and kept away from the outside world in case the power was to be abused.

"Eventually, magic and otherworldly things fell out of favor with the advance of scientific inquiry, experimentation, and observation. While there are still practitioners of some of the old ways—readers of the planets and the stars, for example—magic went underground and was feared and considered the power of dark, evil creatures. The Xaviers couldn't escape their reputation, so they altered their name to Zatavier. It's an open secret, as the name isn't so different. But people have left us alone, for the most part. And while Zataviers know of Fire and what it can do, they generally don't practice using it anymore to ensure it's kept away from the world."

"So how do you know how to do that?" Nell asked.

"I learned it from my older relatives in Sindalia."

"What do you do with it? You don't just make pretty things."

I didn't mean to pipe up, but I did. "He helped heal Grandma from her stroke."

Grandma's hand flew to her heart, but she said nothing.

Andresh looked to me again, as if for guidance, and I gave him a little nod. Then he faced everyone.

"I want to prolong life. I want to end death. Since Fire is the energy of life, I thought if I learned about it, I could save people. But I couldn't figure out its workings. That led me on a different magical path—alchemy. And alchemy is protected as much as Fire, although it's hidden by metaphors and images and rudimentary science. I needed help with it, as it's considered *the* way to immortality."

"But alchemists were cleared out, called frauds," Father said. "For at least a century. They were never able to make gold out of base metals. Do you know what happened to the last alchemist in Brinn? Banished to former colonies."

"Alchemists can't turn metal into gold. That is true. But it was never actually about that. It's all a metaphor for something much bigger."

I wondered how much he was going to say next. Would he outright mention Isabelle and the demons? Would he mention the Magnum Opus?

"It gets very complicated, so I'll only say this: I made a mistake. I went to another realm to cross through the Four Gates of Alchemy. I only made it to the first Gate, though. And I was supposed to sacrifice a part of me that I can't bring myself to give up. The Guardian of that Gate, who accepts the sacrifice, got angry with me and we sort of...fought. He stabbed me in my leg, and he used poison. This poison is changing me. The first thing being my teeth. I don't know what else will change about me, but in order to stop this punishment from progressing, I have to go back and finish what I've started."

Nell shook her head. I didn't know if it meant she didn't want Andresh to go, or if she didn't understand what he was saying. She looked sorely confused, her eyebrows turned up in a perplexed manner.

"Other realms. Gates. Poison," Father said. "I can't grasp this, Andresh. What trouble are you in? Why on earth did you think you could end death?"

"I'm in the gravest of trouble," Andresh confessed. "And though alchemy promises the way to immortality, I've learned the weight of the cost. The thing is—once you start the Great Work, you have to finish it. It could kill me if I don't."

"What if it's killing you now?" Nell asked, her voice slightly above a whisper.

"I don't have an answer for that." Andresh sighed. "No matter what happens...I want my days to be peaceful."

I thought he was about to say *final* days, as though he were giving up. It startled me and I had to swallow to ease the tightening of my throat.

"What can we possibly do to help you, Andresh?" Grandma asked. "Are we even strong enough to? You've gotten yourself involved in incredible, forbidden things. Things we never knew existed."

"I'm afraid I'm the only one who can solve this. And it might mean walking away from you. From all of you. But I don't want to think about that now. Ever since I've been wounded, I've been so tired. I'd like to go upstairs and rest, if I may."

Grandma didn't really respond to that. Nell continued to stare at Andresh, her stunned look replaced by a withered, forlorn expression. Father rose to his feet and patted Andresh's back.

"What you've done is dangerous. Many would say unnatural; possibly evil. It must have taken a lot for you to share this with us. I appreciate your honesty. But I can't condone the choices you've made."

Andresh gave him a pained half smile. "I understand, Mr. Bellamy. It's all been one mistake after the other, and all of them dire." He lowered his head to everyone and headed upstairs.

Father had uttered something that never occurred to me: *evil.* I couldn't picture Andresh that way, and yet even I had to admit he crossed a line as soon as he started working with demons. Had he done something evil? Did it make him an evil person?

And...would that make me evil, too? I did the world no favors when I made a deal with Aineiron and freed him. He could be out there driving people insane for pleasure, for all I knew. If I was the cause of that...well, I would be a candidate for evil for certain.

I took a quick glance at everyone, and even though their expressions differed, the earlier shock on their faces had left a residual impression. They still couldn't believe what they'd seen or heard.

"Lily," Nell began. "How long have you known about Andresh?"

"Since we were children. He's been able to use Fire for a very long time. But even I don't know the extent of his power or what all he can do."

"So you've kept this secret for years?" She almost sounded annoyed. Perhaps even jealous.

"I did so to protect Andresh, and to protect the magic. I was surprised he told me anything about it." A part of me wanted to bring up that I could do it too—just a little—but I was sure everyone would keel over at that. One enormous secret revealed was enough for a while.

Grandma got up from her chair, steadying herself with her cane, and trudged over to Father. "We will have to keep our mouths shut, too. If the wrong people learned of Andresh's power, he could be in grave danger. The church. The chemists. The doctors. Who knows who else would seek him or study him, or how far it could go."

"We should keep him out of the shop," Father said. "People won't be able to handle those new fangs of his. And if he changes further—I don't even know what we'll do. We'll keep him here in the house, I suppose. But perhaps, for our safety, we should move him to the cellar."

"The cellar? Do you plan on chaining him next?" I asked, a little more angry than I meant to be.

"What if his changes make him *monstrous*?" Nell asked bluntly. "What if he loses himself and turns on us? Would you kill him, Father? Grandma? Lily?"

She shocked me with those words. "No, I won't kill him! I'll get him to the Gate before that happens."

"You don't sound so sure of yourself," Nell said.

"*I'll* kill him," Father said, grabbing his crutch and rising from his chair. "I may not be as strong or as whole as I used to be, but when it concerns the safety of my family, I'll summon all that I've got within me to protect you. Even if it means the very worst."

"You—you can't mean that," I said. My vision blurred at his words, and I was ready to cry.

"I do, Lily. This is very serious. If he changes, and if he hurts *anyone*—he is finished."

The family meeting ended there. We each went our own separate ways, though I went up the next floor and listened outside of Andresh's room to see if he was sleeping. The soft, not-so- unpleasant sounds of snoring permeated the door, and satisfied, I went to my bedroom.

Well, I wasn't truly satisfied. I wanted answers. I wanted to save Andresh.

I guess I'll have to be evil, too. Look at me, consulting with demons.

I had a large hand mirror I kept facedown underneath my bed, and had nearly forgotten the curse was gone until I thought of contacting Andresh's demon. I reached under my bed and pulled out the mirror and gave a gentle knock on the glass, as if it were a door. "Isabelle," I said, my voice soft, gentle...and with a slight tremble.

She was there, waiting for me, appearing in a second. Her black, inky eyes unnerved me as she looked at me, unblinking. She grinned, revealing her own fangs.

"Hello, Lily. I want to help you, but I'm so hungry. I haven't been fed for days." She pouted.

Something about how she said it made my skin crawl. "What is it you eat?"

She smiled even wider. "Fire."

I knew she didn't mean ordinary flames. It made sense for a demon to consume life energy—they were demons, after all.

"Open your palm, lilac," Isabelle said.

I winced, as that was what Aineiron had called me.

She continued. "Open your palm, open the gate, and let a little flame out. Just a little one. A year will suffice. Then I'll tell you what you want to know."

I hesitated, but only for a moment. If it meant saving Andresh's life, what would the loss of a year matter?

"How do I get my Fire to you?"

"Open with this." She held up a sharply clawed finger and drew a sigil on the mirror:

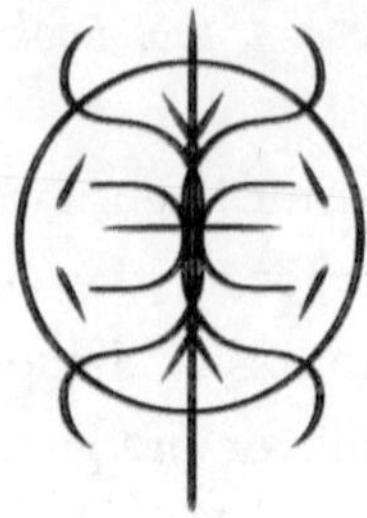

The lines were more complicated than I expected even though it looked deceptively simple. I traced over her mark with my finger, directly onto the mirror—circle first, the intertwining lines, and the four single marks.

I remembered from Aineiron what I would have to do next. Except, I wasn't letting Isabelle out—I was simply going to put my hand in.

I was able to call the Fire out of my hand immediately when it came to saving Andresh. Would I be able to do it this time?

I opened my hand to Isabelle, and a small trickle of Fire came and sputtered out.

"Let me try again," I offered.

It seemed I couldn't open the gate in my hand, or I could, but couldn't keep it open long enough for a decently sized ball of flame to come out. I closed my eyes and thought the words *OPEN OPEN OPEN* when the fiery orb appeared in my palm. I thrust my burning hand into the mirror, right where I traced the sigil.

Isabelle seized my wrist, and a long, pointed tongue escaped her lips. She lapped at the fire in my hands like a kitten slurping milk as a treat, her tongue flicking back and forth. She didn't touch my skin until the very end, when the last trace of my Fire remained, and her tongue lightly brushed against me as she gulped down the last of it all.

She let go of me, and I yanked my hand back through the mirror. Her tongue was scratchy, with tiny little spikes on it like a cat's, and I was sure that if she kept on licking my hand, it would hurt.

"Is the... Is the mirror closed?" I asked.

She drew her sigil in the air and then an 'X' over it, a simple act of crossing it out. "Now it is."

I ran my hand over the glass and tried to push into it. Everything was solid, and nothing moved.

Isabelle laughed. "You can trust me, Lily. I love you."

"Yes, you've said that." It still made me uneasy to hear it.

"You're here to save Andresh," she said.

"Yes. What can be done?"

"He was stung by the scorpion's tail. It will be many decades before the first doctor creates an antidote, so he cannot be cured of its poison. It will slowly change him until he dies. Unless he finishes the Magnum Opus, where he can be refined and remade into something pure and powerful, he won't be saved."

"There's no way to stop his death unless he becomes immortal."

Isabelle nodded. But a wide smile stretched across her features, showing her pointed fangs. She looked positively gleeful. "There is another way to immortality. Not invincibility, but life long-lasting. I love Andresh. I will save him. He was meant for a long life. I've always known it. I'll give it to him when he comes back to Nigredo. I will wait for him there."

"You can grant eternal life?"

"My domain is '*hidden things, amongst paupers, amongst kings.*' I possess the knowledge of all secrets. I will show him what to do."

"You could show me, too."

She shook her head. "It's too big for you. I cannot reveal it unless we make a pact. And you cannot make one with me without my true name." She grinned again. "I will not tell it to you. Search for it, if you are desperate, and call me by my name. This will be the last you see me in the mirrors, Lily. I am Andresh's Isabelle, not yours."

She was gone before I could figure out how she'd left.

So, this was the last help I would ever get from her, unless I found out what she was actually called. I had no idea how to go about securing that kind of information. I'd have to go to the library, or perhaps search even the church's old tomes, to find the books categorizing demons by name. She did give me a clue when she mentioned her domain, but was that enough for me to find her?

I shook my head. Why would I want to make a pact with a demon, anyway? She told me she was going to save Andresh... did I need to know how it was going to happen? I'd heard somewhere, perhaps even from Isabelle, that demons do not lie. Should I trust her? Andresh certainly did.

I needed to share with him what Isabelle told me. I knew I had left him sleeping, but it was possible he could be awake. I headed up one floor to his room and waited outside of it, listening.

There was no snoring. I knocked on the door. "Andresh, it's me."

After a second, the handle turned, and he opened the door slightly. "Lily. Come in. I'm afraid to show the others yet."

I followed him inside, but I already noticed what he was talking about. My gaze found one of his hands, the faint trace of blood on the fingertips, with newly erupted black claws where his fingernails used to be. It wasn't that they were long —on the contrary, they grew perhaps a half-inch above the tip of his finger—it was the fact that they looked incredibly sharp.

They came to striking points that suggested they could easily shred anything in a heated moment.

"The pain woke me up," he said, this time openly showing me his hands. "They burst on through while I was sleeping. Completely shattered my nails as they came out." He pointed to the bed, where there were small streaks of red. "I'm sorry I got blood on the coverlet. I know you get stuck with the laundry at times..."

"It will come out with cold water," I said. "Don't worry. Are you in pain now?"

"There's a residual stinging. But...I can't go out like this. The teeth are bad, but there's something disturbing about these claws. I'm becoming a monster."

CHAPTER 16

Andresh stared at his fingers, wearing such a sad expression that my heart seemed to fall halfway down in my chest.

"Father is really troubled by all of this," I said, trying to be as careful with my words as possible. "He wants to move you down to the cellar. For our safety, he said. And if he sees your hands, he'll hasten that decision."

"I'll stay down there freely. I don't know how far these changes are going to go. I couldn't bear it if I hurt anyone, especially with these." He bent his fingers, emphasizing his new claws.

"When we visit the dental surgeon, we can ask him to do your nails as well as your teeth—file it all down."

"I don't think I can go, looking like this. How are we going to explain this away?"

I thought about it for a moment. "Father's pretty capable. What if we got him the tools and he did your teeth and nails instead? I can run out and get them. I'll secure a file for your teeth, and something else for the nail file."

He nodded. "Could you, if you don't mind, deliver my supper to me tonight? I don't want to show them these claws yet."

Supper! I had forgotten about it! "Oh, I didn't help Grandma at all. I hope Nell did." I glanced at the clock on his writing desk. "I'm late!" By almost twenty minutes, too. I was surprised no one came after me, but perhaps the shock of Andresh's story distracted everyone.

"I'll see you shortly," I told him, as I hurried down the stairs to the kitchen.

Grandma, Nell, and Father were at the table already, and their food was nearly gone.

"Only soup tonight," Grandma said as I entered. "We take it you were with Andresh."

"Yes," I said, and noticed that while there was a placement for me at the table, the one for him was missing.

"Your dinner needs reheating."

"That's fine. It's my fault I'm so late. And Andresh won't be joining us. He's... Well, there was another change. You'll see it eventually, but right now, he's keeping to his room."

"What happened?" Nell asked.

"He's got claws now. Sharp, black ones."

"I knew it. He's turning into some kind of animal."

"We'll move him to the cellar tonight," Father said. "I hate to treat him this way, but we'll probably have to lock him in when he isn't out here...which will be rarely."

"He's turning into something," I said weakly. "And he is ashamed of it. I already told him we'd be moving him, and he agrees wholeheartedly." I looked to my sister. "Nell, will you help me set up a spare bed down there for him?" In truth, we didn't have an actual extra bed frame, but we had plenty of bedding and a spare mattress. "I'll finish supper, feed Andresh, and have you help me carry things down. Is that alright?"

Nell nodded.

"Father, I think it's still safe enough for me to bring Andresh his food. I'd like to do that."

"He hasn't tried anything with you? He hasn't tried to hurt you?"

"He's been his normal self with me. He just feels a great shame, and more unsure of himself than ever before."

Father looked at me a while, his eyes narrowed as he seemed lost in thought. "I will bring his meals starting tomorrow. I'd rather something happen to me than anyone else."

My heart sank at that. He was being far too strict. I was almost afraid to ask for the next thing. "Father, I need your help. Tomorrow I'm going to get files for Andresh. Can you work on his teeth and nails? We need someone strong and sturdy with a precise hand to get those filed down."

"I can do it, but I have to be very, very careful. I'd prefer a surgeon, but I know privacy is of the utmost importance."

"Thank you."

The rest of the family cleared out of the room, with Nell speaking before leaving. "Come and get me when you need help."

I went to the fireplace, to the small cauldron of soup and stirred it. It was still warm, but not hot. I lowered the soup so it would be a little closer to the fire and heat up quickly. When it was ready, I served Andresh's first.

I liked my soup to be a little cooler, so I set mine aside and headed upstairs to Andresh's room with his bowl. "Father's going to work on your hands and teeth tomorrow after I pick up the files," I said, handing him his food.

One of his claws brushed along the top of my hand as he accepted the meal, leaving a thin red line behind. It didn't hurt until the blood rose to the surface.

"Lily! I'm so sorry!" He almost dropped the soup as he set it down on the ground. From his pocket he pulled a kerchief, and wrapped my hand with it, careful not to accidentally scratch me anymore.

"That doesn't bode well for us," I said. "Father is convinced you're going to do something bad to me, or to someone else in the family. I'll have to make up some sort of lie about how I got this."

Andresh's eyes teared up. "I never expected anything like this to happen, that the family I love would grow to fear me, though for good reason. Lily. What if your Father won't let me see you again?"

"Then I'll find a way to sneak out to see you. Now, hurry up and eat so I can change your dressings." Over the days that passed I had always done it, and I was clumsy at first, but now I could do it quickly, as adept as a nurse. "Can I sup with you? Then I'll get to the bandages after we eat." I would tell him about Isabelle then, since I missed my chance earlier.

Andresh nodded. He grabbed his bowl from the floor and moved to the writing desk to eat, while I leaned against the wall and guzzled my soup down instead of chewing the bits of meat and vegetables in it.

I thought perhaps we would talk then, but we were silent as we ate. Occasionally Andresh's new claws would clink against the ceramic of the bowl, despite him using a spoon to eat.

I reached out to him when he finished. "All done?"

He nodded. He went to hand me the bowl, but drew his fingers back, trying to avoid scratching my skin again.

"It'll be alright," I said. "I'll be careful."

I took his things, dipped out of his room and down the stairs, where the dishes were left for me. Oh well. I'd get to them after cleaning Andresh's wound. He was my priority.

I went back upstairs to the bathroom to grab the bandages,

adhesive, and salve for Andresh's thigh, then headed back to his room.

Andresh was waiting for me on the bed. He had dutifully removed his pants as usual, and his wounded leg remained uncovered while he hid the rest of himself with the blanket to avoid being immodest.

As I unwrapped his leg, I said very carefully, "Andresh. You might not like this, but I talked to Isabelle in my room."

His eyes widened. "I'm the one who named her. How did you summon her?"

"Oh, I called to her at the mirror, and she came." I made the split-second decision to hold back telling Andresh I gave her my Fire. "She says she can save you. She needs you to go back to Nigredo Gate." I paused. "I'm...thinking I should believe her. Has she ever harmed you?"

Andresh shook his head. "We're in a pact. As long as she has the name I gave her, she is subservient to me. And she's served me loyally. She's always helped me when I've asked her to. It seems like you beat me to it this time." For a moment, he looked frightened. "What name did you call her by?"

"Isabelle. That's the only name I know."

He looked relieved.

"Why does she want you to go back to the Gate?"

"The lower Gates are guarded by demons. It's a punishment for them, to eternally wait there. The Nigredo Gate, as well as the Albedo Gate, are located in part of the underworld —it's easy for demons to congregate there. She probably wants to see me again, but in person this time."

"She wants you to have a long life, she said."

Andresh let out a short laugh. "She's always telling me that. She says that's all she can see for me. And she can see a lot."

"Demons can't lie, can they? This isn't going to be some trick?"

"Demons can't lie, but they can be deceptive in their own ways. I've been careful, Lily, trust me."

I put the old bandages on the writing desk, then grabbed the salve. I rubbed it on the wound, which was healing nicely. I knew not to rush it, though, as he still sometimes felt twinges of pain on contact. My hand brushed against his rough, scarred skin and I applied the medicine slowly and carefully.

"Andresh. What will you do if she is lying to you?"

"If she tries to hurt me—if she tries to hurt *anyone*—I'll kill her."

He sounded extremely determined, but I had to say something. "You tried to kill the Guardian and it didn't work. How would you take down Isabelle?"

"I'll admit, the Guardian was a misstep. I didn't think that one through. But now I know what to do—blow out their light, like you would a candle."

"That sounds too easy," I said. I decided in that moment that I would follow him. I wouldn't tell him that. I wasn't sure what I would do, but I would protect him, somehow.

I wiped my hands off and proceeded to wrap Andresh's leg with the new bandages.

"When will you meet her?" I asked, suddenly scared he'd be gone from us the very next day.

"It will have to be soon. In a couple days, I think. I don't know how else I'm going to change, or if I'll become something dangerous. I've hurt you already. If I do something worse, I'll never forgive myself."

A couple days was far too soon, but I understood. "You can't just disappear on me, Andresh. I'll never forgive you. You need to say goodbye before you leave."

I secured the bandages with the adhesive strips and

walked over to the desk, piling everything up to take away. "Andresh. Whatever happens...I love you."

His eyes glistened. "I love you too."

"Nell and I are going to set up your bed downstairs. I'll come and get you when it's ready." I paused. "Father wants to start locking you in the cellar after we leave you. He says it's for our protection."

"I agree with your Father. I don't know how far all of this is going to go."

"This'll also be the last time we share a meal. He's taking over giving you food, too. In the meantime, I'll bring some books for you to read—"

"And I'll need a mirror. A small one will suffice."

I nodded. He'd still need to talk to Isabelle if the situation became more dire.

I did as he requested, and as I said I would do. Nell and I managed the bedding, and then I secured the books and mirror. Then Andresh followed the both of us down the stairs to the very bottom of the house, which was quite sparse except for the casks of wine in the far corner of the room.

"Goodnight, Andresh," I said, and Nell echoed my words.

We both turned to head back up the stairs when a rhythmic clacking sound greeted us, a slow approach. It was Father's crutch, followed by his slow, gentle footfalls.

"Hello, girls." He reached into his pocket and pulled out a key. "This is for everyone's protection, Andresh. Please, don't take this as an affront to your person. We all still love you and care for you very much." He gestured for Nell and I to go.

"I love you all too, Mr. Bellamy," Andresh said, his voice sounding fainter as I left him behind.

"I'll bring you your breakfast in the morning," Father said. The last sound I heard was the click from the turning of the lock in the door.

When I got to my bedroom, I cried myself to sleep.

~

This wasn't going to work. Father might keep Andresh locked in the basement at all hours of the night and day, but he couldn't separate us. I wouldn't let it happen.

But Father knew I was going to try to get around his orders to keep away, and as I snuck into the shop early morning to get the skeleton key from the third floor of the counting desk, I noticed he had taken it. Damn it.

I trudged back up to my bedroom.

I had woken up at sunrise for who knows what reason, as I was still tired from the day before. But with new determination, I came up with a ludicrous plan. And it involved Isabelle.

She said she wouldn't talk to me again, but this time, she just *had* to. I had something too delicious for her to pass up.

"Isabelle!" I kept my voice softer, but it still came out louder than I intended.

"There's something different about you, Lily," she said in the glass, appearing without showing me how or when it happened.

"I'm determined to get your help," I said.

"Call me by my name, then give me a new one, and I shall be yours."

"Isabelle, I name you Catherine, now please, make a deal with me."

"My name is neither Isabelle nor Catherine." She looked slightly offended and made a small *tsk* sound. "Go find it in the grimoires and call back to me."

"I'll give you ten years of my life if you show me how to be a Key."

"You are a Key, it's true," she said. "But it'll take fifty years of your lifespan to show you *that* kind of magic."

"That's how much it costs? Can you see when I die, or something? What if I don't have fifty years to give? And if I do, what if I only have ten years of life remaining after that? It's not worth it to me."

"Then our business here is done."

"Just give me a way to talk to Andresh. My Father is stubborn and is keeping me from him. He and Andresh say it's to keep me safe."

"If Andresh meets me at Nigredo Gate, all will be well. I have found the way to protect him from the Guardian."

"I need to talk to him before he does that. Is there anything that can be done?"

"If you give me the ten years you first offered, I will let you walk my Mirror Paths. Do you remember my sigil?"

I shook my head. "It was a bit complicated."

"Commit it to memory now."

She drew on her side of the mirror her special mark:

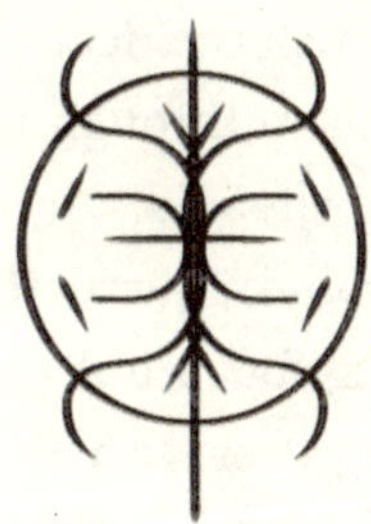

"Practice drawing it," she said. I traced over it several times with my finger until I could draw it in the air without making a mistake.

"Good. I will make it so you are the only one who can see this mark on the mirrors and in the Paths. Wherever you see it, just walk on through. When you are in the Paths, be careful not to stray. Do not venture outside any Path with different sigils. Stay only on mine. Then you will easily go from your mirror to Andresh's mirror, and you will be able to talk to him. You will even be able to step out of the mirror into his room, if you so wish."

"That's incredibly generous of you," I said. "And it sounds terrifying."

"If you wander off, it will be." She licked her lips. "Hold open the collar of your nightgown so that I may see the Fire in your heart."

I remembered Andresh saying the Gate there had to do with emotions. Well, emotions were definitely taking over my senses and decision-making abilities. I lowered my collar and widened it, holding it open with clenched fingers.

"Citrinitas," she said. "Open your Gate."

"I—I've never done this one by myself before," I stammered.

"Put everything you've got in you—your love for Andresh, your frustration with your father, your disappointment in your mother, the sadness from all the death and destruction—take all of it and push it right on through with the power of your Will. The Gate will open," she said.

Images flooded my mind. I pictured Mother seated at her mirror, combing her long, beautiful hair; I pictured Andresh and I in the forest clearing after we had danced, and him giving me my first kiss; then I saw myself kissing Andresh on the pier before he left for Sindalia. I flashed through all of his letters; the ring on my finger circled in the air in my mind; and his command: "Never take it off." The love I felt for him kept blooming in my chest, and then came the last image of Father telling me I could no longer see Andresh until everything was finished, which drew such a sharp pain from me I almost grunted. But then, there it was—a large lilac flame bursting from my chest, singeing the corners of the fabric, but not burning me.

"Come here, Lily," Isabelle said, and I stepped so close to her I was almost right up against the glass.

"Draw my sigil and open it," she said. As the light purple blazed above me, I let go of one of the corners of my nightgown and did as she said. I remembered what it was like with Aine-iron—I had to put my hand into the mirror and pull it open like a door. I did it, and Isabelle came halfway out of the mirror, clutching my shoulders and eagerly lapping up the flames at my chest.

I continued to hold the collar of my nightgown open for her, but tried not to watch how animalistic she looked as she devoured my Fire. She made little noises here and there, of guzzling and grunting and swallowing, and all of it sounded like she felt pure delight.

She held me in place for what seemed like forever. When my Fire started to diminish, she flicked her face up to mine. "You need to hold it for three more minutes. I'll tell you when to close the Gate."

When the third minute passed, Isabelle let go of me and let out the most ecstatic-sounding exhalation of air I'd ever heard. My Gate must have known to shut immediately as soon as she had taken her hands off of me.

"Oh, darling," she said. "I am so grateful for that. Come, I'll walk you to Andresh's mirror now. No, wait, not now."

A knock on my bedroom door startled me.

"Lily? It sounds like you're talking to someone," Nell called out to me through the door.

I didn't say anything more to Isabelle. I just nodded at her.

"Enter the mirror at will. Look for my sigils. They will take you to him," she whispered, and disappeared without showing me the act. She was there, and then simply, she wasn't.

"Come in, Nell," I called.

I looked down at my nightgown collar, burned in random spots. I wasn't sure how to explain that. I dove into bed and pulled the covers up all the way to just below my neck.

Nell let herself into my bedroom and came over and flopped onto my bed. She had something in her hands, something square-shaped and silvery.

"Found this in the waste bin in the shop last night," she said, passing it over to me. "It looks fancy. Sorry I didn't get it to you sooner."

It looked like an invitation, and it was clearly addressed to me. The sender was written simply as "Caliday."

I tore into the envelope none too carefully.

> *Dr. Caliday, Mr. Caliday, and their daughter Miss Adanya Caliday cordially invite Miss Lily Bellamy to formally debut at the annual Celestial Ball at the Caliday mansion in North Highgate. Miss Bellamy is allowed to bring one guest to the event. Costumes and masks fitting the celestial theme are required. Please confirm attendance with the enclosed card and envelope.*

On a small, folded sheet of paper that was haphazardly shoved in with the invitation, a fluid, looping script stated *Andresh is welcome to come. – AC.*

I pulled the blank envelope and response card out and handed Nell the original invitation and small note. Her eyes nearly bulged out of her head as she read silently to herself. "Lily! The Celestial Ball! For your debut! This is huge!"

"Why was it in the trash, then?"

Nell's expression changed from excitement to sadness. "It

must've been Father who threw it away. I don't think he wants you to go. I don't think he's ready to let you go."

"The Season is one big marriage mart, true. I do *not* have marriage on my mind right now. And besides, everyone knows by now that the only one I want is Andresh."

"Maybe he doesn't want you to leave Andresh behind," Nell said.

"That's funny, given he won't let me see him, either."

"He has fangs and claws, and looks like a vampire," she said. "His changes are scary. What if they get worse?"

"Has he tried to hurt anyone in this house since changing?"

"Well...no. But that lie you told about that scratch on your hand hasn't convinced anyone. We're all pretty sure he did that to you."

"On accident." I reached for the Caliday invitation once more. "When is this ball, anyway?" I looked for the date and time. "*Tomorrow?* How long has this been in the trash?"

"I just found it last night when I was emptying all the bins."

"I wouldn't be able to go anyway. It's a masquerade. I don't have a costume or anything else."

"That's too bad." She shifted her weight on the bed. "I heard the Farradays are having their own party tomorrow. Rosalind Farraday was talking about it to Father. As long as you bring some food to donate to the poor, you can come to the dance. You don't have to wear costumes, but the theme is 'Black Mask.' So...it's kind of like a masquerade, but simpler. Everyone will be wearing similar masks. The Farradays rented out Market Square for it and are putting the musicians' platform up tonight. Would you like to do something like that instead? There isn't an age limit like how it is for the Season's galas and balls."

"Sounds like you're the one who wants to go."

"I'm fourteen. I should be old enough to handle myself at a dance."

"I'll talk to Father on your behalf. You know that he won't let you attend without my supervision, right?" Going to a party would be taking time away from Andresh, but...I wondered if I could work out some way for him to secretly attend. It was a masque, after all. We needed to do something fun and pleasurable before he took on the Guardian again, even with Isabelle's help. We needed to feel like a normal, loving couple for once, out in the open, and without shame.

"Thanks for bringing the invitation to me," I said. "You can put it back with the rest of the trash. It was generous of the Calidays to offer, but I don't think it's going to happen with such short notice. I'll focus on the Farradays' party. I'll work on Father, but you have to work on him, too."

"Yes," Nell said, sounding optimistic. "I'll trust you to help me out!" She hopped off the bed and landed with a little thump on her feet. "You're not staying in bed, are you? I mean, I know it's still really early."

"No, I'm awake now. I'll get ready for the day. You can have the bathtub first," I said.

"Thanks!" She was at the door when she asked, "Are you going to make breakfast for everyone?"

"Might as well," I said. "But not quite this early. Give me thirty minutes before coming downstairs."

"Sounds good," Nell said.

When she left the room, I pulled my mirror off the wall. Suddenly I was very frightened—what if Isabelle was tricking me? She took so much Fire—she could've eaten and then disappeared. Nonetheless, I was going to try the Mirror Paths anyway.

I drew Isabelle's sigil on the glass with my finger, and to my surprise it actually left a glowing mark behind, a greenish color decorated with bits of smoke. I laid the mirror on the ground and took a step—

And fell on through. I landed hard on the ground, roughly hewn black rock that was lit by a mysterious green light from which I could not trace a source. It looked as though I was in some sort of cavern, similar to the scene from when we first saw the Guardian at the Gate in the mirror.

I rose none too gracefully to my feet. Ahead two paths diverged, and one of them was marked with Isabelle's sigil. I followed that one, and the texture of the landscape changed slightly. Down the black rock flowed molten silver, as if the mercury and mirror were melting down the rock. I didn't dare touch it, for fear that it would burn me. The silvery material caught the green light, which brightened the pathway.

I spotted another sigil and turned a hard right, and then, almost as if it was nailed to the wall, a large oval shape hung in the darkness. It was like looking through a window—I peered through it and recognized the wallpaper to the bathroom. Nell opened the door to it and I hurriedly walked away from what had to have been the bathroom mirror so I wouldn't violate her privacy.

To the left, I caught another sigil and followed it down another rocky, silvery, green-lit corridor. The window in the wall was a square shape, and tiny. It must have been a hand mirror. Written in glowing green on the stone was the phrase, "Pull on the sides to make it bigger – I." Did the glass stretch like an accordion? There was only one way to find out.

I decided to make the mirror taller first, then wider, comparable to the huge mirror hanging in the bathroom. I simply tugged on the edges, and the mirror did what I wanted.

Now that it was big, I recognized the wooden planks of the basement ceiling. I was overjoyed to have found it on the second try. Andresh must've placed the mirror on the floor, or on his bed, but thank God it was lying faceup.

"Andresh!" I called to him. He didn't answer. Perhaps he was still sleeping. "Andresh!" I tried one more time. Silence.

I grabbed the edges of the mirror on my side and stretched them all the way to the ground so I could walk through. I tried to remove the mirror from the black stone wall first to step through it that way, but it was tight and secure there. Secure enough to not come off, but weak enough to be moulded like clay. That didn't make sense to me, but why should I have expected any of this to?

I tried to walk through the mirror and slammed into it, then remembered I needed to open the door like a Gate. I drew Isabelle's sigil, then reached my hand through, and pulled it open before stepping through.

I crashed into Andresh, who woke instantly and jumped backward out of bed like a frightened cat—he nearly hissed at me like one, too. I was so happy to see him, but what stopped me from running to him was the next change.

His hair had turned completely white.

CHAPTER 17

I stared at him in a bit of a stupor. He didn't look bad at all. And it didn't age him, despite the shocking change of color to his braid and crown. He looked like the Winter Prince in the fairytale of the Queen of the Snows.

"Lily!" Andresh crawled back onto the mattress to rush to my side. "What did you do? How did you get here?"

"You're going to be so angry with me," I said, "but I don't care. Father took the skeleton key and is watching over you so closely, and he won't let me see you! So...I talked with Isabelle and she showed me the Mirror Paths. I can talk to you in mirrors just like she does. And I can step out of them, too. As far as I know, I can only do it in this house. Unless I wander off inside the mirrors."

Andresh's pale white face took on some rosiness, then full-on redness. Yes, he was angry with me to be certain. "And what was the cost of that?" His voice came out flat.

"Fire."

He buried his face in his hands. "I never should have showed you Fire. Never should have told you about it. Every time you give up Fire, you risk giving up too much and shortening your life. How much did she take from you?"

Suddenly I was afraid. Not of Andresh losing his temper with me, not that he ever did, but that I had made the wrong decision and made things worse. "I'm not ready to tell you that yet," I said, my voice coming out small.

"Oh, Lily." This time his voice wavered, like he was going to cry.

"It was worth it to me to do it," I said. "I wanted to see you before you went off to the Gate. And I have a selfish request. As risky as it is, I want you to come with me to the Farraday party tomorrow. We need to do something fun before everything we know comes to an end. And to what end, I don't know. But I want to enjoy myself with you."

"I can't go out like this," Andresh said. "Your Father found some tools in storage late last night, and he tried to fix my teeth and nails...and the files broke in half. I can't hide them. And now, my hair..."

"I can conceal you enough. The party's theme is Black Mask. We'll all be wearing them. I'll just get you one that covers your whole face. Add to that a pair of heavier gloves, and you keeping silent for the night, and no one should notice your affliction. And if anyone asks, I'll say you're my cousin from the Winterlands."

"It sounds incredibly risky."

"Not with the Mirror Paths! I'll come to the cellar tomorrow just before the party, and we'll exit through a hand mirror I'll place in the alley just outside the house. In and out we'll be." Then the next thought hit me. "Oh, that's right. Nell wants to come. What do we do about her?"

Andresh was looking at me with a curious expression on his face. "You really want this. I never took you for someone who wanted to dance all night at the ball. You weren't enthusiastic about debuting, as I recall."

"This won't be a debut. That's the great thing about it."

"...Tell me how to walk the Mirror Paths. You should be able to share this without any sacrifice. And I'm sure Isabelle won't mind if it's me."

"What do you plan to do?"

"You and Nell will go to the party. I'll meet you there separately, and I'll just...I'll ask you for one dance, and then I'll come back here. I don't want to risk more than that when these changes keep coming."

That was fair. "You draw Isabelle's sigil on the mirror, and then you push your hand through the glass and open it like a door. Then you can step through it. Isabelle marked the paths to all the mirrors from the house with her sigil, and it glows in the darkness so you can see where to go. She warned never to go off the paths or away from her markings."

"She showed you her sigil, then. Lily, you've been given a lot of trust and power. She must feel something for you," he said quietly.

"Did she give you her sigil, too?"

"I had to use the grimoire to find it."

"Oh."

The sound of slow clunking down the stairs, and the rattling of keys on a chain, alerted us to stop talking.

I searched for the hand mirror I had brought for Andresh. It was too small for me to just jump into. I drew Isabelle's sigil in the glass with my finger and then, on impulse, tugged at the edges of the mirror to see if they would spread. Just as within the Mirror Paths, they did, and I stretched it enough that I could take a step forward and fall into the glass like I had with the mirror in my room.

I turned and gave a startled Andresh a quick peck on the

lips before I disappeared into the hand mirror. When I landed on the hard rock of the Paths, I saw him staring into the glass from the other side as I reshaped the mirror to its original size. "See you later, Andresh."

I WASN'T sure what Father wanted to do in Andresh's room, considering I hadn't made breakfast for anyone yet, but somehow I avoided him when I made it out of the mirror and back into my bedroom. Nell had finished her bath, and I went ahead and took mine quickly, then dressed for the day in a cotton gown dyed Pomona green. I rushed down the stairs to the kitchen, stoking the fire to smoke some kippers with our breakfast of toast and warm porridge. I wasn't good at making any of it, but I had been craving something a bit heartier than our normal fare.

Father trudged up the stairs from the cellar and into the kitchen, and he beckoned to me to come over to him. He gave me a quick kiss on the cheek and sat down at the dining table.

"Been a while since you made kippers," he said.

"I know. Thought we could use a treat." I wiped the oils from the fish off of my hand after splitting them open like butterflies. "You know, Father, Nell said that one of the Farraday daughters talked to you about their party. Nell and I really want to go. It's for a good cause—the Farradays are collecting food for the poor. We just need to bring something with us that won't spoil, and then we can attend. It's in Market Square."

"There will be a hundred people there at least, then," Father said. I couldn't tell if that bothered or reassured him.

"I won't take my eyes off Nell. She's too beautiful. All the boys—even some men—may want to dance with her, but you know me. I'm like a bulldog. I'll bark and make a fuss and scare them away if any of them have untoward intentions. And I promise we won't be out all night."

"I know you're supposed to debut this year," Father said carefully. "I'm sorry that there have been no invitations thus far." What a lie.

"But this is just a dance. A country party. It's technically not a Season debut. Children will be at this party—there will be no marriage market as far as I know. I think I'll be safe." I lowered my voice. "Besides, you know who I'd choose, anyway, if asked."

"I do. And I would be of the mind to give you to him, if he cures his affliction and stops his dalliance with dark magic."

I nodded. "For now...may Nell and I go to the Farradays' party?"

Father sat there for a moment in thought. "Fine. But I can't let Andresh go with you. He's changed again. Nothing frightening, but highly noticeable."

"What do you mean?" My turn to lie.

"His hair has gone completely white. Like snow. I've never seen anything like it. It came on him in the night. Most of his changes seem to occur at night or when he's sleeping. Since the dance is at night, I can't risk him changing, let alone in public. He'll stay downstairs while you two are out."

"I understand. But won't you let him come up from the basement for breakfast this time? The air down there gets stagnant."

"I'll let him out when it's just me in the house, and Grandma safely in her room asleep."

I knew he would be stubborn about it. I'd have to use the Mirror Paths again once I got more details about the dance from Nell. But at least we got permission to go.

TWENTY MINUTES BEFORE THE FARRADAYS' party, I sat in front of the vanity in Nell's bedroom. She insisted on doing my hair for the dance. I was wearing my dress for the party already, a short-sleeved empire gown dyed barbeau blue. My white gloves rested in my lap.

Nell was already put together in her finest dress—a morone-dyed gown of a brilliant red color that made her shining gold hair, freshly curled around her face, look striking. My reddish-brown hair was still a work in progress.

"I know your hair fell out of its style, but I'm going to put in so many pins, it will have no choice but to stay put," Nell said. "Be sure to avoid lightning."

I laughed. "It's not supposed to rain tonight; don't worry."

Curling my hair had already been a disaster. Nell had me part my hair in the center and wrap the hair framing my face around pieces of fabric, and she made me sleep in it the previous night, hoping the curls that were supposed to come from it would match the styles popular with the gentry. It looked wonderful at first when she unrolled it from the fabric earlier, but it collapsed into long waves, then...nothing. Straight and boring.

She decided to pin it all back into a low-hanging chignon. It was *not* the style, but, "I'm not sure what else to do," she admitted.

I had gone into town yesterday afternoon to pick up our masks from the local craftworks shop in Market Square. The musicians' platform was almost completed when I got there.

Nell and I had half-masks that looked like they were made out of heavy lace, and they were to be tied around our heads with a thick black ribbon. The masks still showed skin, but were busy enough in their design to conceal who we were. My mask also hid the large scar that bloomed across my forehead, unless you were to carefully scrutinize the spot.

Nell held my mask up to my face. "It looks good with your hair, but we need something else." The dress I had picked out tonight was also the best one I owned, a barbeau blue that flattered the color of my hair. "I know what will look good! Hold on a moment!"

Nell ducked out of her bedroom and thumped down the steps. I wasn't sure where she had gone until she returned with two peacock feathers she'd taken from the shop.

She took the long feathers and cut them into four-inch pieces, making sure to preserve the colorful peacock eye. She pinned the two smaller pieces into my hair. They weren't all that subtle, but they matched my gown nicely.

"Cosmetics, and then we can go," Nell said, her excitement leaking out into her voice.

Nell went more into the red territory when it came to her lips and cheeks, which, while one could say it bordered on the distasteful, actually looked nice with the color of her dress.

I chose lighter colors. Pink and coral for me. I lined my eyes with kohl and then did Nell's, and at last we were ready to leave.

In my reticule I had stuffed an unassuming little hand mirror, and then Andresh's full-face mask, which was made from papier-mâché glossed over in such a shiny way it looked ceramic. When Nell and I had bid farewell to Grandma and Father (Father teared up at the sight of us, and we hugged him goodbye), we took the side exit from the house, away from the shop. The alleyway was right there.

I needed to get rid of Nell. And the perfect reason appeared. "Nell! We forgot our donations! We can't attend without them!"

"Wow, we must be easily distracted. I can't believe we both

forgot," Nell said, but she smiled and went back into the house. I scurried to a corner of the alleyway and set the mask and mirror in a spot that hopefully didn't attract attention.

I rushed back to where I'd been standing, and upon Nell's return she handed me a basket with several pieces of dried jerky, and she carried a jar of pickled plums, which I had never liked and was secretly grateful she was donating them.

When we got to Market Square, an entryway had been built so that the donations could be collected before allowing people into the dance area. Nell and I happily rid ourselves of our donations and, holding hands, we beelined toward the musicians' platform. A quadrille was playing and dancers had already assembled at the base of the platform.

We were told upon entry that the rule of the night was to never turn down a dance, unless, for safety reasons, someone felt threatened. I agreed with the rule. "Remember, Nell, lots of men can't control—well, they see someone beautiful and they can't help themselves. The second you feel uncomfortable, find me. Although I plan to be close to you, anyway."

As soon as I said that, a young man, maybe sixteen, asked Nell for the first dance, and off they went to join the quadrille now in action. I stood nearby and watched them for a while, until a tap on my shoulder alerted me to a half-masked gentleman who I recognized as the butcher.

"Mr. Davies! I didn't think you would come here!"

"Is that you, Miss Bellamy? You're not supposed to recognize me!"

"You're not supposed to recognize me either."

"I thought tonight was for a good cause, though. The wife is here, too." He gestured to a fully masked woman who towered over all the other female guests on the dance floor. She was dancing with someone else. "Well... I was wondering if you would like to dance the next one with me."

I felt myself blush. I didn't expect *anyone* to ask. "Of course, Mr. Davies. But we need to stay close to Nell and her partner. Er, partners. She'll have a lot tonight. I need to make sure she's safe."

"You're quite a dutiful sister, Miss Bellamy." He smiled.

The next song to come on was the cotillion, and Mr. Davies was my only partner for the night, and only for two dances. The songs alternated between country dances, reels, and the ever-so-scandalous new one, the waltz.

And through all of those dances, I waited for Andresh to come, as everyone but Mr. Davies ignored my presence. Even Nell seemed to forget I existed as she flirted with a variety of teenaged boys and young men.

I chose to sit down by the platform for the country waltz as I observed Nell step on the feet of her partner—twice—but continue the intimate dance anyway. The boy she was dancing with was so enamored with her, he didn't seem to care that she was more awful than adept.

There was not quite a commotion at the entryway, but some kind of acknowledgement (gasping, murmuring) at the appearance of the young masked man with the long snow-white hair that cascaded down his shoulders to the small of his back.

I smiled. I couldn't help it. And then I felt tears come. I didn't take my mask off, but wiped my eyes, and headed straight towards him once he made it through the entrance.

He spotted me immediately. "Lily."

"Andresh." My voice wavered when I spoke his name. "Thank you. I was really hoping you'd be able to make it tonight."

"I'm afraid I can only spare one dance," he said, and for a split second, I caught the glimpse of one of his fangs. "Let's make it count."

The musicians struck up a new song, the waltz—*not* the country dance version, but the intimate one—and Andresh whisked me away to the floor, where we joined couples gracefully sweeping around the dance space in a circle. He supported my back with one hand, while the other gripped my own.

"You look beautiful," Andresh said.

"So do you."

He let out a little laugh.

We continued to whirl around the other partygoers, and I could only assume the Humble Father and Holy Mother must have blessed us, because Andresh and I were no dancers, but somehow we were in perfect sync with each other as we glided through every step.

Andresh squeezed my hand through his gloves, a gentle gesture of assurance, and then a second time, to the point it hurt.

"Andresh, you need to let me—"

He fell to the ground, landing on all fours. His howl broke through the music, and his head darted in every direction, quick movements that suggested a panic had overtaken him.

The musicians stopped and people started running up to us. "Are you alright?" an older gentleman asked, crouching on his knees to bring Andresh to his feet.

Andresh swatted him away. "Get away from me." He crawled back from the swarm of us gathering around him, and I tried to get closer to him, but people pushed me back.

"God!" a woman shouted. "What's wrong with his eyes?"

"Lily!" Andresh cried in desperation. "Lily!"

"Andresh! I'm coming! Let me through, damn it!"

I heard Nell come up behind me. "Did you say Andresh?"

I fell to my knees and crawled toward him, ignoring everyone. "I'm here, I'm here." What was happening? Did he change again? What did someone say, something about his eyes?

As I approached, I heard him whimper, "Burning! There's too many colors. I can't see!" He jerked his head around, and my heart fell in my chest because he looked so frightened. "Lily! Where are you?"

I made it to him, and he grabbed onto my shoulders. "Lilac. It is you." And he looked up at me with the most horrific eyes. The blue was gone. The white was gone. All that colored his eyes was an oily, inky black—like a demon's.

He grabbed onto me desperately, pulling himself upright to his feet. "I can't see anything but Fire. Fire burning all around me." His voice held a tremor, and I thought he would start crying in his fear.

I held my arm out, gesturing for the crowd to get out of the way. "We're alright. I'm taking him home."

I walked him out of there, holding his arm, and Nell followed us. We were practically all running at that point.

"Lily! Andresh! What happened?" she called to us.

I whirled around, still gripping Andresh. "Go home, Eleanor." When I said her actual name, she knew I was serious.

She paled. "But what about—"

"Go home. I'll explain everything later. *Don't tell Father or Grandma yet!*"

She looked frightened, but I was grateful she listened to me, and hurried off in the direction of our house and shop.

"We should keep running," I told Andresh, as there were plenty of couples from the party taking the air. "We should keep running until no one can see us."

I dragged him along as quickly as I could manage, but by the time we got to an alleyway that was still too far from home, Andresh squeezed my arm.

"Stop, Lily," Andresh said. I let go.

He pulled his mask off his face, and the blackness of his eyes startled me against his pale skin and white hair. He was crying, and his tears were the color of coal.

"I know what I have to do now," he said. "Lily."

He raised both arms to me and stepped forward. He reached awkwardly toward my face, felt the mask there, and patted the back of my head until he found the ribbon. He untied my mask and let it fall to the ground.

His hand touched my cheek, but he had to feel around it, going lower until he found my lips. Once he had, he kept his finger there and leaned in to give me a kiss.

"I love you," he said, pulling away from me. "This is goodbye."

He took a few steps backward from me.

"Andresh?" My voice was filled with alarm. My heartbeat quickened.

He burst into turquoise flames, the Fire escaping from the doors he had shown me on the human body. He was silent at first, but as the Fire intensified, he moaned, and he let out a painful scream. His entire body was engulfed.

I didn't have a single thought in my head. I ran to him, and wrapped my arms around him, pulling him into a tight embrace. His Fire burned bright and hot, and overpowered us both, until my screams joined his.

CHAPTER 18

I felt the entirety of my body blow away like dust in the wind, reconstituted as some smoky substance, and suddenly I was whole again and naked, lying on my stomach, the cool ground an instant comfort.

Isabelle and the Guardian were waiting for us. The massive, jet-black moon gate, whose open space shimmered, as if the air in the hollowed-out circle had substance, indicated we were at Nigredo Gate. The Guardian stood in front of it, as still as a statue, unmoving, unblinking, and barely breathing.

I gasped when I realized that Andresh's monstrous transformation was so similar to the Guardian's appearance. They almost looked the same, if it weren't for the massive scorpion tail the Guardian possessed.

It looked like we were in a massive cave tunnel, and a mysterious light of pale green coated the scenery, but I could not find the source of the glow. It illuminated all of us, making it seem like we were in another world. My stomach knotted with unease.

The chignon I'd worn for the ball had unraveled into a

loose knot; I ran my fingers through it and pulled it apart, bringing my hair forward to cover my breasts as I rose to rest on my shins. My hands flew to hide the spot between my legs.

"Andresh. You brought Lily," Isabelle said casually.

Andresh was behind me, and he rose to his feet. He didn't care to cover himself and stepped forward to Isabelle. "That wasn't supposed to happen. And you won't lay a finger on her, you or the Guardian."

"I promise," Isabelle responded in her smooth, beautiful voice. "But in case she should try anything"—Isabelle took a step toward me, her black panther foot padding the ground, and she raised her hand to me—"Burden. Kneel."

My body felt like hundreds of burrs stuck to it, and I froze, then lurched forward as I bristled with a dark energy that forced me back to the ground. I prostrated myself before them all, my back flat and forward; my chin on my knees and my face turned downward; my breasts smashed against my thighs; and my hands outstretched on the floor.

There was something about the way she spoke the word *burden*. Her voice seemed to gain the weight of an anvil, the word fell heavy in her throat, and there was a slight echo to it. The word reverberated in my mind, and it hurt for me to try to move out of my position.

I couldn't see Andresh's face, but I heard the shock in his voice. "Is that... That cannot be her True Name, can it?"

"My domain is hidden things. You know this, Andresh. And a burden is surely something to keep hidden."

Andresh shook his head. "Take it back, Isabelle. Or I'll sever our contract."

"We're at the point in the plot where I almost don't need you anymore," she said. "Let's get on with my promise. I will save you from the Guardian. I will grant you eternal life. We have one more change, and then we can proceed." She smiled, her teeth like little daggers. "Oh, looks like it's about to start."

I turned my head to the side as soon as I heard Andresh fall to the floor. He curled up in a fetal position, and yet he also couldn't stop moving, rolling to the side, and *something moved near his spine.* His lower back pulsed, and Andresh screamed as something white and segmented exploded out of him right at the tailbone. Blood spattered everywhere; his new tail trembled and thrashed, and the stinger on the end of it glistened with fresh red.

He finally stopped moving, though his breathing was rapid and pained.

"All done now, Andresh. You did good work." Isabelle helped him to his feet. Andresh remained bent over, but he was still standing as Isabelle gestured to the Guardian—now Andresh's twin.

"Cendelamon," she said to the Guardian. "You are relieved of your duty and can be with me at last."

Cendelamon's own scorpion tail shuddered, and made a cracking sound like pottery smashing, as the tail disconnected from his body and broke into hardened pieces. They looked like pearlescent stone and were scattered about the side of the Gate. Two long, black horns, like those on a bull, sprouted from his head like a fast-blooming flower—a painless transformation as opposed to Andresh's own. The pallor left Cendelamon's skin as he grew into a dark tan, and the white seeped out of his long, straight hair, changing it to the color of a dark, pine green.

I tried to get up from my spot to rush to Andresh's side, but I was still weighed down heavily in my kneeling position. What sort of spell had Isabelle used on me?

"Isabelle," Andresh said, his voice sounding pained, "I hereby break our bond. Bello—"

Isabelle's voice overpowered him and she cut him off. "Mirela. Be quiet."

Andresh went silent. He didn't make a single sound, no struggle to stand at his full posture, no whimpering from pain.

"Please, Isabelle, I beg you—let me up," I cried.

"You seem aware of what I can do. You may rise," she said.

I didn't care about being naked anymore. I rushed to Andresh's side. Black tears dripped from his equally black eyes and ran down his pale white face. He gripped my hand, but said nothing.

"Andresh, this is my final gift to you. You did not complete the Magnum Opus, but once you start it, you cannot stop. You are a part of it now, as the new Guardian of Nigredo Gate. You will live forever, feeding off of human desire, and prevent unsavory and unworthy people who wish to abuse the Opus from crossing over." Isabelle approached us, her panther tail swishing back and forth, and she felt Andresh's face. Her fingers discovered his lips, and she gave him a quick kiss, so fast that I couldn't move to stop it.

"What have you done?" I sobbed.

"Andresh wanted to become a god. In this way, he is," Isabelle said simply. "Unless someone kills him, he is eternal. Exactly what he wanted."

Andresh shook his head rapidly and raised his scorpion tail to stab Isabelle. She grabbed the top of Andresh's crown and said, "Oh subjugated one, I give you a new name: *Stultus.*"

Andresh's tail immediately dropped.

"You're a fool for ever making a deal with a demon. It never comes out exactly as you wish." She gestured to the Gate. "Take your place, now."

Andresh strode over to where the Guardian used to stand, and posed powerfully, his arms crossing his chest, his tail raised above his head, ready to strike. He, too, looked like a statue, a carving that would never move until the time to feed or defend came.

"You don't belong here, Lily," Isabelle said. "The Guardian knows no companions. He stands alone. I've waited centuries for this. He can finally come home." She patted Cendelamon's shoulder and pointed to Andresh. "Say goodbye to Stultus, and Cendelamon will send you back. As a Guardian of Gates, he can open and close them, too."

"Andresh!" I shouted at him. He didn't flinch.

"That's not his name anymore, love. He will not answer to it."

I frowned so hard I bit my lower lip and tasted the faintest trace of blood. "Fine. Stultus!"

Andresh turned to me, but didn't leave his spot. "Nigredo," he said. His voice had changed. It deepened and sounded both gravelly and echoey all at once. "Give me your desire."

More tears fell from my eyes and I started to approach him when Cendelamon drew a fiery circle in the air and pushed me through it. My last words at Nigredo Gate: "I promise I'll come back for you!"

I was in my bedroom.

THE MORNING CAME, and I was wearing the nightgown I had grabbed randomly when I was returned to my room. Nell had called to me through the door, and I answered, "Don't come in. I'm not ready. I'll tell everyone what happened at breakfast."

And what exactly was I going to tell everyone? I could hardly process what had happened at the Gate, and I knew sharing the whole story would frighten everyone. They would likely forbid me from trying to save Andresh. I had to keep things as simple as possible: get right to work at getting him out of there.

But I was angry, too. Something in me boiled my blood, and if I could give it a name, it would be Isabelle. I was going to kill her and rescue Andresh.

I drew her sigil on the mirror and reached inside the glass, my hand making the motions of opening a door, but this time, nothing happened. There was no movement or sensation, and in the next second, it was like the mirror *spat* my hand back out.

Wasn't I a Key? Couldn't I open anything? What was the point of being something worth fifty years of Fire and magical knowledge if I couldn't do anything with it?

My shoulders shook and I sobbed terribly. I was inconsolable, letting out short little wails broken up by gasps where I tried to catch my breath. I was helpless, but I couldn't afford to be.

Once I dried my face and calmed down, I walked downstairs to the kitchen, where Grandma was serving eggs.

Nell looked on edge. I couldn't tell if she had blurted out what happened or not. But then Father trudged up the cellar stairs, and he looked furious.

"Where is Andresh?"

"You don't have to worry about him anymore, Father. He's gone."

I explained that Andresh went to the party to spend one final night with me, and he was whisked away to the Gate to take care of things once and for all. I did not tell them I had accompanied him, and I hoped Nell hadn't figured that out on her own or said anything about it.

"How did Andresh leave the basement? He's been locked in there all this time!" Father said, his face turning red.

I shrugged. "He's a magician. He used magic."

"If he could do that at any time, then what was the point?"

"He willingly stayed down there because he thought he would endanger us."

"Well, now that he's at this Gate...has he?"

"No. No one is in danger anymore." I wouldn't elaborate beyond, "I know where he is, and I will get him back. I need to figure out how to get there. In the meantime, please leave me alone to grieve."

My family looked crestfallen and were helpless to make me feel better. Father confessed he didn't want me to involve myself in Andresh's "darkness," but I could only say, "I love him. And Andresh has never hurt me."

I stopped sleeping in my bedroom and essentially moved into the cellar to sleep on Andresh's mattress. Every time I crawled into his bed, I prayed for a lingering scent, some trace of him, but it was like everything about him disappeared once he became the demon Stultus at Nigredo Gate.

Over the next two weeks, I tried what I could. I drew a handle on my mirror and mimed opening it, to see if that would work, but it seemed like I needed some type of demonic connection, like a sigil. That was how I opened the door for both Aineiron and Isabelle.

Now that Andresh had become a demon...did he have a sigil, too? Could I use that to get to him? How would I find out such a thing? I couldn't ask Isabelle without wanting to kill her on the spot, but I knew someone else.

Aineiron. Right. He was out and about in the world, but...

The hand mirror I'd left outside for Andresh to use had been taken sometime during the Farradays' party. I looked and looked for it, but never recovered it. So I journeyed back to my bedroom to call on demons once more.

I cleared my throat and stood in front of my mirror. "Aineiron. Come to me."

"Why hello there, Lilac."

Why could demons do that? Just...*be there.* I could not see how he appeared; only that he was there as if he always had been.

Aineiron was sitting on my bed, staring at me, with human eyes in a human figure. But he bore an odd scent, like a dash of smoke. Not sulfuric, but the hint of something that burned.

He was dressed fashionably, in rider's boots, pale tan pants, a gold and cream crosshatched waistcoat, and a jacket the color of pine needles. All he was missing was a hat, but honestly, it would have hidden his marvelous gold, curling hair.

"You've done well for yourself," I muttered.

"Thanks to you," he said with a smile.

"You should be able to see me properly now," I said. "Not a figure of flame."

"Yes. But I remember you best by your Fire." He gave me a pouty face that would've looked stupid if he wasn't so unnervingly handsome. "I'm hungry. You stopped feeding me, and I miss it *so much.*"

"I know you're not Isabelle, but...could you tell me something that's been hidden from me?"

"Give me a dab of Fire, dear. A teardrop at the tip of your finger, like the small flame on a wick. I'll tell you what I can."

I concentrated with all I had within me, but I could not call the Fire out. I gritted my teeth, clenched and unclenched my fists, and no pale purple burst from my hands.

"This is painful to watch. You have to give me permission, but may I use my magic to call it out?"

I took a step back from him as he rose to his feet. "You know how to call things?"

"Only some. I know the True Name of Fire. When I was stuck in that dark realm of mirrors, I couldn't use my magic or my powers to get myself out. I was blocked from speaking the ancient words. But now that I'm free...I can access a little magic of my own. Let me coax it out of you."

"So...you're not strong enough to use Magic by Will." I felt a little safer.

Aineiron looked offended. He shook his head, seeming disappointed. "No. Never got that far. Magic by Word is all I have, and all I have are a handful of words. But I have the most important one. I'll speak it in front of you, so you may learn it. But you must swear not to harm me."

"You must swear not to harm *me*," I shot back at him.

"That's fair. Come here, my love. Give me your hand."

I took in a deep breath. What could happen to me would be nowhere near as awful as what had happened to Andresh. I needed to be strong and unafraid in order to save him, and I would use Aineiron how I wished, since he was *not* a guardian of secrets, or knower of hidden things.

I took two steps towards him and extended my hand. He took me gently by the wrist. "Give me some of your flame." He lowered his face towards my hand, his lips ever so close to my palm, and said the name smoothly and beautifully. "*Hirutânvolya.*"

I committed it to memory.

A small flick of light purple Fire hovered above my hand. As Aineiron had said, it was the size of the flame at the end of a candlewick. His tongue shot outward, like a human's but slightly longer. But his tongue retreated to his mouth so fast I could barely see him ingest the flame. It was like watching a frog catch a fly, but with more grace.

He grinned contentedly, a smile stretching across his face; then he licked his lips. "You taste like buttercream, my love."

It annoyed and unnerved me that he kept calling me that. "Stop it. I'm not your 'love.'"

"I don't know how else to express my affection and appreciation for you," Aineiron said, that ridiculous pout returning.

"Help me already! Tell me what I need to know. How do I get back to Nigredo Gate?"

"Do you remember how you got there in the first place?"

"Well...Andresh was burning and I grabbed onto him, and I burned, and quickly felt myself drift away, like ash on the wind..."

"That's the trick. Your body has to taste death for a little bit. You need to sublimate."

"Taste death? As in, *die*?"

"A little death. One of many. Burn your body away with your Fire, and with Magic by Will, use intention to navigate to the Gate, and rebuild yourself. Sublimation is the way to travel between worlds, you know."

"What is sublimation, though?"

"Sucrendus the Alchemist put it plainly: *the body first made spiritual; the spirit then corporeal.* You go from being a physical body to a spirit of the air, and back to a body again. You can't do it if your Will isn't strong enough."

"There's no direct door to Nigredo that I can open, seeing as how I'm a Key and all? I have to sublimate?"

"I do not know of any other way. Perhaps you should ask the demon whose domain is the hidden. This is hidden knowledge, after all."

"Damn it," I muttered, sounding a little like Andresh. "It all comes back to Isabelle, doesn't it? Well. I knew I'd see her again, anyway. I have my own plans for her."

Aineiron actually looked a little shaky at that. My words must have come out in such a way to convey my hatred for Isabelle, for her betrayal. I planned to kill her, but not before saving Andresh.

"Andresh was given a new name, a new identity," I said.

"He's a demon at Nigredo Gate now. How do I change him back? Do I need to know his sigil, if he has one now?"

Aineiron sighed. "Will you make a pact with me? I've got such a craving...I'll tell you more then."

He looked so desperate that I thought about giving in. But what good did a pact do for Andresh? And if I thought about it carefully, Aineiron had given me plenty of information for a good while.

"...No, I don't think I will," I said evenly. "Not today."

Aineiron's eyes seemed to darken. His whole demeanor changed. He even somehow seemed *taller* than before, as he walked away from me. "You bitch," he spat out between clenched teeth, giving me a final glare. Just as he was there, he wasn't, and a scent like a gentle aftertaste, lingered—the smell of burning.

Since that strange day, I took weekly walks to St. Rinnea's Abbey ruins. I prayed to Our Lady of Knives, asking her to fill me with the spirit of vengeance—something strong enough that would allow me to kill Isabelle. Not only to punish her for what she did to Andresh, but to prevent her from tricking any other human ever again. If Isabelle still existed as a demon, she might never let Andresh go. He might be at Nigredo Gate forever, just as she had intended.

I always brought an extra set of clothes and shoes with me when I visited the abbey. My goal was to call out my own Fire and let it burn me until my form changed to something new, something that allowed me to permeate the walls of other worlds to take me to Nigredo Gate, like it had when Andresh and I went there together. Sublimation—just as Aineiron had told me.

I remembered how Aineiron spoke Fire's True Name. I would whisper it in case someone listened or watched nearby, and the Fire would leave my hands. I tried to open the other Gates in my body, but couldn't go beyond my palms, so I couldn't get the flames to spread over and consume me, no matter how much of my Will was behind it. I did not have the power to bend things my way.

After the fourth week of trying sublimation, I was exhausted. When I returned from my last visit to the abbey, I fell facedown onto Andresh's old bed in the guest room and let out the longest, saddest-sounding exhale. There had to be some kind of clue related to alchemy—Andresh knew how to sublimate, he knew Isabelle's True Name, and he had been to Nigredo Gate more than once. I couldn't wait any longer to find out what these things were, and if such forbidden knowledge in the end could help me.

I didn't know why I hadn't done it earlier. I stripped his bed of all its sheets and blankets, then lifted the mattress off of its frame, searching to see if he had shoved anything underneath or in between. There was nothing there. I moved on to the wardrobe, finding his other clothes hanging untouched on their pegs, and felt around in all of the pockets. Nothing. I fruitlessly searched his satchel for any hidden compartments, and it was all empty.

Lastly, his desk. He had saved the letters I'd sent him over the years and roughly stacked them in the main drawer, along with a talisman with a red stone in it. I'd never seen him wear it, and I wasn't sure if it was magical or not. I was afraid to touch it, so I grabbed it by its cord and moved it aside.

I felt around further inside the desk and found a mechanism far against the back of the drawer and twisted it around until I heard a click. A door to my right under the top of the desk revealed itself once it opened, and I spied three small books resting there. They were dated, and it was the third book that caught my eye. It was only partially filled in, and it looked like it was from Andresh's time at university.

I had to save him. No matter the cost. Even if that meant walking the same path, and this was the only way to learn. I opened the book and began to read:

The Diary of One Andresh Zatavier, Master Sorcerer and Alchemist, 1819—

ACKNOWLEDGMENTS

There are so many people to thank for this one. First off is Tanya Anne Crosby, who discovered I was writing *The Name and the Key* and making it a trilogy. I was pretty loud about it on social media, on my blog, and in multiple interviews for my debut, *Son of the Siren*, but had never disclosed anything directly to my publisher. Lo and behold, she found out, and offered a contract for it. Thanks to my agent Rick Lewis for helping with that, too.

This is probably the most magical thing to happen to me in publishing thus far. I had worked on *The Name and the Key* since 2010, first as a graduate thesis (completed in 2013), then as an ongoing project living in the back of my mind for years. It always begged me to make it into three books, and it's finally happening. I'm so delighted you've picked up the first book in the trilogy.

Next, I'd like to thank my editor Kim Ostrom who gave me reassurances about the book even as I was drafting it. I was venturing into a lot of new territory with this one—upping the romance, journeying into darker places, and also...writing something that differed in length from *Son of the Siren*. Her editorial focus really helped me bring out more tension in the novel and helped me fix a lot of issues with it after drafting.

My proofreader Kate Gleason also deserves a shout-out for her marvelous proofreading work on the manuscript. She caught so many errors, from the silly to the serious, and made this book so much better with her eagle eyes.

I also need to thank my beta readers, Mia Sanchez and Jay Barlow—two talented writers in their own right, whose intial reactions to the novel helped me get it ready to send off to my publisher. They had very different opinions, but readers always do, so it helped prepare me to write the best manuscript I possibly could and to keep in mind how reading will always be subjective.

I want to thank artist Ecem Karslı for designing the unique demonic sigils used in the book, and artist Juhaihai, who has worked with me for years, for making beautiful promotional art (and fun chibis!) of the characters in *The Name and the Key.* I hope to work with both artists again as the trilogy continues.

I want to thank my family and friends for their unending support. I know it can be like a rollercoaster with me, when I share the highs and lows of writing a book. No matter how all-over-the-place I was with it, the love and guidance you gave me was consistent throughout. Thank you.

To my readers—it's been quite a ride. Thank you for being there.

Also by Kristina Elyse Butke

The Darkening Gate

The Name and the Key

Standalone

Son of the Siren

About the Author

Kristina Elyse Butke is the author of the YA fantasy *Son of the Siren*, (2024) published by Oliver Heber Books. It was a finalist in the Young Adult Category in the American Writing Awards in 2025. Since then, she has thrown herself into writing her first trilogy, *The Darkening Gate.*

She earned her MFA in Writing Popular Fiction from Seton Hill University, which allowed her to teach English composition as an adjunct professor. Soon after, Kristina moved to Kumamoto prefecture in Japan to teach English to high school students for six years through the prestigious JET Program. Upon return, she was back teaching college again, once more focusing on composition.

Not only has Kristina lived abroad in Japan, but she also briefly studied overseas in Wales as an undergraduate. Her time in both countries–the Dragon Lands–serve as creative inspiration, and her experiences abroad have changed her life and her perspective. The fantastical settings and creatures she creates are often sourced from her time in Japan and Wales.

When Kristina isn't reading, writing, or cosplaying, you can find her wandering languidly through dark forests, the more whimsical, the better.

~

Follow Kristina on the web: https://linktr.ee/kristinaelysebutke

Sign up for Kristina's email newsletter for exclusives: https://colossal-artisan-9806.kit.com/2ed842dd9b

A small press bound by the belief that every voice matters.

Sign up for our newsletter to learn about new releases and more.

Buy directly from us to save on ebooks, book bundles, and special editions.

Follow us on social media:

facebook.com/oliverheberbooks
instagram.com/oliverheberbooks
tiktok.com/@oliverheberbooks
bsky.app/profile/oliverheberbooks.bsky.social
youtube.com/@OliverHeberBooksPublisher
oliverheberbooks.substack.com
amazon.com/oliverheberbooks

www.ingramcontent.com/pod-product-compliance
Lightning Source LLC
LaVergne TN
LVHW091301150826
845673LV00006B/1502